The Playboy SEAL

Also by Rachel Robinson

The Playboy SEAL

THE REAL SEAL
BOOK 2

RACHEL ROBINSON

Cover design by Allison Martin
Edited by My Brother's Editor

The Playboy SEAL was originally self-published as Hero Hair in 2017
by Rachel Robison.

Paperback ISBN 979-8-89567-175-7
Ebook ISBN 979-8-89567-174-0
LCCN 2025943789

For my hero and his $40 haircut.

The Playboy SEAL

Prologue

TAP. *Tap. Tap.* "Is this thing on?"

"Carina is going to be frustrated if we mess this up."

"Greenleigh. You're trying to blow her cover. Amateur move, Teala."

"Oh, stop. Can you be quiet for a few seconds so I can figure this out?"

"That red light means it's on. It's rolling. Happy to help."

"How do we delete? I don't want her to hear us arguing."

"Honey, she's writing our story. She's going to hear things a lot worse than us arguing. Remember?"

"Oh, god. Why did I agree to this again?"

"Because it's a good story. And Smith was in a fucking movie. I want to be in a movie too!"

"Macs. Our love story is not Nicholas Sparks caliber."

"*Twilight?*"

"Oh my gosh! Give me a few more seconds, please. I can't think clearly with your questions. She wanted me to start talking about something specific." *Papers rustle.*

"So, is that a no to *Twilight*? Because I'd really love to bite your neck right now."

"I'm not responding to that."

"Lick. Fine. I want to lick your neck right now."

"You're embarrassing me."

"Romance novel, remember? Sex. We're going to fuck all over these pages—leak cum like overused commas on this shit."

"No. Just no."

"Don't turn me down. I'm a goddamn Navy SEAL."

Sigh. "I wish she could hear my eye roll right now. No one would believe you're a SEAL. It's the whole point of this."

"Why? Because I manscape?"

"Partially."

"Because my hair products cost more than your makeup?"

"That factors in."

"My Gucci wallet?"

"And your collection of Armani T-shirts. Yes, Macs. Yes to all of the above."

"Hey, I was single when I spent money on those things."

"Ahhh. When you were single. That's where we're supposed to start."

"Shit."

Giggles. "On a shingle."

"I can't help the things I did before you."

"Neither can I. That's where we're starting, though."

"It's not really the beginning. Most stories start at the beginning."

"You're right. It's sort of the middle. When everything went to hell."

"Including me."

Scoff. "Oh, and the rest of the world? You're so self-referential sometimes."

"A world I'm trying to save!"

"You say potato, I say po-ta-to."

"I'm not even going to start that conversation again."

"Because I'm right. Now get on with it before you put Carina to sleep."

"Greenleigh."

"Seriously? Just go, Macs. Talk."

"Okay. It was a dark and stormy night, and I was about to fuck shit up. I had awesome hair and big, throbbing muscles…"

"Oh, Jesus. It's going to be a long night, isn't it?"

"Only if you let me lick your neck."

END RECORDING.

CHAPTER ONE
Teala

MY FATHER IS AN ASSHOLE—A fact that has taken me twenty-five years to accept. It's easy to turn a blind eye to bad behavior as a child and even as an indifferent teenager. It's when the adult vision focuses that the haze you've believed as truth is exposed as an impostor. Aunt Patti, Aunt Christine, and Aunt Jessica were not fucking aunts. My mother needed him financially and emotionally in some twisted way, so we stayed. I blame her for being weak, for letting me believe their lies for so long. I forgave her easily once I realized how warped her sense of self actually was. I'll never forgive him. He is not a good person.

I don't blame my lack of long-term relationships on my father, though. That's on me. I have a very distinct type of man I like to toy with, experiment with. The bad ones. They are usually good-looking and know it. They'll have some personality flaw that keeps them from committing, which typically is vanity with a side of boredom. They don't spend the night, and if they do, they're gone before the sun rises. In other words, the kind of men who don't know what the word *together* means.

When you think about it, together is such a strange,

complicated word. Everyone is familiar with what it implies in any language around the world. If you peel back the surface, you find the true meaning. Together is only several degrees away from separation. Things and people wedge themselves between together. They ache to tear apart, steal, and covet that which doesn't belong to them, that which seems better than what they themselves have. Together doesn't last forever.

Can a human ever truly belong to another human? Can together stay that way long-term? In my experience it's always temporary, a fleeting feeling of lust and happiness. Kisses start to taste differently once the newness has worn out its welcome. There is less desire, more comfortable indifference. I'm not unhappy being single. I'm merely indifferent, existing in the spaces in between. That's where I'm at now. In between experiments, searching for the next man to warm my bed and show me exactly why together doesn't work.

I blow out a long breath, exhaling things like nonpermanence and bad fathers. "Take it down to lotus," I say, my voice low. "Set your intention for class and for life." My yoga studio is a ripe one hundred and four degrees Fahrenheit. The participants in my class are fresh. We're only seven minutes into practice.

Using my best soft voice, something I'm always told doesn't come naturally, I guide them through several poses and end in downward dog for a long stretch. I know Judd is staring at my ass right now. He always does. It's partially my fault because I went out on a date with him, but I figured once I told him it wasn't going to work out, he'd take classes with another of my yoga instructors. His persistence is noble but goes unrewarded. There's nothing wrong with him. He's handsome and intelligent, and I know we'd at least have yoga in common. It's probably the red flag. Having things in common with someone generally leads to more than I want.

I flip from the pose and sit, facing the room lined with colorful mats. Judd looks away quickly. I quirk a brow and speak the next move in a monotone voice, reminding them to focus on their intentions and to let their egos go.

I should take my own advice. Judd should take my advice. I pull a face when he lifts his gaze and then cowers back to his position. My watch vibrates on my wrist. A text from my friend Carina. *I got you a date*, it reads.

"Take another Vinyasa flow if you feel the desire or stay in downward dog." I stand and approach the stereo system in the back. "Inversions are next. Grab some water. Stay hydrated."

I try tapping the screen of my watch a couple times with sweaty hands and end up having to towel off. I send her back a quick thumbs-up. Moose is the guy's name. He's the best friend of the man Carina is seeing. He's tall, bulky, and has dimples and eyes that would make you want to smack your mama. He's also a Navy SEAL, which automatically puts him in the bad boy category regardless of his dating tendencies. I bite my bottom lip to halt a smile and return to the front of the room.

Judd moves his mat behind another woman. I hide my disgust with a sigh and lead the class in handstands. My body is lithe and tight from a lifestyle devoted to clean eating and exercise. There isn't another option when your business and livelihood is a yoga studio. I built it from the ground up, and three years in, my classes always sell out. When I'm not here, I'm working out at boot camp classes or home sleeping. It's not as if I have much free time to spare when you break my life apart piece by piece.

Thirty minutes later I end the class and leave the

studio with the lights low and my class reflecting on their time spent here. I grab my water bottle from under the front desk and towel off, tossing the towel on the seat of the chair before I sit down. My front desk girl is gearing up to go clean the studio before the next class arrives.

I pull my cell phone out of the drawer and call Carina now that I'm free. She answers on the third ring.

"I'm good, right? Call me matchmaker Carina. You want his number or do want me to text it to you?" she gushes.

"I can't believe he agreed. Did you tell him what I look like? Why would he agree to a blind date without knowing I'm not a troll?" Men like Moose have standards. Usually high ones for actual dates—people who will be seen with them in public.

She pauses. "I don't think he's like that. He seems like a good guy."

Oh, fuck. Not one of those. The monkey in the desert. Monkeys don't belong in deserts. Everyone knows that.

"I told him you were pretty, though."

She may be one of my best friends, but Carina's as wild as one of my eyebrow hairs. She's introverted for the most part, so it makes sense. She's also an author who writes all day, in the dark, in her pajamas. Granted, her books are popular, but she needs to live a little, in my humble opinion. I think this new guy is good for her.

"Pretty is not how I want to be described, Care. I appreciate the compliment, though." I laugh.

"What should I have said? That you're a sex-crazed, lust-longing lion ready to attack their next victim? Like I said, I'm not sure that's what he's after. A fact that *should* make you happy."

I grunt. "Give me his number."

"You're welcome," Carina grumbles.

I take down his digits with a pen on a sticky note, and

we make plans to work out together with our friend Jasmine. I hang up the phone, a little disheartened. Judd winks at me on his way by. I do my best to nod and smile instead of flipping him the bird.

That wouldn't be very Zen of me, would it?

"Tell me again why you don't have a girlfriend?" I ask Moose.

He's sitting next to me on a barstool. It's early, so the bar isn't loud and crowded yet. I'm less interested in his reason than I am in watching his lips move. This man is beautiful in the rogue, *I want to destroy your vagina* kind of way. Except his personality doesn't quite match up. Carina was, unfortunately, right.

He coughs, smiles, and pushes his lips to one side. "I haven't found the right woman. I see no sense in entering relationships until I'm sure they'll work out. It's a conscious choice, not something that has come about because I have some enormous flaw. That's why you're asking, right? I promise you I'm not saddled with too much baggage."

I smile. "I would never insinuate that a man as good-looking as you has a flaw," I admit, flirting my ass off. "Isn't that the whole purpose of dating, though? To figure out who works for you and who doesn't?"

Moose has dimples—tiny little check marks on his cheeks any time he flashes his bright white grin. It's mesmerizing. I swallow hard.

He takes a swig of his dark beer and drains his second pint tonight. Alcohol problem, perhaps? That would make sense. I start my mental man checklist.

"I think I know what I want." He signals the

bartender with a finger and points to the bar in front of him.

Oh, alcohol is definitely going on the list.

His honest reply shocks me.

"You do?"

Moose nods. "Yeah. Impossible standards, really."

I take a small sip of my gin and tonic. This drink is about one hundred calories. His beer arrives, and he drinks half straight away. "Slow down. Or do you think I'm such horrible company that you need to be wasted? You're going to have to explain those standards a little more thoroughly." Color me intrigued.

He swivels to face me and takes one of my hands in his. "Listen. I'm not really ready to date. I'm kind of hung up on someone. More than hung up. I agreed to go out on a date with you to...appease my friend. Throw him off."

I widen my eyes. Someone starts the jukebox in the corner, and an awful rap song blares through every speaker in this dive bar.

"Which friend? Certainly not my friend," I say, bringing my free hand to my chest. "Carina wouldn't have cared either way. So it must be Smith? Why would you care about appeasing him?"

Smith is Carina's boyfriend. She told me all about their date and how Moose showed up and agreed to go out on a date with me.

"It's just semantics. Don't worry about the details. The fact is you're a beautiful woman, and I'm glad we're hanging out right now because I'm lonely, but I can't have a relationship. Not now. Maybe never."

I shake my hands and my head at the same time. "Carina didn't tell you the most important fact about me. She's too soft and nice. I don't do relationships, Moose. Is that your real name, by the way?"

His brows knit together in confusion. "You're a frog hog?"

I laugh. "No. No. You're the first of your kind I've ever had the pleasure of drinking with. I just don't want a relationship. I'm too busy and, frankly, they're never worth the pain at the end. I want nights. That's it. Your name?" I ask again. If I distract him from my whore tendencies, I might still have a shot.

"Ryan Perry," he says, extending his hand, sliding his half finished beer to the edge of the bar. "If you're saying what I think you are, then I'm finished drinking for the night." His dimples show. "We share a mind with regard to pain and endings. That's for sure."

"Teala Smart," I reply, letting his large hand engulf my own. "It's nice to officially meet you, Ryan Perry." Reaching across him, I grab his half finished beer and down it in five large gulps. "Looks like I'll be burning some calories tonight after all."

His eyes twinkle with mirth. "It's Moose," Ryan Perry replies.

I lick my lips. His gaze darts to the lower half of my face.

"Want to get out of here, Moose? My apartment is only a few blocks over."

He said he was lonely. It's a foregone conclusion I'm going to have my way with him.

He presses his lips into a firm line, but his eyes are full of excitement.

Oh, this is going to be so much fun. I'm practically delirious with desire. It's been months since I've had an orgasm around a real man. I tilt my head back and finish my own drink and stand.

Moose slams cash down on the bar and grabs my hand. "I'll be gone by morning," he says, trying to warn me off.

"Fuck no, you won't," I reply, looking at my watch. "You'll be gone by eleven thirty p.m. Let's get going."

Moose shakes his head but follows me out into the night and the few blocks to my historic apartment in the Gaslamp District of San Diego. We make small talk but never say anything of consequence to each other. He smiles a lot, and I think it's because he knows I like to look at his dimples, but Carina was so right. This man is a good man. Nothing like my usual suspects, and for a tiny moment I wish I could be the girl that someone like him is hung up on.

He holds my hand, and I can almost envision I am that girl. Especially when we get back to my apartment and he fucks me so hard and with so much blissful intensity that I'll feel him in between my legs for days on end.

He cradles my head. He kisses me senseless. He closes his eyes and calls me Megan when he pulls off the condom and comes on my rock-hard abs.

I'm not mad. I don't even mention it to him after. I asked for this.

I always ask for this.

CHAPTER TWO

Macs

"YOU OWE ME FIFTY BUCKS, dude. That chick swiped right!" These guys should know better by now. I'm an expert in a lot of things. Hot chick retrieval and capture is one of those things. Pursing my lips to the side, I flip my iPhone to show them. They always demand proof. "That's as good as mine." I shake the phone back and forth in their faces. I'm getting a mental stiffy thinking about it. If I swipe right on a woman's picture and she swipes right on mine, we make a match—a sex date is as good as promised.

I've never, not even once, had a relationship. I don't spend the night with women. They don't spend the night with me. It's almost as if this swiping app was developed for my personal enjoyment. It works for me. It works for them. It's a symbiotic relationship. The give and take is equal, and no one ever ends up hurt. Unless my cock gets a mind of its own and does a little punishing, but we can't get upset with him, now, can we?

Tahoe scoffs, and Moose rolls his eyes. "How the fuck do you do that? You don't even look that good in your photos. You look like a tool. I commend your hobby, but I still don't understand."

13

A swipe-right match is the equivalent to Pavlov's dogs for someone like me. It's sex. Fucking. Plain and simple. This app isn't for people seeking forevers or potential spouses. It's brilliant.

"Chicks like tools," I say. Well, the chicks I want like tools. For a moment I'm scared I am actually a tool. No, no. I can't be a tool. I'm a motherfucking Navy SEAL. I play a part to get laid because playing a part is easier than being myself in a relationship. Truths. Questions. Honesty. Sharing a bathroom. No. Not when a swipe right gives me everything I desire.

"You know, Macs, I know someone you should probably meet. When we get back from Colorado. Let me be your swipe right," Moose says. He won't meet my eyes, but he's smiling like he's lost in a memory.

"What the hell does that mean? I'm not swinging that way this week, bro. Maybe when we're deployed." I clap him on the back.

Tahoe laughs.

"Fuck off. I know a woman you need to meet. Our date didn't…ahhh…go as planned. I think you're more her speed." He looks at the gym exit.

We're sitting on a bench bullshitting. Moose watches Smith run on a treadmill at full speed. That man works harder than all of us in this gym. He's a fucking beast. With his awesome scars, he's basically the Godfather of the SEAL Teams.

"What does she look like?" I ask, breaking my gaze from Smith's feet pounding rubber. "If you're passing her off, I bet she's not my style."

Tahoe wanders off, mumbling under his breath, a towel slung over his shoulder.

"She's your style. Trust me," Moose says, finally meeting my eyes.

"Ah shit, buddy. You fucked her, didn't you?" I'm not

opposed to having sloppy seconds if she's as hot as he's insinuating. "A good fuck, or just hot as shit? Either one is fine by me. Sometimes hot as shit is better than a good fuck because I get more ammo for the spank bank."

"You're twisted as fuck. You know that, right?" Moose groans.

I stand, turn, and glance at the floor-to-ceiling mirror.

I run my hands through my long, sweaty hair. "Someone has to do the job. Answer my question." This already seems like too much work. I'm a busy man. The effort must be at the most minimal level if it's going to work out. I bought a house recently, and fixing it up takes more time than I ever thought I could devote to something that wasn't my career.

My number one priority will always be my job. Sex is just a necessary evil to keep my head straight. I need it as much as I need water—oxygen. I'm not even embarrassed to admit it anymore. The first step is recognizing you have a problem. The second step is telling yourself it's not a fucking problem.

Standing, he shakes his head. "She's both. A solid both." Moose groans. "I'm already regretting opening my mouth. You make us look bad."

I could resent that statement, but he's right. SEALs are known for our philandering ways. We take too many trips. We are away from home too frequently. Cheating on a girlfriend or spouse is too easy. It falls into the excitement category. Some have described it as a thrill—a rush. I think deep down they feel guilty afterward, but they would never let that show. Others call it sex addiction, plain and simple. They love their wives and children, but they require the thrill of the chase as much as I require sex to thrive.

When you understand those facts, I'm one of the good guys. I don't have anyone at home to hurt. I'm alone.

There's no woman to call or text a million times a day. I don't check in with anyone. I open an app instead.

"Is that code for she sucks awesome dick?" I flex my bicep. The lighting does awesome things for my muscles. They're tan and rigid, angles and valleys glistening with perspiration and rippling muscles.

He pushes me, and it breaks my gaze from the mirror.

"Fine. Fine. I promise to be a gentleman. For the first half of the date, anyway. She's DTF for sure?" I'm surprised Moose has been with a woman like this. Typically he's known as the good guy. The one who would never slum with a one-night stand.

His eyes widen. "Oh, yeah. She's DTF," he replies.

Wow. That fucking good?

"You had a weak moment, bro?" I tease, making my way to the locker room attached to the gym.

I hit the urinal, relieving myself with a long groan. Moose does the same next to me.

He finally responds, "I don't know what the hell I was thinking. I guess I thought trying something new might be a good thing. Break up the monotony, you know?"

"Sex is always a good thing." I make an inappropriate joke that would get me banned in all fifty states, and Moose merely rolls his eyes. I start one of the shower-heads and wait until the water turns lukewarm and grab my bottle of soap.

We thought Moose was gay for a long time. He's probably the best-looking guy on the teams, behind me, of course. He doesn't sleep around at all, and I think I've only seen him date one blond chick like five years ago. His mother set him up with her, and she looked absolutely terrified at the beach party our command throws yearly.

"Do you sleep around a lot?" I ask. Curiosity wins out in the end. Is he a closeted version of myself?

I glance sideways to glimpse his face. He shakes his head, his eyes closed as soap streams down his face.

"You know I don't. Carina set me up with her friend. Smith was there, and I couldn't reasonably say no. She owns a yoga studio. Her head is on straight."

For the moment I squash the image of fucking a woman with her legs bent behind her head in humping dog position in favor of learning more about my friend. "Carina's friend? So she is most definitely hot as fuck?" Well, sort of learning something about my friend, mostly worried about my prospects.

He cranks the water off. It halts with a groan. "Of course she's hot. I just told you that. She isn't looking for anything serious. Her morals line up with yours. She's serious."

"Now I see why you couldn't say no. Alcohol involved?"

He shakes his head as he wraps his towel around his waist. It barely makes it around. "Teala knew what she wanted before she took one sip. And she didn't want a second date, or even the possibility of more. Trust me, I asked."

Teala. I like her name. It's different. I grew up in Florida, so the Caribbean was always where my family would vacation. The teal blue waters quickly became what I associated with my family and being together. I still head down to an island when I run into time off.

"I asked multiple times, actually. It was hard to believe," Moose says, eyebrows raised.

"Jesus, Mother of Mary. She really is me in woman form. I appreciate you thinking of me, buddy. I'll call her tonight. What about you, though? Going to swipe right and keep up your awesome streak?"

Moose doesn't have the app on his phone. He would never. I wonder why he even agreed to the date with another woman when it's so obvious he's hung up on someone else.

He laughs. "Not for me. You hold the lion's share in that market anyway. I wouldn't want to steal your panty-dropping thunder."

He closes down—the wall he builds around his personal life slams into place. I accept the closure and prattle on about an upcoming trip and how I'm working on built-in shelves in my living room. He gives me a few tips and tells me about how his cousin's television slopes to the right because he fucked up his own shelves so thoroughly.

"You're so supportive of my DIY obsession. Please, only tell me stories if they end with perfection," I bark, smiling at my friend.

"Just fucking with ya. His shelves came out perfect," he counters.

Moose and I make plans to meet at the gym tomorrow morning before work, and we go our separate ways.

The sun sets in the distance on my drive home. I pull up to my house and admire everything I've accomplished on the outside. The stucco is fresh, and the shutters are newly painted. I had to replace every single window in this fucking beast. The bay window in front is in the shape of a half moon. My kitchen is on the other side of it. Every single tiled shingle was installed with my own two hands. I'm in the mindset of if you want something done right, you do it yourself. Even if you have no fucking clue what you're doing. I learned as I went. Friends taught me. YouTube was there for me, and that's the end of the story.

There would be no way I could afford this house if it wasn't a fixer-upper. Southern California real estate is something of a unicorn. Everything is overpriced. Even the shanty shack bungalows down by the Mexican border. I got this for a steal. It's in a great neighborhood, and I even have a little bit of land. My neighbors are far enough away that I can't smell their morning dragon breath. It's a luxury.

I unlock the door and disarm the security system. It smells like paint, wood, and sawdust. I'm pretty sure I'll be cleaning up sawdust for the better part of a decade after I'm finished with the renovations.

Tossing my keys on the farmhouse table I built last week, I head for the fridge. It's not a kitchen. Not yet, at least. No cabinets or drawers exist, but I do have beer and eggs. I pop the top off a Sam Adams and head for the sliding glass door in the rear of the house. My view overlooks a canyon, and the sun is setting over the ocean in the distance. If I had unlimited funds, I would have bought a small condo right on the water so I could surf every morning and all weekend, but something inside me urged me to buy the bigger house and tackle all the projects that came along with it.

Once the burnt orange sun disappears completely, I take the last swig of beer and head inside to the sofa in my living room. Using the remote, I click on the over-sized TV sitting on the floor. I can't help but hear the way the news anchor's voice echoes through my empty house. I need more furniture. Or another beer.

Beer is probably the answer.

Sometimes the silence I've created is too fucking loud.

CHAPTER THREE
Teala

"ALL RIGHT, Mom. I'll come see you this weekend, okay? I'm about to head into the grocery store," I say into my cell as I make my way through the parking lot. She asks me if I'm baking for my weekly friend get-together. I may talk to my mom more than most people. I blame it on my singleness. "Yes. Jasmine wants me to bake something with chocolate. I told Carina I wanted to do this Paleo recipe I found online, but she just about beheaded me over the phone." I'll end up trying to say goodbye at least three more times before this conversation ends. It takes about twenty minutes to get off the phone with Mom.

"Are you making Grandma's fudge brownies?" she asks.

I smile. "How did you know?"

She's my best friend. Of course she knows. Some people argue that mothers and daughters shouldn't be friends. We are living proof that not only does it work, but it's possible for daughters to grow up and be productive citizens of society. Her parenting never interfered with our friendship. Especially after my father took off.

"Because you wouldn't be my Teala if someone said chocolate and you didn't make the brownies. Will you be bringing home the guy you had a date with last weekend?"

Oh, god. The one subject we don't fully talk about. I tell her about a date here and there, but she has no clue how many sexual partners I've had and how few real relationships I've been a part of. Sometimes I tell her I'm dating someone just to throw her off my trail. I'm sure she reads through the lines but doesn't want to talk about my sex life without my prompting it.

Currently, she's talking about Moose. I thought about him for days after, and I almost called him. He gave me his number and took mine. "Oh, that didn't work out, Mom. We had fun, though. I might see him again," I tack on in hopes of not crushing her spirits completely.

"Oh, I was looking forward to meeting one of your men, honey." She sighs.

My heart clenches. I swallow down my pride. "I'm sorry. You don't want to meet one of my men, though. I won't bring just anyone home. I want you to meet the one. When I'm sure I've met the right guy, then you'll meet him."

"That makes sense."

It shouldn't. I made the whole thing up. If I told her that I feel attachments are only a hindrance and love is too messy and painful to even attempt, she would think less of me. Or worse, that it was her fault somehow.

"How about you? Any dates lately?"

She laughs, and the gleeful noise makes me grin. It's like I'm ten and it's still a forbidden question. "Oh, Teala. You know I don't have any luck with men." She's beautiful. Stunning. She passed enough of her beautiful qualities to make me okay-looking, but Viola Sebrof is anything but ordinary. She has flawless skin, a head full of beautiful dark raven hair, and blue eyes. "You show me yours, and I'll show you mine?" she asks.

I envision her full lips pulling to one corner as she smiles, and it causes a pain of homesickness. "The studio is my boyfriend. Want to drive down for my class the week after next? I'll save you a spot."

She lives about thirty minutes away from me, and we see each other as frequently as possible. My mom has always been supportive in anything I wanted to do—within reason. The studio is a venture she agreed with almost immediately, and I haven't looked back. It provides me with a beautiful, full life.

"I really do have to go now, though. I don't want to annoy the grocery patrons. People seem to frown upon the pitch of my voice." It's a trait I've gotten used to. I wish the world would, too.

"Nonsense, honey. Your voice is lovely."

I scoff. "You're biased. Plus, it's about two octaves away from being identical to yours. Your compliment is moot."

"A mother's compliment is never moot. We always tell the truth."

I agree with that. She confirms she will come to my Saturday morning class next week and tells me to buy a certain brand of chocolate. I have to stay on the phone with her for a few more minutes while I catalog all of the chocolate options in front of me.

"Bye for real. Love you, Mom."

"I love you too, baby girl. Call me tonight."

She calls me in the morning, and I call her at night. Sometimes we talk midday if I have a question or if she wants to see what I'm up to. She knows my schedule, so she's never a nuisance. My father forced our ironclad bond. The love that dissipated for him after she finally left him and transformed into something else. It seeped away from him and traveled over to my mom. She did everything by herself and never let me see her sweat. Viola is strong and brave. She is beautiful and fierce. She takes challenges head-on. She loves me more than any person can possibly love another. Growing up, my needs were met, and my fond memories revolve around her laugh and smile. It's the time she spent with me that leaves the most impact.

I hang up the phone with a smile on my face. With the red basket hooked on my elbow, I make my way to the next aisle to gather the rest of my supplies. My shoulders are back, and my head is held high. I'm a confident, independent woman. My life is full. There's no room for anyone else in it.

Why the hell do I feel the need to keep convincing myself of that?

We're sitting around Jasmine's kitchen table, our wineglasses securely in our hands. Dessert plates look like tiny battlegrounds. Nary a soldier survived. My confection was the first to disappear.

"Who is up for a workout tomorrow? I need to get my cardio in for the week," I say. To keep workout diversity, I like to do boot camp classes. It involves lots of free weights and treadmill sprinting. Yoga can only take you so far. If you want weekly dessert nights, wine, *and* abs, you have to do the time in the gym. My offer is directed at everyone, though I'm already certain who will join me.

Charlotte groans. "I'm in. Yeah. I'm probably only

agreeing because I just ate my weight in sugar and chocolate, but pencil me in anyway. Ten in the morning tomorrow, right?"

I nod, and she drains the remnants of her red wine. Carina agrees as well. Jasmine says she'll meet us there if her hair appointment doesn't run over. Jasmine's hair appointments always conveniently run over.

"Where is the commitment, Jaz? Hamstrings before highlights!" I exclaim, shaking a finger in her direction.

She rolls her eyes. "You're one to talk about commitment," she replies. It's lighthearted, but I still cringe a little. Mostly my friends don't mention my lack of a boyfriend. Charlotte is fresh out of a long-term relationship. One would think she'd be more understanding.

I laugh it off. "Listen. I have commitment. It's a staunch commitment to not committing. That's respectable, right? It's not as if I don't commit to anything. I have my studio and my fitness. I just don't see the worth in committing to something that has the ability to commit less to me. My commitments are unwavering." See what I did there? No one can argue with that logic.

Carina shrugs, checks her phone, and stares off in the distance. She's distracted by a man. A taken one.

"You don't know what you're missing, though. Just once I want you to try. Keep your heart out of it if you want. Try to date a man. No bagging and tagging and high-fiving. Stay the night. Go on more than one date. Don't have sex on the first night," Charlotte says.

Someone laughs and covers a cackle with a giggle.

Jasmine nods her approval of the ludicrous plan. "I couldn't possibly. Who could be worth that?"

"Who has been your best sex lately?"

I shake my head. "I can't call one already on the list. I need a new guy if we're going to do this properly." Maybe it's the wine talking, but this plan gets better and better as the seconds pass. Haven't I wondered what it might be like to have someone to come home to every night?

Jasmine screams. "She's considering it. Dear baby Jesus, she's going to do it. The female gigolo is doing a man more than once."

Blinking slowly, I hold a palm out. "Don't seal this deal yet. I'm considering it. To prove all you bitches wrong." I take another sip of my wine. "It means I'll have to deviate from my usual type. That may pose a problem with chemistry."

"Valid point," Charlotte says. "How will you ever stand tolerating a man who respects you for more than what's between your legs? The thought is horrifying."

She forgot about my boobs. I paid good money for those. I rid myself of my flat chest as soon as Flying Lotus, my yoga studio, started bringing in a steady income. They aren't huge rocks bolted to my chest, nor are they so small as to not be noticed. I needed to be able to practice yoga without being hindered. My silicone bags are the absolute perfect size. If there is one thing you can find without fail in Southern California, it's a plastic surgeon with precision skill. We have the best in the world.

Readjusting my bra strap, I glare at her. "It's a mutual understanding that all we both care about is what is between our legs. Not just the men. I'll have to change my mindset, too. When I've submerged myself in this type of situation for so long, you have to realize how... awkward it will be." I let an actual date flit through my mind. One in which we talk and laugh. We share our interests and learn about each other with the sole intent being to get to know each other to see if our personalities jibe. It's horrifying.

When you've never opened the door to this, it's hard

to understand what it truly means. How can so many people date? The probability that you'll end up alone and hurt is high. Almost certain, actually. People don't have to like each other to have sex. Not even a little bit. You just have to want sex and find the other person physically attractive. The simplicity of it makes anything other than this mindset absolutely boggling. Perhaps I could find someone worth keeping around. I wouldn't be so lonely. My mom would finally be able to meet someone in my life other than my girlfriends. The thought makes my heart race.

My friends start a casual conversation about my sex life. I don't balk. It's not normal for a woman to lead a lifestyle where boyfriends don't exist. Even if I don't agree with their choices, I understand why they think I'm strange. It is strange. In college it was perfectly acceptable as long as you used all the proper precautions. Suddenly in our late twenties, I'm an oddity.

"Let's make it interesting," Jasmine says. "If you can have a normal relationship with a dude, then we all pay for your share of the girls' vacation. It's Vegas this year, so you know how awesome it would be."

I smile even though I'm still nervous and confused as sin. Never one to shy away from a bet, I say, "You're on. Get out your Gucci wallets, ladies. I'm going to crush a relationship, and then you'll all wonder why you can't find the right one."

"If she doesn't win and fails miserably, like we all predict, then she has to buy drinks and dinners the entire vacation," Charlotte says, her tone victorious.

I stand, place my hands on my hips, and cock my head to the side. "Oh, ye of little faith, you have yourselves a deal." Who the fuck am I going to find to participate in this experiment long enough to garner a free trip to Vegas? "How long does the relationship have to last?"

I shake Charlotte's hand because she's closest and because she's smiling so wide it's almost a snarl.

"Months. And you can't sleep with him until at least the fourth date," she says through her teeth.

I widen my eyes as I glance at each of my friends one by one. They nod in agreement.

"That's an average amount of time, Teala," Charlotte replies. My expression must be alarmed. "Four dates is actually on the lower end. I usually don't sleep with a guy until, like, the fifth or sixth date." She must wear a chastity belt made of solid steel and swallow the goddamn key.

I sit down and put my head in my hands. I don't want them to see me sweat, but damn. Admitting I have no idea what I'm doing is hard.

"I'll need advice. I don't know if I can wait that long. There are actual decent-looking men out in the world who will wait that long for sex? Four dates?" Incredulity seeps into my voice. "A relationship. Sure, fine. That's something I could manage, but waiting four dates for sex is like torture!"

"If he really wants to be with you, he will put in the work and time. You can't use sex to keep a relationship going," Charlotte explains. "That's lesson number one."

I nod.

"Find common ground."

Common ground for me has always been deciding who goes downtown first.

I glance at my quiet friend to my right. Carina scoots her chair closer to me.

"Teala, what's the worst that could possibly happen?"

Leave it to the writer to ask the open-ended questions —the questions I don't want to answer. She makes me feel things I'd rather never feel.

Looking at her big brown eyes, I realize what she's trying to force me to understand. "I could like it," I reply.

That would be so much worse than anything else. It would be terrifying.

From across the room, I hear my cell phone chiming with a new text.

CHAPTER FOUR

Macs

TEALA DOESN'T RESPOND to my text right away. This is already more work than swiping at my cell phone screen. Maybe she has no clue who I am, so she's ignoring me. I text a little more detail. *Moose gave me your number. I work with him.* There, now she'll know exactly what she's working with. Literally and figuratively. I'm not lazy. It's quite the opposite. I'm one hundred percent constantly. Keeping things like women and dates less complicated is a requirement for my sanity. I drum my fingers on the side of the cabinet as I let my imagination get the better of me.

After a daydream moves from me killing a bad guy while fucking a bottle blond, I realize there's still no response. If Moose hadn't told me she was worth it, I wouldn't have even bothered with explaining. I tap my foot to the beat of the music as I alternate my gaze from my cell phone to the kitchen cabinets I'm currently trying to put up in my dust bowl of a house. My friend Tahoe is outside with the table saw and a cooler of beer. For a drunk Saturday, he's gotten more accomplished than he usually does. He's the one friend who knows how to do everything. He's a kickass SEAL, and he built his own house from the ground up.

He lumbers through the front door with an armful of unpainted molding and drops the stack on the counter in front of me. "Time for paint," he says, wiping his brow with a tattooed-covered forearm. Tahoe is his nickname because he's built like a motherfucking SUV. He has everything, including that third row in the back that most other trucks are void of. Picking his beer up, he polishes off the contents in a few seconds flat. "What the fuck are you doing in here?" he asks, his brow furrowed at the accumulating molding.

I shrug, finish my own bottle of beer, and set the empty down in front of me. "I'm exercising," I say, flexing my bicep as I make a show of popping the top off another brew. "Painting will be quick. You're doing the time-consuming part outside."

"Fair point. Maybe we should trade places." He scoffs and digs for his cell phone in his pocket. A huge grin breaks out on his scary face. He flashes the screen my way.

"Nice rack," I say. "Is it new?"

Tahoe is a bigger player than I am, but his game is a little sketchier than mine.

"I don't know. I don't have this number programmed into my phone." He smiles widely.

I shake my head. "I don't know how you keep them all straight. You need to tighten your game."

Licking his lips, he sets off to text back. "Nope. My game is airtight, bro. Watch this. 'Those are the most beautiful tits I've ever seen. I want to test their density. Meet me tonight? Where?'" Tahoe reads the text aloud, then makes a show of hitting send.

"What if her face doesn't match her rack? What then?" I ask.

He cracks his neck, tilting it from one side to the other. "Then I fuck her doggy style while holding on to the prettiest part of her body."

I grimace. "Fucking dog."

"Dog. Yes. Doggy style. You're finally getting it. You swiping any pussy tonight?" His question reminds me about my unanswered text.

I glance down at my own phone.

"You're such a modern playboy. I'm too old-school for that shit," he drawls. A man like Tahoe can procure women however he sees fit. He's just leaving my avenue alone. Brotherhood runs deep. Sort of.

Teala is texting back, the gray bubble forcing excitement down to my cock. "Looks like I might be doing it the old-school way tonight, bro. A chick Moose set me up with."

Tahoe raises one bushy brow. "Moose? As in *I don't like women, Ryan Perry*?"

"One and the same," I reply. I don't want to give away any of Moose's secrets, so I don't say anything more. "Friend of a friend or something," I explain when he flicks a confused look my way, then focuses his attention back on his own cell when another text message pings.

Teala finally responds. *What did you have in mind?* She's a grammatically correct texter. That's a good thing. I have a few pet peeves outside of the typical ones, and grammar is one of them. Women who can't be bothered to spell out the word "you" annoy me.

What do I have in mind? Well, thanks to Tahoe, doggy style is edging to the top of my list. I pick up the pile of molding and bring it over to the bench in my living room and spread it out—no need to return the text right away when she took her time. Tahoe comes over, a shit-eating grin still on his face, and starts painting the long pieces of wood a bright white. He's humming some melody as he works, only he manages to make it sound creepy.

I run my hands through my hair and take a sip of beer. The room swims a little. I'm not sure how best to convey exactly what I want the outcome of our date to be. I pick up my phone and see she's writing again. I text before hers comes through. *Whatever you want. Free tonight?* That's vague enough. It's also pretty clear.

Dinner? Her reply is swift.

Ah, dinner. That's more than I usually do. I'm buzzed, and this isn't my usual circumstance. I can be a good guy like Moose. At least for an hour or two. *Sure. La Samba at eight,* I reply, glancing at the clock. It's four.

"I'm off alcohol for the rest of the afternoon," I proclaim, draining my beer, one finger in the air to drive my point home. "I'll head outside to sand," I reply amid Tahoe's sudden outburst of booing and cackling. I have to be somewhat sober if I'm going to fuck her properly. You see, there must be rules if my game is to stay in tip-top shape. Inebriation in any form past buzzed isn't allowed from either party.

Despite what it may seem, I do care if women are satisfied. It's not just about me. Well, it sort of is, but my perfectionist ways swing into my sex life as well. I spend hours upon hours training to be the best at my job. It's cutthroat—the balance of life or death perched between my forefinger and the cold metal trigger. Some of the drive to be successful is bound to drip into my sexual escapades. The need to be the best isn't something that can be dulled. In truth, it would make my life a little easier if I could subdue that instinct.

The pile of wood that needs to be sanded is large and looming. I set to work with the bright sun beaming down on my neck and bare back. Tahoe has given up humming his death tune in favor of singing Elton John. I shake my head. Crazy motherfucker.

My hair is fucking perfect. I slide my fingers through the sides one last time before I turn off the bathroom light. My bedroom and bathroom were the first rooms I finished remodeling and furnishing. If I keep the door shut, I can pretend the rest of my house doesn't look like a war zone of dust and unfinished edges. My OCD is at peace in here. No one else sees inside this room. Every small detail says something about me or my personality. Be it the finer details or the weird way I need the bed to be made. These are things I'm not comfortable sharing with anyone—personal sanctities attached to people are forced to part with.

My father always said that attachments hold people back from fulfilling their full potential. I was never quite sure what that meant until I grew up and realized he was talking about my mom. And me. His obligation was to his family. He never knew we saw the desperation in his eyes when he turned down a business trip or a round of golf with his partners in favor of whatever activity my mother had planned for that weekend. I can't say his thoughts had any effect on the way I've chosen to live my life, because I give my decisions more credit than that. I control them. No one else does. But maybe some subconscious Freudian shit slipped in and forced my hand a little.

I grab a couple of empty beer bottles and toss them in the large trash bin outside before driving downtown earlier than I need to. After I park in the lot adjacent to the La Samba, I respond to a text, confirming a meeting for early Monday morning on base. We have a lot of planning to do with the upcoming deployment. Many training trips are on the horizon. That means lots of variety between my hotel bedsheets along with adrenaline-fueled activities. My life is razor-sharp awesome. I have to be careful the blade is always facing away from me.

Someone sends a dick pic in the group text thread and gets banned from our conversation by way of a quick group vote. That happens at least once a week. Typically someone tries to be funny, and it ends in a two-day punishment ban for bruising our eyes. I'm chuckling under my breath as I enter the restaurant. It's busy. The drone of noise and chaos sets my teeth on edge for a moment or two until I gain my bearings. I love the food here but hate everything else about the location. Everything is too close together.

The bar is crawling with people, and I curse Moose for his brief description of Teala. *"She's hot. Small. Darkish hair. Big lips and a big smile."* At the time it was all I needed to know.

As I survey the gaggle of women in front of me, it's not enough. I'm in Gaslamp. It's a section of San Diego where the young and beautiful roam in full force: they own every street and trashcan here. I make my way closer when a quick survey doesn't produce any results. No one looks like they're waiting for anyone. There are eight brunettes, all caught up in conversation with other men.

With my hands in my pockets, I debate sending her a text message. This feels like the worst idea I've ever had. Meeting her here without having any idea what she looks like puts me at a disadvantage. My only hope is that she hasn't arrived yet. The last thing I want is for her to see me looking desperate. Snaking up to the bar, I order an import beer. With a wink to the cute bartender, I let my gaze wander.

A stunning woman with dirty-blond hair catches my eye. She's talking to a man, but she's eyeing me over his right shoulder. A smile creeps across her full, glossed lips. *Teala.*

"Darkish hair, my ass," I whisper under my breath. I tilt my chin up in a greeting, and I'm rewarded with her full smile. Her eyes crinkle in the corner as she tamps down her glee by biting the corner of her mouth. I watch her intently, taking a sip of my beer as she excuses herself from her company. I stay right where I am. The perfect view of her body as she makes her way toward me happens to be exactly where I'm standing.

She sees another guy she knows and leans over to kiss the dude's cheek. Her gaze meets mine once again as she approaches me, winding her tight body through the packed crowd, a lowball of clear liquid in one hand. It's almost full. Even in heels she's about five foot five… maybe six. Moose didn't lie. She's a stunner. Not unlike my usual woman, though. You can tell she works out a lot. Her skin is pale—flawless. She heeds the doctor's warnings to stay covered in the sun. She cares about aging well, which means she cares about the rest of the superficial things. Like waxing every important part of her body. I'm keyed into everything at once, dissecting every nuance of her body and the way she moves. Reading people is a skilled talent of mine. I use it in my job, but mostly it's put to use in situations such as these.

Teala extends her hand. "Macs," she says, pushing her lips to one side. She has blue-gray eyes. It's a color that's hard to describe. Like a stainless steel appliance wrestled with the ocean and the outcome was a stalemate. I stare a second longer than I should. Maybe she is a touch more beautiful than my normal woman.

"That obvious, huh?" I reply, taking her hand in mine to place a cool kiss on the back. She smells like a vanilla creamsicle—a dessert I want on my cheat day.

She shakes her head, tossing her hair, already on to my overt game. "Ryan told me enough," she replies, using Moose's real name. "Plus, I could tell you were looking for someone." The problem with that statement is she wasn't looking for anyone. "I'm Teala," she finishes, letting her eyes wander from my face down my body. Hot chick retrieval is officially in progress.

"Sorry to interrupt." I lift my chin in her companion's direction. I raise my beer as an excuse. "I'm good if you want to continue your conversation." I clear my throat and take a quick swig.

She watches my lips intently.

"I'm hungry. Let's have dinner," she says. "That was the plan, right?"

"Well, Teala," I say, tasting her name on the tip of my tongue. "Usually plans are made with the probability of destruction. That's life." I catch sight of my reflection in the shiny material of the glass behind the bar and smile. "For the sake of your stomach, let's stick to the plan and see how it ends." And then the plan I have for after dinner.

"Oh, man. He didn't tell you, did he?" Teala says, blinding me with white teeth.

She sips her drink, and my gaze dips to her exposed cleavage. It appears silky soft. I want to put my face in between her tits and rub myself against them like a cat.

I sigh. "Didn't tell me what?"

"Your game won't work with me. I'm better at it than you are," she replies, her voice decisive.

Raising my eyebrows, I nod at Teala and signal for the attention of a waitress. I let her know we're ready to be seated. I called ahead for reservations, and now I'm glad I did. I'm intrigued. As we make our way to a booth in the corner of the room, I glimpse Teala as she nods and waves to several people. My heart rate speeds up. The upper hand. She has it. And I can't fix it. Not tonight, at least.

After we're seated and I've examined her ass from every angle as she slides into the booth, she sets her glass down in front of her and pins her lips together with her teeth.

"You're really hot, Macs," she says. "I assumed you would be, but I have to say you've surpassed my expectations, and that's an awful thing."

I raise one brow. "Awful?"

She can't possibly be one of those chicks who date down. Not with her looks. I slide closer to her until I'm sitting right next to her. My leg is mere inches from hers. I peer down at her.

"Anything but awful. I think you're beautiful. Stunning even." Superficial talk. This is comfortable territory. "Even if every other man in this restaurant shares the same sentiments with me."

Without taking her eyes off mine, she says, "I own a yoga studio. Half of those people take classes there. I see them regularly. You're in *my* neighborhood, remember?"

I zone in on what she didn't say. "The other half?"

"Are men I have been with." She lifts and lowers one shoulder. A gesture to signify this is already old news to me.

Fuck. "A plus for honesty. Sounds like we both know what we want then?"

She smiles, but it fades quickly, and a mask of confusion transforms her features. I swallow hard. That's not a promising sign. Fuck.

The waitress comes and takes our orders. We've both frequented this restaurant enough to know exactly what we want to eat and drink. To the degree that I'm wondering why I've never seen her here before. She scoots away from me, edging her way closer to the exit of the booth.

"Here's the thing. You're my type," Teala says.

I grin. "Funny you mention it. You're my type too."

She shakes her head. "You see, the problem with this is that we don't know anything about each other, and we're able to determine this based on superfluous, meaningless attributes."

I hold my hands out to the sides. "I still don't see a problem with that. If you're trying to explain through thinly veiled statements that we'll blow each other's minds while naked, then yes. I agree. Let's do that. Mind. Blown."

She watches my mouth, her own lips part, breaths pushing through a little more rushed now that I've exposed the elephant in the room for what it is. Sexual chemistry.

I set my hand in between our thighs. "Come on. What do you say?"

Teala looks down at my hand and back up at my face. "I'd usually say, let's get out of here, but I can't."

I blow out a long breath. Our food arrives, so I have time to figure out how to remedy this situation. I drain my beer and notice she hasn't taken a sip of her own drink since we've sat down. She's purposely staying sober. Why? Because I'm so appealing and she's trying to hold back, or because she wants to be completely sober when I make her legs tingle? She chews slowly, politely, but keeps her eyes on her salad and far away from me. I'd think it a shy gesture if everything else about this woman didn't ooze sex and seduction. We talk about mundane things for a second or two. She asks my age, and I answer truthfully.

For the most part, I let my food sit untouched in front of me. During a lull in the conversation I tell her what I'm really thinking. "I want you," I say, my voice just loud enough for her to hear me. "I want to fuck you. Let me fuck you into oblivion, Teala."

Her fork clanks against her plate. My cock hardens under the table.

Swallowing the mouthful of food, her steely eyes flick up to meet mine. "Tell me about yourself instead."

In this moment, I've never wanted to fuck a woman more. This isn't insta-love, or even insta-lust. I want to insta-fuck. Plain and simple.

CHAPTER FIVE

Teala

HIS DARK BROWS KNIT TOGETHER in confusion, and his full lips twist in wry amusement. Even in amused confusion, his face remains in complete symmetry. Macs may very well be the most beautiful man I've ever laid eyes on. If it weren't for his overtly large muscles, his appearance lends to that of a high fashion model. The type of man you see in magazines or in movies. You get to look, but never touch.

If there is a God, he has a messed-up sense of humor. Why is it that men, the species that barely contributes to procreation, get better looking with age, and women, the ones responsible for giving birth and harboring monthly periods for fifty-plus years, wilt? Literally: tits, ass, thighs, slowing metabolism—the works. Women have to work harder at the gym every single year. Looking at Macs, who is the same exact age as me, forces displaced anger and discontent. It's not fair, and there's no one to blame except genetics.

He runs a hand through the side of his perfectly sculpted hair, and it draws my gaze up from his mouth. He shakes his head, his bottom lip caught between his teeth. "Typically I don't talk about myself. Why don't you tell me about yourself if you're so keen on talking *instead?"*

I want instead, but I can't have it. Not tonight, anyway. It's a shame. Perhaps the biggest shame on the planet.

"It's obvious you didn't want to actually go on a date with me," I deadpan. "Not a real one, anyway."

He shrugs. "It's obvious you want more than a date with me," he counters. "I can make this a *real one* pretty quickly." His lips twitch.

Puffing my own lips out, I release a held breath.

I turn away from him. I see a couple of my yoga studio patrons staring in my direction, so I force a smile to my face. It's still on my face when I turn back to him. "You want to know about me? You actually care to know trivial details of a person you just met?" I ask. One glance tells me all I need to know about Macs. He has a single-minded focus with regard to the opposite sex. I can't be upset about that. It's a sentiment I share fully.

He has a mouthful of food sliding around his mouth. "I asked, didn't I?"

Oh, he's such a charmer. He's used to getting whatever he wants, and I guess it's obvious at this point he isn't getting me. Not tonight. Even if I'd love nothing more than to take him home and show him exactly how amazing I am at "sex and sayonara." I think it would impress him. Maybe.

"I'll take it you've learned basic details about me from Ryan. Hopefully not too much," I end with, suddenly embarrassed. I've had sex with his friend. Why doesn't he find that unappealing?

Macs throws a finger in the air and signals to the waitress to bring him another beer. He uses a lewd, dimpled smile to thank her. I shiver. It's an automatic response.

"Moose," he corrects, "told me a lot of things. Now I'm

hesitant to believe anything he told me is truth." Oh, fiddlesticks. He does know sexual details. "By all means, tell me anything you think I should know about you." Using the side of his thumb, he traces his bottom lip back and forth.

Sliding my head from one side to the other, I bring up a hand to cradle the back of my neck, a nervous gesture warranted in this new foreign territory. I'm sticky with a light sheen of sweat. "To be honest, you're making me nervous," I say, averting my gaze.

"I get that a lot," he replies, his voice sending a wave of desire coursing through my veins. A mere voice, something that is usually innocuous, affects me. This is going to be harder than I anticipated. Who cares if I win some stupid bet with my friends, anyway? Is it that important?

"You didn't let me finish. I'm nervous because I'm not sure I've ever met someone so self-absorbed." Now I look at him. If I was hoping to offend him, even mildly, I've failed. His beatific smile and his motherfucking dimples tell me the opposite is true. "I get it. I do. But you can turn off the charm. It won't work on me." These aren't small, cute dimples like Moose has. These are *melt my panties off* hot.

"Turn it off?" he asks, palming his wide chest with one hand. "I haven't turned it on yet. Charm me with details about yourself."

The waitress drops off his beer and scurries off when I send a disenchanted look her way.

I take a sip of my untouched drink. Watered down vodka. "What I would usually tell a date is that my apartment is within walking distance to this restaurant and I expect you to be out of my house before morning." I press my lips together and wait for him to respond.

He raises one brow. "Moose didn't lie then."

No, I'm a sexual deviant with a penchant for jumping bones at the first sight of muscle.

I shake my head. "He told you the truth. That's my usual protocol, but tonight is different," I reply. My heart thumps against my chest in excitement. "Unfortunately. I'm turning over a new leaf, and ding, ding, ding, you're the winner!" A tiny, uncomfortable laugh escapes my mouth. "I mean, you lost in actuality. Now that I've met you, I know you're my old type. I need to find a guy who wants to date like regular people and not have sex until the third or fourth date." At his wide-eyed stare, I continue. "It's completely insane. My friends think it's important for me to find someone normal after my life full of meaningless sex." I shrug and play at nonchalance. If I don't make a huge deal about this, maybe he won't embarrass me too much.

"Can you start tomorrow?" he asks, rubbing his arm with a large, solid hand. "I'll make tonight more than worth it. I promise."

Oh, fuck, would he ever.

"I'll make tonight everything."

My panties are soaked, and he hasn't even touched me. His voice and appearance are enough to force faltering resolve. He mistakes my silence for acceptance.

"Let's get out of here," he whispers, leaning in closer. He brushes my hair behind my ear. His fingers sweep the skin at the nape of my neck. "I want you so bad, Teala. Please. Let me have you. One night." His words are a direct hit. He touches on everything that makes him desirable. There's only one way to squelch this before it goes further. Honesty.

I sigh. "I have a business degree, and I hated college. My yoga studio is my life. I'm almost always there. I don't have pets because I'm still working on houseplants. I'm sort of messy, but particular with certain things like refrigerator organization. I don't eat salad on dates because I'm worried men might think I actually love it. The color teal is not my favorite color…it's actually red or orange. I talk to my mom every day, sometimes a few times a day, because I love her. She's the reason I have any sort of good attributes to my name."

Macs doesn't move away as I speak. His breaths are heavy against the side of my neck.

"Go on," he demands.

I swallow, my neck working. I'm baffled. He doesn't want to know more. How annoying must it be to pretend to care about the inner workings of another person. Especially one you just met. "If I humor you, you need to back off a bit. You're coming on stronger than a category five hurricane."

He growls. An actual audible noise of frustration and lust. "Every word you say makes me even harder. I'm not backing off. Quite the opposite. I will listen to everything you have to say until there is nothing left to say. That's when actions come into play, and, Teala?" he asks.

I nod, a quick gesture to signal him to go on.

"That's when I'm going to show you what you're doing to me. Up close and personal."

Dirty talk that isn't confined to bedroom walls is always the hottest. I can make eye contact with a stranger while Macs promises me nasty things. Do I know that it's not normal to desire him so quickly? Yes and no. Any hot-blooded woman would desire him. Most would never act on their desires. Would a normal woman be offended or put off by his forward suggestions? I'm not sure I can answer that affirmatively either. I want him, and I'm blinded by it.

I realize Macs is complicated. I'm probably even more so. This is a player meeting a most worthy opponent. There cannot be any winners tonight. The longing multiplies with each and every breath I take in his proximity, and you can taste the want in the air between us. Looking him square in his dreamy eyes, I go on. "Most days I don't take off my workout clothing. I enjoy reading when I have spare time. Or baking. Chai tea is one of my favorite drinks."

"I could get you out of your Lululemon any day of the week." His statement momentarily breaks my focus. "Naked is more comfortable than any clothes can be."

I bite my lip to stifle a laugh. A quick appraisal of his clothing tells me he's also well dressed. He's so attractive that trivial things like his clothing take a back seat. I wonder, briefly, what he would look like wearing tattered clothing suited for under a bridge of a highway. As I study his high cheekbones and chiseled jaw, I conclude it wouldn't matter. Not one bit. I would fuck a homeless man who looked like Macs.

I smile to cover the uneasiness my realization has brought. "You like workout clothing? Are you a spandex-Lycra blend connoisseur?"

"Tight ones that hug perfect curves? You could say I'm down with them. I spend a lot of time at gyms." He raises his brow as if to insinuate the fact should be obvious. "I'm skilled in the art of gym clothing."

I push my plate away and down the rest of my drink. Looking at the ceiling and the bottom of my almost empty glass, I try to ignore my cell phone vibrating on the bench next to me. "Well, that's one fact I can add to the list of things I know about you. Something we have in common as well."

Backing away from me a bit, he tilts his head back a touch and looks at me down his straight nose. "I have a quote for you, Teala. It will tell you more about me than any basic conversation."

I swallow. "Getting a little hipster-emo on me? Can't say I expected that."

His tongue darts out and wets his bottom lip. My heart rate responds immediately. What would kissing him feel like? What would his lips on my skin do to me? Would I even survive his brand of passion mixed with attractiveness? I'd survive just fine, I realize. I'd want more. A taste—a night—would never be enough.

"I can't say I expected to tell you anything about myself," Macs replies. "I expected we'd be fucking right now."

I don't respond with words, just a face that probably looks pretty similar to my orgasm face.

Tipping his head back, he drains his beer. I think he might have an alcohol problem, too. From the little exposure I've had to Navy SEALs, I'd be willing to bet that most of them can either drink like fish and still remain highly functioning, or they're all raging closet alcoholics. "I don't plan to see you again. I can be emo if I want." His posture changes, and he scoots away from me even farther. The spell has broken, and this frog prince doesn't need kissing. He needs an escape route.

His honesty catches me off guard, and I can't help the sting of disappointment even if I expected it. "Of course," I say, nodding. "Quote your life. I'm intrigued. For mere entertainment purposes at the very least. We might as well finish our dinner and make the most of it." I'm embarrassed as I think of the mundane, stupid facts I told him about myself. He doesn't care about them or me.

"Tay-la," he says, pronouncing it in two syllables.

I glance at his face.

His lips press into a firm line. "No one ever got to the top of their ivory tower, gazed out the window, and said, 'That was easy.' Open the door to the back stairwell. It's teeming with blood, sweat, tears, and piles of steaming bones."

My mouth pops open a touch, and his gaze darts down. He catches himself and brings his eyes to meet mine. "I get it. That is basically the soundtrack to my life."

"Then don't look so disappointed."

I glare at him. "I'm not disappointed."

He raises one brow. "No?"

My phone vibrates again, reminding me of why *I am* disappointed. I grab my iPhone with the intent to silence it completely, and I see at least a dozen texts from my friends. Most of the texts look to be inspirational quotes they've mutated to resemble "don't have sex" instead. The most recent is from Jasmine. It reads, *Hang in there, baby. Don't make one.*

Rolling my eyes, I toss my phone into my bag. "Fine. I'm disappointed I'll have to face my friends tomorrow empty-handed so to speak. Not that I'm not bringing you home. I mean, I guess there will be a little bit of remorse because you're so good-looking and I'm sure you'd be a good lay, but it's mostly that I'll have to start over. How the hell am I supposed to find a guy who doesn't want sex?"

Macs laughs. "You really are serious, aren't you?"

"I'm considering bringing you home and lying about it. That about sums it up?"

He shakes his head. "I won't damn your soul to hell if you fib." He's all white, straight teeth, scruffy jaw, and fucking dimples.

I blink a few times to clear the haze he creates.

I'm going to do it. I have nothing to lose. "Or you could pretend to be my boyfriend for a little while, and I promise I'll blow your mind at the acceptable time." I tell him the whole deal. About the trip to Vegas and everything. I spill details that are messy and immature. He isn't put off at all. At best, he is completely amused. "I promise, dear God, I promise to make this worth it for you."

"Isn't it kind of a lie still? If I agree, we're pretending anyway. Why couldn't you pretend but still let me fuck you tonight?"

I turn my face to the ceiling. "Because maybe pretending with someone will prepare me for a man who really wants me forever." I return his honesty with a dose of my own. "Maybe my friends are right. A relationship might be worth it. Even if it is pretend."

He swallows, then cracks his knuckles one by one. His eyes fixate on each finger as he goes. His hands are rough and soft at the same time. The backs are smooth, with a speckling of hair. Perfectly shaped fingers—not too skinny or too fat. His palms are rough and calloused, but not so much that it would be considered a detriment. I can't tell what he's thinking, but I can tell he's closed himself off completely.

"It's a stupid idea. This is a first date. You just met me. I'm insane. My god, I'm insane. My mother would be mortified if I told her. Forget I said any of this. I'll pick up the check for dinner, and we can be on our way. My friends have made me insane."

"Here's the thing. I've never been in a relationship. I wouldn't know how to pretend properly. I will admit that I'm intrigued by the idea because of that fact and nothing else."

Well, that stings a little.

"What would it entail exactly? And how long until I get you naked?"

My face must register shock, because he continues. "I'm always up for a challenge. Don't read into it. You are hot. You proposed a situation I've never been propositioned with before. If we're going to do this, we have to do it right. Hand me your cell phone."

Hesitantly, without taking my eyes off his, I find my phone by touch and lay it on the table in front of us. He opens it with a swipe to pull the camera up. He smiles when he reads the text messages bubbling up on my screen. He scoots next to me, so close that I smell the sweet musk of his cologne, and he raises the phone. "Smile, Teala. It's our first selfie!"

A smirk is all I can force before the flash blinds us. He hands the phone back to me.

"Send that to your friends. Challenge accepted."

I don't want to send the picture. I want to keep him to myself for a little longer. A man like Macs can't be kept by anyone. Not even the most attractive woman in the world and definitely not a messed-up, commitment-phobe like myself. I hit send and anticipate the onslaught of texts back. I glance over at Macs. His own cell phone is in his hand, and he's swiping left faster than I thought was possible.

CHAPTER SIX

Macs

CALL IT A MOMENT OF WEAKNESS. A moment of curiosity so strong I was compelled to give in to the beautiful woman sitting next to me. Call it sexual chemistry so strong I know it will be worth the wait. We're hashing out the details, and for the first time since I met Teala, she seems happy, or excited at the very least.

"Four dates and then sex?" I confirm. I keep my cell phone in hand as we speak. I know it's rude, but after the tension tonight, I'll need a release stronger than my right hand can provide.

She nods, not even looking in my direction. "Maybe three. I have to confirm with them. They had some weird timetable I'm not familiar with."

I can't say I'm familiar with it either. My friends are either similar to me in promiscuity or married. When Teala remains quiet, I look up from my phone. Her gaze is directed at my cell.

"And what about seeing other people?" she asks.

Ah. This may be a point of contention.

"Well, you can't sleep with anyone until the third date, so I don't think that's a factor, right?" I avoid the point completely.

"And what about you? We are pretending, I guess." Her reply is a touch sarcastic. "Although if you wanted to get the full experience, maybe you should...refrain, too."

She's not shy, and it's a turn-on added in her favor. Teala's eyes are curious, and her body language suggests she's already comfortable around me. I wonder if she's this comfortable with any attractive man. I'm probably nothing special in her eyes. She laughs as she sees the text messages pop up on her screen.

"Jasmine said she would break the bet if she were me."

Jasmine. Who is Jasmine, and where can I find her? "Jasmine has a good point."

She ignores me. "First kiss is second date."

"Heavy petting?" I ask.

Teala sighs. "Let me ask," she groans. She taps out a text, and her friend responds almost immediately. "No and yes. Varied responses. All of that is reserved for the date in which sex takes place. Ludicrous." She shakes her head, her eyes narrowed at her phone.

"You like a challenge as much as I do," I remark. It's the reason I wanted to be a Navy SEAL. So few can actually make it. It's hard, and I love to do hard things.

She hangs her head and brings one hand up to cover her face. "You'll have to meet my mom and do exactly as I say. This is too much to ask from you. It's too much to ask from a friend, let alone a stranger."

"Just because I want to charm your panties off and make you forget about your friends and mom and, fuck, even your own name, doesn't mean I can't play nice and meet your mom. Parents tend to like me. Maybe you should meet my parents as well. That might get them off my back, too. There's a possibility this could work for both of us equally. My reputation will garner a black mark, though. Which is why I may need to keep up my, ah, swiping." I flash the screen her way so she can see the app I have opened and exactly what I'm doing.

She puts the tip of her thumbnail in between her teeth. "That's fair. But it can't interfere with our dates."

"You have to take me to Vegas on the trip, too," I interject, her mouth distracting me from any lucid conversation.

Her eyes widen. "Why would you want to come with me? With my friends? That would be a nightmare for you."

As an explanation, I flash her my screen one more time. "Spearmint Rhino, Teala," I say. It's my all-time favorite strip club. I may not even need an app to get what I want once I saunter into that beautiful brick building.

My words don't faze her. She nods and holds up a small palm to halt the conversation. Her eyebrows bunch in confusion. "If my friends find out this was all a lie, they'll be furious. Jasmine will disown me. You'll be careful? The whole point is to convince them."

"Careful is my middle name. I wrap that shit up every single time. I'll bring you with me to the strip club. We will have a raucous time. The best time ever." My joke garners a small giggle and a white, charming smile. I sigh in relief. I didn't know it was possible to have a woman accept my lifestyle with such ease. One who wants to fuck me, too. Two for one. We both make an effort to finish our dinners. The waitress clears the table and lingers longer than Teala is comfortable with. She's judging my actions. My every move. She's learning, an observation I've never watched firsthand with another woman before. This experiment in self-control and deceit will be good for my womanizing tactical skills.

Teala stands from the table in one lithe move. "By the way, that's not what I meant about being careful, and you know it. Condoms aren't careful. They are mandatory. You and I both know that." She excuses herself to use the restroom.

On the way, she swings by another table with a few men. It's obvious they're having a guys' night out. One of the men, a handsome fellow with an expensive business suit, wraps an arm around her waist and pulls her into an awkward side hug.

My phone pings on the table, alerting me of a match. Then it pings again. I don't look at it to see which woman is responding to my swipe. I study Teala. Her personality is effervescent. She's a chameleon in any circumstance. She smiles and laughs. She plays the game. The men look at her like she's dinner, but she's not giving them any appetizers. Teala handles the attention like a well-seasoned pro. Gliding out of their grasps easily and joking like it's the most natural thing in the world. From this angle I can appreciate every goddamn curve on her tight body. The slope of her back at the bottom of her spine transitions into a stunning, solid ass. An ass that squats. An ass that I could bounce quarters off of. An ass that gives me wood with clothes on it. I don't know her well, but even the small amount I've learned has led me to believe she truly is a full, devious package.

I want her body. I want it more now that I see that other men want her body. No one can deny the caveman response to others desiring the same thing.

And as a testament to how much our shady deal and date mean to her, Teala doesn't glance my way once as she mingles with other men. This is one of the reasons I don't date. Even if you don't want it to be, things become complicated. Do those men think she's with me? Do they think I'm the type of man who lets my woman get groped by other men? I close my eyes and breathe while I wait for her to return.

Teala doesn't make any stops on the way back to our table. Her eyes are all mine. So is her smile. It's equal parts sweetness and mischief. An unfamiliar stirring in my chest alerts me to the fact that I'm wasting my time right now. I'm not getting laid. And my dick is steel hard, lying uncomfortably against my leg. I need to wrap this up quickly so I can move on to a more advantageous situation.

I pretend to be involved in a text message when she sits down.

"I'm probably keeping you. If you want to get going, I understand. The least I can do is cut you early," she says. The smile in her voice forces me to look at her. She sizzles like fire as I rake my gaze over her neck, lips, and then her huge doe eyes. She bites her lip.

As silently as possible, I groan. "You're not holding me up. It's fine." It's not, but I can't control my words when I'm this turned on. I look at my watch. I know what time it is, I just saw it on my phone. I only raise my wrist to show off my designer timepiece, an accessory I'm very proud of. "It's getting late, though."

She puffs out an irritated breath. "Especially if I'm not getting laid," she whispers. "I'll walk you out?"

That's right. She lives within walking distance. More importantly, she wants to get laid. I place a couple bills in with the check and make a gesture for her to lead the way out.

It's dark. I can't see her as well outside. "I could walk you home," I offer.

She clears her throat. "My friends are there."

"I feel like we have babysitters."

"They don't trust me. And for good reason."

It must be a bitch to be friends with women. Teala seems to be on a whole different wavelength than her friends. It makes a little more sense why winning this bet means more to her than it should. I'd tell my friends to fuck off, but then again I don't have anything to prove.

She walks next to me, careful not to brush my arm as she goes.

"This is me," I say when we reach my car. "I feel like it should be the other way around. Me walking you to your car." And then fucking you in the back seat doggy style, with your face pressed up against the glass. Then I'd make you clean off the makeup smears. Yes, I fancy that plan quite a lot.

"You do have dating instincts!" Teala quips. "Gentle-manly ones."

I shake my head, laughing. "I don't. But that's okay. It doesn't make a difference for what we're doing." She's silhouetted by a street light. Even in the dark I can see her face fall as she averts her gaze. "Look at me, Teala."

She doesn't. Probably because I told her to. I like that and hate that at the same time. "Look at me now," I say, lowering my voice. "Look at me now, uh." I thrust my hips forward and clasp my hands behind my head. "Look at me now." I flash her a hip-hop smile, minus the grill.

She laughs and looks at me. "Oh, god. You're one of those people!"

"What kind? The motherfuckin' awesome kind?" I ask, bringing my arms down to cross over my broad chest. Her gaze skims my muscles. I flex a little harder.

She swallows—an audible noise.

Her smile is electric. "The kind who quotes rap songs in everyday conversation. I have a friend who does that. She drops down to get her twerk on wherever we are at the mention of dropping something. It's ridiculous."

I lift my chin. "Yet, you're laughing. Maybe you're right, though. Cool people quote rap songs. It makes life less boring."

I take a step toward her. I'm in her space. She wants

me in it. Nothing has been more obvious. Her lips part, her hands in fists by her sides.

Teala's shoulders loosen a touch. "Are you okay to drive?" she asks, glancing at my car.

She's underestimating my alcohol tolerance. It's fair. Everyone does. I have the ability to drink more than anyone I know and still function on a level most would consider normal.

Bending down, I wrap one hand around the back of her neck and pull her head toward mine. I stop before her skin touches mine. Against her lips I say, "Only if you're okay going home by yourself."

I can taste the desire in her breaths as we trade air. She's putty in my hands, head limp and ready to go anywhere I want it. My dick raises its hand. It wants to be called on.

"Until next time. You really should firm up what's acceptable on the second date," I say, backing off a little.

Teala slams her eyes shut. The motion wrinkles her brows.

"Why did it have to be you? Why are you my type? Why couldn't I have shown up tonight and found a nice, normal guy? One who actually wanted to date and not fuck. Someone less good-looking. Someone more...more decent."

I've never looked at myself as a bad person, but if you break it down in the terms she did, I'm the definition of a bad guy. "Every guy wants to fuck. Don't delude yourself," I reply. Slowly, brushing the side of her neck as I go, I release her, giving her head freedom.

She steps away. "You're right. I guess. I assumed the same thing, but I was told differently," she replies.

Teala brushes hair off her cheek. Her hair is beautiful, long, and shiny. She takes care of it. I'll be able to wrap it around my hand a couple of times. My phone pings from my pocket. The noise draws her gaze to my crotch. When she realizes what she's looking at, she takes another step back.

"This is going to be hard."

"It's not the only thing that's hard," I reply, grinning. "Joking aside, it's not that difficult. We're both consenting adults." Since my first submersion into the SEAL world during Hell Week, the rest of my life has seemed easy. Surely she's dealt with more difficult obstacles than refraining from sex.

She sighs. "I should go. You have my number. We can make plans for another date. That is, if you're absolutely sure you want to jump into this charade with me."

If the end goal is me getting into her pants, I can do that. I'll look at this the way I look at my swiping. It's just taking longer for her to swipe back. I'll continue doing me in the meantime. She's worth it. Moose says so.

"Tomorrow? I'll come up with a date. As an equal contributor, it's only fair."

She smiles, bites the corner of her lip, and nods her head. "Until then. Good night."

With a small wave, Teala walks away, showing me what I'm missing out on—what will be mine very soon. This is a fun game. Something to conquer. I never thought something like this would appeal to me, but it does. So much so that I know I need to make our next date something amazing. Panty melting. Scorching.

I'm so engrossed in my ideas and how I can win this competition I forget all about the girls in my pocket. For a little while, at least.

CHAPTER SEVEN
Teala

I TAUGHT three hot yoga classes before noon. It's two in the afternoon, and I haven't heard from Macs. Not that I'm the type of person to wait for a phone call from a man, but for the first time in a while I'm excited to hear from a man. I'm also excited to tell my mother I'm dating someone. To tell my friends he called for a second date.

"It's fake, Teala," I tell myself as I glance at my watch for the third time in one minute. I tap on it to see how many calories I've burned and sigh. I'm meeting Jasmine for a workout at our boot camp class across the street. If he hasn't called by then, I may have to lie.

The girl who works my front desk pushes a Greek wrap across the desk. "Eat. You've already burned more calories than you can make up today," she says. "We might need to hire another teacher so there's backup when someone gets sick."

"It's fine. I have it, it's no big deal." I don't have to pay an instructor today. As inconvenient as it is to be here on my day off, I don't complain too much. Owning my own business has taught me more about life than I can quantify. Running a good business and making money isn't an easy task. I've managed to create something successful that funds an exceptional life. I've helped my mother out a time or two when she hit a rough patch. Nothing makes me happier. "She'll be back tomorrow. Just one more class and we're done for the day. You should get certified," I offer.

A double-threat employee. She can run things and teach classes. A woman can dream. She laughs and brushes off my suggestion with a lame excuse. That's a millennial for you. I had to fire the last twenty-two-year-old desk girl after she brought her small dog to work. I told her it was unacceptable. Twice. She told me it was a hostile work environment. A yoga studio. Hostile. I laughed while I paid her in cash from my own wallet just to get her out of my sight.

Rolling my eyes, I eat the wrap in four bites, inhaling quickly without tasting the food.

She stares at me with huge eyes. "I don't know how you can do that."

I shrug. "It's food."

"You're going to teach a class after eating that in thirty seconds? I'm not sure that's a great idea."

Smiling, I crumple the wrapper and toss it into the trash can across the room. "I'll take it easy this go-round." My watch pings with a text, but it's just Jasmine confirming our meet-up. "Ugh," I moan. "Is the room clean? I'll head in and fold cold towels."

She nods, so I head into the warm room, my bare feet sticking to the dark hardwood floors. I do a few stretches on my mat in the front. I prefer the low lights in here to those in the real world. Everything is so bright and harsh. I hear the soft waft of the door behind me.

"Teala. How are you?" I recognize his voice right away and shiver despite the warm room.

I turn to the side to glance at him in the mirror. "Gavin. I'm well. How are you?"

"I had no idea Trudy was out today," he replies.

I sigh. Let's call Gavin specimen A. A man I slept with who could have been more if he wasn't such a dickhead. Speaking of—specimen B. It's his dick. It's long, pink, and strong. I laugh.

"What's so funny?" Gavin asks, eyes narrowed.

I shake my head. I subconsciously quoted a rap song. There's no hope for me. Macs did call people who do it awesome, though.

I stop laughing. "Nothing, Gavin. Just thought of something." And now I want to crawl in a hole because I care what a man like Macs thinks of me.

He shifts his weight from one foot to the other. I'm making him self-conscious. Good. Let him think I'm laughing at him. He deserves more than embarrassment.

"I don't know why you don't find another studio to practice at."

He's a lean and handsome businessman who travels to San Diego frequently. We had a passion-fueled night a few months ago. For a brief amount of time he made it seem like he wanted more than just a night. I thought a regular hookup might be better than a bunch of new ones, but I was so wrong. He left and put an envelope of cash on my pillow.

"I don't need your money here either," I deadpan, turning my gaze to my knees for a stretch.

"I'm sorry. I tried calling you and emailed the studio. I freaked out," he explains and unrolls his mat next to me.

I close my eyes. After my night, the last thing I need is Gavin this close to me. My watch vibrates. I look down and see a message from Macs. I smile. *The playground is where I spend all of my nights…Balboa Park. Meet me by the monkey bars at 6.* I keep smiling—a goofy, face-bending smile I can't control. I forget where I'm at and whom I'm talking to.

When I finally glance Gavin's way, he's eyeing me down not so subtly. Standing, I head over to the towel fridge and begin rolling the wet squares of fabric. "You can stay for class, but I don't want to talk about it, Gavin. I'm over it. I'm seeing someone else now." Saying those words feels sweeter than I thought they would. Even if it's a lie. Using my cell phone, I set the music to low, electric mood music and send back a thumbs-up to reply to Macs.

I screenshot his text and send it to my friends in our group message. They all reply with generic congratulations and jokes. None of them suspect anything. Not to my face anyway. How could they not speculate given my history? They know me too well. I'll have to keep the false pretenses and my guard up.

Don't stalk me there, please, I text back to my friends. I ask what's acceptable behavior for a second date and receive mixed messages. Some say a kiss is okay. Others say making out is completely acceptable. No touching below the waist is what they agree upon in the end.

A few more yoga patrons trickle in. Gavin ignores my eyes studiously. He watches me, though, when he thinks I'm not looking. I know the look on his face, and it makes me feel validated. He knows he fucked up. But I'm not a woman who can be kept. He did himself a favor by changing his mind. I'd never tell him that.

It's a forty-five-minute class. With my head in the clouds, daydreaming about what tonight might hold, it passes by in an eyeblink. Gavin's loaded gazes become background noise.

Stepping outside after my instruction has finished, I call my mom and fill her in on the details. I haven't heard her this happy for a long time. I make a mental note to lie about my relationship status more frequently. I envision the smile she's wearing, and a pang of loneliness hits me.

I pull my feet up onto the bench in the locker room. Not loneliness for myself, but for her. I ask about her friends, and she reluctantly tells me she has a date in the upcoming week. Her excitement for my own date morphs into dread.

"Mom, you can't stay locked away forever. Dad has moved on. You deserve to be happy. I'm not a little girl anymore. It's a shame no one is enjoying your sugarloaf."

People enter, their hot bodies secreting warmth into the air in this small space. I called her to calm my nerves, but somehow it's made me even more anxious about everything. I slide by sweaty bodies in the hallway, grab my sweater and purse from under the desk, and wave to the desk girl on my way out into the parking lot. As I go, I tell my mom all the reasons she's such a fabulous catch.

"You're doing the single men a disservice," I say, finishing my lecture. I'm surprised she's humored me this long.

Mom ignores my sentiments. "I'll bring a loaf when I drive down. Can I meet him then?"

Him. Him. My heart thumps out a staccato, thinking of him. His body. His dimples. His dark-rimmed lashes. The way his neck works when he swallows, the way his fingers brush my skin and light a fire from the outside in. A him that will never be mine completely.

Will she call my bluff if she meets him? Can she tell it's just wild, lying chemistry? Macs said he would meet her. "I'll ask him, okay?" I tell her I have to meet up with Jasmine. "I'll call you in the morning and let you know how it goes. Love you."

"Be yourself, honey. The weird, lovable, honest self you hide from," she whispers. "I love you, too," she tacks on quickly so I don't have to respond.

I'm always myself. Unfortunately, this time it doesn't matter who I am. This isn't a game I can win.

Even though it's summer, the air is always cool at night. It's a San Diego kind of thing you can't explain unless you've been here. Macs told me to wear my workout clothing. After my boot camp workout, I showered and put a clean outfit back on. That's not a rare occurrence, actually. It's my lifestyle.

I see Macs immediately as I cross the large field of grass leading to the gas lamp-lit playground. Only a few of my friends have kids, so I'm not around them or their haunts very often. Did I think it odd this is where he wanted to meet? I've been subjected to weirder things in my twenty-eight years of life. He's doing pull-ups on a set of monkey bars that look too high to be considered safe for children. With him on them, they look like anything except an obstacle for a child. He's a playground for every grown-ass woman on planet Earth.

Macs is shirtless. Sweat is trickling down his chest, rippling over his abs, and disappearing into the waistband of his black workout shorts. I tighten my slinky sweater around my shoulders and shiver. With a sigh and my resolve steeled, I approach him. He watches me carefully as I near, his eyes on me as he lifts and lowers himself over and over. It's automatic for him. The movement of hoisting his body weight is as effortless as walking is to a normal person.

He blinks sweat out of his eyes a few times. When I'm standing in front of him, so close that I could reach out and touch the most obvious bulge hanging in front of my face, I stop. The scent of sweat and bodywash and unadulterated male mingle in the night air.

"Like the view?" Macs asks, his voice labored. Sort of how it probably sounds while he's fucking.

I have to tear my gaze from his body to focus on his face. My heart races with the promise of lust. Maybe I'm sick—something's wrong with me for not feeling anything except desire. There are no emotions attached to the present, just the need to have my way with him in any way I see fit.

"I love the view. I feel a little overdressed, though," I reply.

He bites his tongue in this carnal smile that sends shockwaves to my core. I take a step back.

He drops down from the bar and lands right in front of me with a slight thud. A gust of Macs hits me, and I suck in a breath and hold it. I can't be this near. His face. The sleek, stunning features are prominent under the lights overhead.

"We could fix that," Macs says, stepping toward me, his eyes roving my body.

His chest is heaving, and his muscles are fucking perfect. Not that I'm an expert in this field, but I've seen quite a few fit men in my fitness journey, and Macs Newstead takes the golden trophy in every single way.

Ignoring his sentiment to take my clothes off, I reply, "Your symmetry is flawless." The compliment comes out of my mouth before I realize what I've done. Never compliment a man like Macs. It will go straight to his already enlarged head.

"You think?" He smiles. Dimples pop.

Well, I've already destroyed any hope of playing it cool. "I know. You work hard," I state. "You...your body...it's insane. In a good way. The best way." I cock my head to the side to angle for a better view of his shoulders. The desire to trace his every perfect curve emerges, and I have to take another step away from him. He notices.

"Thanks for noticing. You work hard as well." In a

small movement, he steps toward me and slides the sweater off my shoulders. It hits the white sand beneath us. He manages this without touching my skin. "You're stunning. What does perfection taste like?"

My breath catches. Taste it. Taste me. Right now. I swallow. "What is our date going to consist of? I could make up details for my friends, but we should do some normal date-like things." My voice isn't at all confident. It's embarrassing and reeks of melancholy.

"Maybe take our perfect, symmetrical bodies, put them together, and fuck right here?" He points a finger down.

Yes. Right here. In the sand, under the lights. Your dick deep inside of me. Your beautiful mouth on my skin. Yes.

"I'm joking, Teala," Macs whispers, his smile still in place. He shakes his head. "Ninja Warrior, of course." He raises his arm behind him to the sprawling play structure. "For time. Because we're both badasses like that."

I quirk a brow. "We're going to work out? I've kind of reached my quota for the day. I'll watch you, though." My arms feel like lead, and my legs are already sore. I roll my neck. "One of my teachers called out sick today, so I taught a million classes and then went to the gym. It sounds like I'm whining, but I'm really not. That's not a normal day for me."

Macs laughs and shows me where he's set up a picnic on a table in a dark corner of the park. "I thought we could work up an appetite first."

He reaches down and readjusts his thick dick without hiding the gesture. I can't help but watch. Meeting his gaze a second later, he smirks.

"We don't have to work out first. You could watch me if you want. Or we could make it interesting. Throw a bet in there for good measure. It's obvious we're both competitive."

Macs and I have something in common, and I actually like it.

Sighing, I close my eyes and pull a knee up to my chest and then repeat the stretch with the other leg. Macs notices my grimace and nods in approval. He says I am a woman after his own heart, and beneath the painful ab muscles, my stomach flutters. We agree to do the course he has planned once before we sit down to eat the salads he's packed for our dinner. Macs bites his lip in between sentences as he explains what obstacle comes next. I'm only vaguely aware I'm supposed to be listening to him so I know what comes next.

I'm dissecting him. With a no-nonsense authoritative air, I can see the person he is when he's not trying to get laid. "Got it," I admit. He's laid out the course. It will take a few minutes to complete. "What are the terms? I'm all for girl power and all that, but I'll never be able to beat your time. Don't you have an obstacle course at work?" I try at nonchalance as I grab my sweater from the sand and toss it over a ladder nearby. His gaze is piercing, following my every move like a hawk.

Hands on his narrow, muscular hips, he tilts his head left and right, lost in thought. "If I win, I get to touch you wherever I want."

I scoff. "That's not allowed. Wait, above the waist is allowed. So is kissing. Second date making out was confirmed as acceptable."

Macs smiles and rubs his hands together. "Fuck yes. Perfect. And if you make it through the course, you get to touch me. Above the waist and lips on lips," he amends, folding his hands together in front of his chest.

Would it bother someone like Charlotte if they shared nothing but a physical connection with a man? What if it's just lust—chemistry? Looking at Macs and watching him look at me, I'm confident it will never be more than that. How do you dichotomize a relationship enough to understand the percentages? Fifty percent things in common, thirty percent compatibility and finding the other interesting, ten percent attraction, ten percent... lust? What is the goddamn formula? Who makes up the rules? Why does this confuse me? I'm a well-educated woman, with smarts beyond the average person, and I've never been able to figure it out.

"This doesn't seem much of a bet," I tease, moving around Macs to climb the small ladder that leads up to the play structure. "Both of the outcomes give relatively the same reward," I explain. Jumping out, I hang on the bar he was just hanging from. My hips are eye level with Macs. He grins. I want his scrutiny as I have nothing to hide.

Out of my peripheral, I watch as he reaches a hand out to touch me and then lets it fall into a fist by his side.

"Give me a little more credit. I'm in the business of strategy. Everything in my life is purposeful, Tay-la," Macs says, growling my name.

With aching, heavy arms, I make my way across the monkey bars with ease. He follows right next to me, walking as quickly as I'm progressing. His presence makes everything below my belly button fire in suspense. The wobbly bridge is next, and this does not look to be built with grown-ups in mind.

He hops up behind me to splay his arms on either side of the metal poles. His chest is so near my back that I feel the heat radiating from his body. It warms me from the chill in the air.

"This bridge isn't holding two people," I say, exasperated.

"Then go," he says, leaning down to whisper into the crook of my neck by my ear.

I very purposefully left my cell phone in my car. I'm

completely in control right now, but at this rate I'm not sure how much longer I'll be able to stave off my desires. He's shirtless, oozing masculinity, and smelling of sweat. Every word spoken is a double entendre. Stealing a deep breath, I push away from his heat and cross the bridge.

After I get to the other side as quickly as possible to avoid breaking anything, might I add, I turn to see him swinging down to the ground. He motions for me to keep going. The monkey bars were the hardest obstacle of his pseudo course. I make light work of zigzag balance stones and climb down a rock wall. My sneakers sink into the sand, and I walk precariously to try and keep the fine white grit out of my shoes.

I'm one of those odd people who hate the beach because of the sand. A quick thirty-minute trip to the beach and you're cleaning sand out of your car for weeks to come. It lodges itself in places sand should never be. I think sand is an awful torture device when placed in a children's playground.

"Course completed," I call out, glancing at my watch. I glance left and right and can't find Macs. I stand in the light of the nearest streetlight. The picnic table he's set up nearby is empty but for the basket of food. I hear chattering on the other side of the park, so I walk around, doing my best to stay out of the sand. I shiver from the light breeze. Surely no one with kids is visiting the park at this time of night.

"You've got to be fucking kidding me," I murmur when I see my friends.

They're circling Macs like he's prey and they're the lions in a zoo exhibit.

Tossing my arms up in the air, I approach them. "Why are you here?" I ask, tromping over the grass to stand near them.

Macs smiles, flashing a devious grin at me, then turns it back to them.

Charlotte turns, and Jasmine and Carina continue staring at Macs, like he's some sort of anomaly they can't quite define.

I snap my fingers. "Hello? Is someone going to answer?"

Macs breaks through their circle of lust to stand in front of me. "You left your phone in the car," he explains. "They wanted to check in. Make sure you were okay."

What a bowl full of bullshit.

Irritated, I grit my teeth and take a few deep breaths through my nose. Macs must see my inner turmoil. He puts an arm around my waist and pulls me to him in one fluid gesture. As simple as it seems, my friends are all but forgotten the second I snake my hand around him and run my fingers along his bare skin.

Jasmine replies, "We shouldn't have come. But they didn't think you were actually going on a date."

Macs holds me a little tighter, pulling me into his side. "This is most definitely a date, ladies." He leans down and places a kiss on the top of my head. Who does he think he's kidding? My friends aren't going to believe I'm with a man who kisses me on the head, like a mother does to her child. It's too innocent. "Now that you're here, though…I'm sure I have enough if you'd like to join in our nighttime picnic."

"No," I say, completely defiant to that idea. "You guys need to trust me a little. I'm pissed. You need to go."

Carina looks down at the grass. Charlotte answers for them, telling me how they're merely concerned for my best interests. If these women hadn't been my friends for over a decade, I'd probably do something rash and stupid. As it stands, I'm going to give them the cold shoulder for at least a week. They tell Macs they don't want to interrupt our date and decline his generous picnic offer.

"I can't believe you're real," Charlotte says, looking at Macs, her eyes traveling the expanse of his chest and rippled abs. "I mean...that is rude. Sorry, but you're really...something."

I roll my eyes and groan in frustration.

I'm not even jealous. I expect him to receive this kind of attention and embrace it. It means he's top tier. Plus, he's not mine, anyway. Macs squeezes my side to get my attention. I swallow down my nerves and look skyward to meet his gaze.

"I'm nothing compared to this lady standing next to me. No one looks at me when she's by my side."

My stomach flips. Macs is putting on a show so flamboyant, I may burst into flames and die of embarrassment.

My friends squeal among themselves, like appropriate, professional adults. Macs leans down, wrapping his other hand around me to circle me in his arms. His skin is against me. I catch my breath a moment before he places a small kiss on the corner of my mouth. I forget to shut my eyes. I forget that my friends are gawking. I forget my own fucking name. He smells delicious. Seeing him this close is what my dreams are made of. His skin is just as flawless up close. He leans away, a glint of something in his narrowed eyes. Promise. That's what I'm seeing. I want it now.

He leans his forehead against mine.

"That was awful convincing," I whisper, my chest heaving more so now than when I did his obstacle course.

"Maybe I wasn't convincing anyone. Maybe I just wanted to taste you."

Macs doesn't take his eyes off mine as he speaks, and

it does things to my insides I can't describe. I'm hot and cold all at once. Warning bells are ringing loudly in my mind. The woman I am without him next to me isn't happy right now, and she's the intelligent one.

"I want more," I say, ignoring my inner thoughts.

He whispers in the ear my friends can't see. "As do I. I want to give you everything. All ten inches of my fat, hard cock. Inside you, filling you up, making you scream. I want to fuck you so good you'll never ask for *more* again in your life. I want you so badly it hurts." To drive the point home, he pulls me against his workout shorts. I feel all ten inches of stone-hard cock throbbing against my stomach.

I close my eyes and step away from his body. "And on that note." I sigh, glancing at my friends.

They're talking among themselves. I hear snippets now that I'm tuned into something other than Macs and his devilishly perfect body and mouth. A small, well-placed kiss has me on edge. Everyone is aware of it, too.

"If you're finished being children, Macs and I will go have dinner. Bring your concerned crew and go somewhere else. Don't you have anything better to do, anyway?" I swing my hands on my hips as I approach my frenemies.

"No one thought you were telling the truth," Jasmine explains. "We're sorry. No harm, no foul."

"I'm not a liar," I deadpan. "I get to decide if there's no harm, and I'm still debating. You guys are awful people sometimes. I. Am. Not. A. Liar."

She shakes her head. "You're not, but you are…" she says, tapping her chin. "You're…"

"A promiscuous woman," Macs replies, butting in from behind me, but he doesn't say it, he sings it.

Sighing, I turn to him. My friends laugh and continue

singing the rest of the song. I hold out my hands to stop the madness.

"I'll agree with that description. In all seriousness, what did you think was going to happen at the playground?" I wave my arm behind us. "When you saw we were here, you could have left. I'm not doing anything indecent in public. Not tonight, anyway." I smirk through my irritation.

Macs brushes my side with his hand as he passes by me and approaches my friends.

CHAPTER EIGHT

Macs

NOW THAT MY hard-on is gone for the moment, I make my way to sweet-talk her bitch-ass friends. They're ruining everything. Despite what Teala says, we *would* be fucking in the sand, at this playground, right at this moment, if they hadn't interrupted. The physical connection between us is palpable. It breathes on its own. It has a life force neither of us can deny. I'm unsure if it's because of the woman or the situation. I've never held back before or not given in to my desires.

It doesn't take much convincing to get rid of the cunt clan. I tell them she's in non-promiscuous hands and that after dinner my only intention is to walk her to her car and bid a good night with a harmless and rule-permitted kiss. They blush. They fall all over themselves. I flex my muscles and flash them *the smile*. It works because it always works. They disappear into the darkness of the parking lot amid laughter and high-pitched squeals. I turn, hands on my hips, to face Teala. Her anger permeates the air surrounding us.

"Your friends are sort of special, aren't they?" I ask.

She folds in on herself and sits on the grass in a small, tight mound. "They have the best intentions. I promise they aren't always so immature and annoying," she says, voice gruff, tired.

She seems oblivious to the fact that her friends are filled with sheer and violent envy. Not because of me, either. They want her life. Their looks poised and controlled, their words of encouragement laced with undercurrents of jealousy. And why wouldn't they? She has what most only dream about. Freedom and options unrestricted by a set of moral, outdated rules. For the first time, I view Teala as an equal. She defends her friends once more by telling me a story about how they saved her from a disastrous date. They came barreling in, kind of how they did tonight, but were so annoying they literally deterred her man-child of a date from getting a word in edgewise. He eventually apologized, because that's what most people do, and walked out of the restaurant with promises to call Teala later. He never called, but he did follow her back to her apartment and tried some ballsy, drunk bullshit. My skin prickles the moment she says it. People like that get punished. According to Teala, Jasmine's presence was the only thing that kept it from spiraling into something more distasteful.

I sit next to Teala, shuddering against the chill in the air now that sweat has dried on my bare chest. "You don't seem convinced of that," I admit, sighing. "Maybe they're just...jealous?"

She shakes her head. "I have to believe they have good intentions. It's the only logical reason people would act so illogically. I have major issues with commitment. It's not a secret. In that regard, they're accurate." Valid point. "Can we pretend to be *more* for a second?" she asks.

I clear my throat. "More what?" My pulse skitters in anticipation. Fight-or-flight response at the most base level. I'm not used to base level. It's odd that it feels the same as when I'm making life-or-death decisions.

I watch her neck work as she swallows. My gaze flits to her lips and mouth.

"You know, like people who care what the other person has to say? They take their words to heart and give advice."

I almost don't catch what she says because I'm envisioning my dick where her words are exiting.

Sighing. "I care what you have to say." Not really. Unless it involves words ordering me to take my pants off or to switch it up to reverse cowgirl. "By the same token, I'm not sure I'm the best person to issue advice. Especially to you. I can listen." I lean over and nudge her with a huge shoulder. Teala almost falls to the side.

With a smile, she nods, but still avoids eye contact. "I don't think I'll ever want a relationship, and I know how bad that is. Even playing along with this charade with you only makes me want you," she says, pausing. Finally, her gaze meets mine. "Makes me want you...chemically. Not forever. I don't think."

Pressing my lips together, I formulate the right words to respond with. Too brash, and I'll scare her away, and getting into her pants won't be an option. Too sentimental, and I'll give her the wrong idea about my own feelings on the subject. I scratch the side of my head and wrap my free arm around her. She's warm to my cool touch. I decide on the truth. "I'll never want a relationship either. There's nothing wrong with that. Or you. If there is, then I can give you a list of hundreds of women who suffer the same affliction," I reply.

Her eyes widen. "Hundreds? You've been with hundreds of women?" An unpleasant noise rolls up from her throat.

I laugh. Giving up the notches in my bedpost isn't

something I'll readily agree to. "Give or take." I tilt my head left and right, subtly, and then smile.

"That's more than me," she whispers, eyes unblinking.

It's reassuring to hear. No man wants to throw his hot dog down a bowling lane. "Everyone places values on different things. I place the higher tags on my career and bettering myself in that regard. Others value a family and their home lives," I explain.

She agrees. Something funny happens next—I begin telling her about my house and all of the projects I have going on. I tell her about the molding and how time-consuming everything ends up. How contractors are unreliable pieces of shit. She asks me if I'm a perfection-ist. I admit that I am. I give her a weakness. I hand it to her so easily. It's something that can be taken and used against me like a weapon.

We make our way over to the picnic table, and I serve her food. She hands me a drink. The uneasiness I feel abates. The casual conversation continues, but it's still full of things I don't usually offer. Facts. Truths about me and my life, and she speaks her truths about life and business. When I stop analyzing the situation, I find myself relaxed in her company.

I watch her take sips of her drink. I trace her profile as she glances toward a stray noise from the street next to us. Her face is perfectly proportioned. It matches her personality. Unlike some women I've been with, who, despite their best attempts, can't seem to line up who they are inside and outside. From the little I know about Teala, I have determined, despite what she says, she does, in fact, want a relationship even though she doesn't need one. Guilt is an emotion I don't feel readily or frequently, but something similar settles in the pit of my stomach.

She won't find it as long as I'm dallying with her with our sex games.

I'll have to be careful. "So, we need to do a spitfire round. You give me lots of facts so we can fool our parents and your friends," I say.

She turns, a huge smile pulling her lips open. I lick my lips. Every woman has a scent—an indescribable aroma apart from perfume and the flowery shit they coat themselves with. Teala's is sweet. I can tell from the small kiss I placed by her mouth. I swallow down a mouthful of saliva.

"We're boyfriend and girlfriend. We know things about each other. What would most people know after forty-eight hours?" My cell phone is in my car. The emptiness its absence causes makes me jumpy. I wanted this to seem like a proper date, but knowing this date will end without me getting it in forces me to twitch with need.

"I told you too many things on our horrible date. Remember?" Remembering it now makes it seem that much more awkward.

Nodding. "Other than being a Mr. Fix-it and a SEAL, there isn't much else. I don't have a favorite color. Or food. I like anything that tastes good. I broke my ankle when I was ten. I'm an only child. I never let women in my house."

"You told me about your house!" she exclaims.

My heart hammers.

"Does that make me special? Will I be granted access to keep up pretenses?"

I do my best to check my emotions. "Come on now, darling. Look at me. Are you special? You tell me. You'll pretend you've seen inside, though."

Her face falls. A scowl replaces her magnificent smile. "You don't have to be so rude."

Shit, that was rude. Tone down your asshole, I chide myself.

"Come on. It's a game. You have something no other woman has had from me before. My complete honesty. You want to go to Vegas, and I want in your pants." That's a truth. Right? I flex my fists, letting my fingertips trace the lines in my palm. "It's a four-bedroom. I can see a sliver of the ocean from my backyard. The sunset is pretty amazing. There's dust everywhere, and my bedroom is always neat. I drink a lot, but not too much. I handle stress by working out and fucking. Those are the only two releases in my life. If something in my life doesn't serve either of those things, I usually cut it out. I have a lot of friends, but we all have our own things going on."

Teala looks away. Her lips purse and her eyebrows draw in. "You're kind of horrible and beautiful. This isn't going to be easy, is it?" she asks.

"The only easy day was yesterday," I quip. Most people know the stereotyped phrases about SEALs. Immediately, I know she's heard this one before.

"Jerry fuckin' Seinfeld has entered the building. Good one." Teala rolls her eyes and leans back on the picnic bench seat. "Humor. Another thing to go into your positive column."

I care more about the negative column. I peek over to her side of the bench, and her eyes meet mine. "If your friends hadn't shown up tonight," I say, trying as a distraction.

"We'd probably be having sex right now," she says, finishing my thoughts. "Not that I'm opposed, but it is against the rules. You have this glamorizing effect, and yet you're a complete and total asshole. I get the draw. You're like the bucket list man. The unicorn you have to land before you settle down with *the one*. You know, the man with the steady job and the stable life? The nice guy." She sighs. "Maybe you're the guy."

I quirk a brow. "Tell me how you really feel. What guy?"

"The guy right before the one."

I pride myself on a lot of things. Never coming in second best is one of those things. In some twisted way she is referring to me as second best.

Standing, I round the table slowly, never taking my eyes off hers. "I'm not in the habit of letting people talk shit without punishing them." I crack my knuckles with my thumbs. "You don't want the one, remember?"

Tilting her head to the side, she urges me on using a look. I prowl, stalking forward until I can barely stand the snapping chemistry vibrating in the air between us. I straddle the bench so we're face-to-face, nose-to-nose.

"I'm no one's guy. You know what I am. There's little to wonder. There's no shady with a chance of drama." I pause for effect.

She breathes in, her eyes blinking slowly.

"I don't have any ex-girlfriends. I have a demanding work schedule."

I peck her lips with my own, letting them linger a second longer than warranted. She's too close. The scent of her perfume and skin is infiltrating my fortress—my reserve is faltering. A sigh escapes her lips.

"And the most mind-blowing sex you'll ever have," I growl. My breaths come faster now, the anticipation reaching a fever pitch.

"Somehow I don't doubt that," she whispers, her words exaggerated so her lips brush mine as she speaks.

My hands are gripping the sides of the wood so hard, I'm fearful I might get a splinter. I want to touch her, but then I won't be able to stop touching her. What makes her so desirable? In the want lies something that doesn't belong, something that typically isn't coupled with desire. I don't want to touch her because I know how it will end.

She'll disappear from my life forever. I'll never touch her again, and I'll want to touch her more than once. Merely looking into her eyes right now confirms that fact.

"Can I see your apartment?" I ask.

Teala's hands are inching closer to mine on the bench in front of us. "Is that a good idea?"

"If you know one thing about me, you should know that all of my ideas are good ones. Remember that." I pause. "I promise I won't fuck you." I waggle my eyebrows. "That's what you're worried about, right? No fucking. Even if that *is* always a good idea."

"When you put it so eloquently, then of course. A nightcap is probably in order anyway," she says.

I edge back to gain some breathing space. She follows my lead.

"This has to be the strangest date I've ever been on. Wait, non-date. Maybe a couple of nightcaps are in order."

"It is a date," I retort. I busy myself with gathering our things and walk slowly toward our cars. I can tell she's skeptical because she's dragging her feet, trying to formulate an excuse as to why I can't come over. "It's a date because I plan to kiss the ever-loving shit out of you tonight." *And then use all my willpower to not tear your panties off and fuck you against a wall.*

That changes her mind. She tucks her hair behind her ears and bites her bottom lip. She gives me directions and the code to her parking garage in case we get separated in traffic downtown. I throw a clean shirt on from my passenger seat. It's a quick drive, and something akin to butterflies invades my stomach as I park next to her vehicle. My cell phone is blowing up in the center console, so I peek at it to see the notifications. There are a few text messages from Tahoe, so I reply to those and ignore the rest. I have matches. Women whom I could be fucking in an hour or less.

Teala exits her car and smiles at me through my windshield. Her workout clothing leaves little to my imagination. I see every ripple of her abs and the swoop of her thighs as they glide to her knees. I swallow as I let my eyes wander up to the swell of her breasts, her long neck, and then wide, pink lips, straight nose, and cheekbones so beautiful my critical eye can't detect an imperfection. The women on my phone aren't Teala. They might look similar, but I want this one.

Carefully, I open my car door and call her over. She ambles over, eyes curious. With my right hand I grab some random change I have at the bottom of my cup holder. I despise change. I'm killing two birds with one stone. I jiggle the coins in my palm and stand to face her.

"Twenty-two cents," I explain, moving my hand down so she can see it.

She smiles. "Big baller."

I smirk back, making sure to use the smile. "It might as well be a million dollars. Give me your hand."

Teala raises one sculpted brow. "Okay?"

I dump two dimes and two pennies into her cool hand.

"If we lose this bet because of me, you get to keep that," I say. I figure this show might endear her to our cause and relieve some of the tension she feels at letting me into her world.

She jerks her chin to the side. "The stakes are so high. How will you ever keep your hands off me, big man?"

She takes my hand and leads me to the elevator. As

we ride up to her floor, she doesn't take her gaze off mine in the reflection of the mirrored walls. Her eyes flicker with mischief. I like it because it's a familiar look.

I also fucking hate it.

CHAPTER NINE
Teala

MY HEART IS HAMMERING in my chest. This is a normal occurrence. I've had many hot men in my apartment over the years. The problem is I called my mom on the way to my house, and she heard it in my voice. The excitement, the nerves, the anxiety. Leave it to a mother to alert you to the fact that you should be more nervous than you actually are. Macs is gazing out of the window, looking down at the traffic and people walking the streets. I'm on the eighth floor, and my view is awesome. It's why I purchased this apartment.

The exterior of my building still has the original swooping curves and gray gargoyles. There's a panel of glass that spans across my whole living room. Off to the right, you can see the bay in the distance, and to the left are the exquisite, bustling city views I've come to crave. I like to know I'm surrounded by people even if I'm mostly alone. My hand shakes as I measure a shot of bourbon into a lowball.

"On ice?" I ask, looking at him over my shoulder. My kitchen is open to the living area.

"Neat," he replies, spinning to make eye contact at the sound of my voice.

I shiver. I nod and hold out the glass for him and set it on the concrete counter. While the exterior is beautiful and original, the inside of my unit is modern and sleek. Cool tones with matte metal finishing touches, only punctuated by the colorful artwork I have dripping on every available wall. I stare down at the twenty-two cents on the counter and smile.

Stalking forward, he slides the glass toward his chest and then picks it up. "Thank you," he says. "You have quite the place here, Tay-la." He takes a sip and closes his eyes. "This is good. Real good."

Watching his lips starts an erotic movie reel in my mind. I close my own eyes, but for a different reason.

"I've been here forever. I love it. The views are perfect," I reply, turning quickly to the bar to make myself a drink.

The liquor bottles are lined neatly on a metal cart. I choose vodka and then excuse myself to change out of my workout clothing. Hesitantly, he agrees to let me leave the room. Because I'm sick in the head, I pray he follows me. He'll walk in when I'm naked, and he'll take me right then and there. I don't have to prove anything to anyone. My friends would never know the difference, and even if they did, I can more than afford my own way to Vegas.

I toss on a black maxi dress with a racerback. It shows off my shoulders and back muscles. If anyone can appreciate those, it's him. As I walk past my low, black dresser, I swipe my chapstick and glide it on. I pick up my vodka from the coaster and join Macs next to the window. I don't keep curtains or shades on my windows. I like the possibility of someone seeing me naked. Or fucking. Or just watching me when I least suspect it. Life is too boring.

Macs's scent permeates my living space. It's terrific.

Man musk, deodorant, and whatever cologne he wears. He coughs on a sip of his drink and cranes his neck when he hears me padding up behind him.

"Trying to sneak up on me?"

"Even I know I can't sneak up on a SEAL."

The smile drops from his face. What did I say? I've mentally noted not to bring up his profession again. That must be an issue for him.

"Unless you want me to sneak up on you?" I add on.

Eyeing me over the rim of his glass, he throws it back to finish in a large swallow. He makes a show of putting his empty glass down on the table next to the couch. "I like your dress," he says when he turns his attention back to me. With his hand still cool from the glass, he traces my bare shoulders with two fingers. "It shows how hard you work."

Exactly as I thought. "Thank you. It's sort of in my job description. You're a pretty hard worker yourself," I reply, placing my hand on his bicep.

Macs watches my hand on his arm.

"So, is this the part where you kiss the ever-loving shit out of me?" I ask, drinking the rest of my cocktail and setting my own glass next to his.

He's wearing a clean shirt, so I've surmised he must have changed in the car. He still has the goddamn workout shorts on. I bet a woman designed them. They're the kind that show a hard-on from six miles away. Macs has one. A big one. Kissing isn't going to help that problem. Well, him kissing me on the lips isn't going to fix that problem. Me kissing him somewhere else would fix it quite easily.

Quirking one brow, he runs a hand through his hair. "I could. Are you going to be a good host and show me the rest of your place first?"

Ah, hidden agendas. Yes.

I nod. "Well, you've seen my living room and kitchen." I wave my arm to the large room we're standing in.

He follows me down a hallway next to the kitchen.

"This is my spare room." I open the door to a teal and white fluffy wonderland. They're my mom's favorite colors. She stays here sometimes, so I decorated the room with her in mind.

Macs bites his lip, uninterested in anything except his main goal. "And your room?"

"For the record, I don't think you're supposed to be seeing my bedroom this early in the dating process." I close the door behind me and show him the guest bathroom. It's solid white, including the hand soap bottle, but for the large artwork above the toilet.

"Also for the record, if we aren't fucking in your bedroom, I don't think it matters what room I'm seeing." He nods at the artwork. "Sloths?" he asks with a smile.

I laugh as the uncomfortable sensation takes over my stomach. No one understands my obsession. Charlotte got me this picture last Christmas. It's probably my favorite.

"You did say they were your favorites," he amends, remembering one of our first conversations.

"Listen. Do something for me. Look at it," I command.

He does, a small smile appearing on his lips.

"See? You can't help but smile when you see a sloth. It's like a happy pill. There's something about the fur, the lumbering limbs, and sleepy faces. Nothing about them makes you upset." Some people have Zen. I have sloths and a yoga studio.

I tug him out of the room, but not before I see his smile stretch a little further. Sloths. Gets them every time. "And this is my bedroom." It's black and gold. Like, shockingly black and gold. "I'm a sucker for a good theme," I explain. The dark bed frame matches my black duvet and the furry pillows perfectly. "Before you ask, no, I'm not a vampire." I tug the corner of my lip while I wait for his appraisal.

Spinning toward me, he quirks a brow. "Do you sparkle?" It's an innocent, funny question, but it doesn't match the feral look in his eyes as he goes back to surveying my bed. "I could make you sparkle," he says, without looking at me.

"I've never been propositioned with that before," I reply.

Macs prowls around my room, touching the surface of my dresser and the tall poster of my bed as he makes his way toward the window that looks out into the office building across the street. I trace the outline of my thumbnail with my ring finger. My nerves are at an all-time high, watching him in my space. He takes up so much room.

"Great views in here too," I say nervously. I do have heavy black-and-gold striped drapes that cover this window. They're open now, the soft glow of the city night flooding my bedroom, casting busy shadows on the black wooden floorboards.

He turns, leaning his back on the thick glass as he does. He slides his hands into the pockets of his shorts, and he visibly adjusts his dick from one side to the other. "I'd have to agree about that view," he says, gaze zeroed in on me.

He lifts his shoulders off the glass and leans back on it again, as if he's testing it for durability. It's durable. A man once railed me so hard against it I was afraid it would break. The building orgasm was so intense, I didn't even stop him. Death by orgasm. It describes everything that's wrong with my life in one sexual escapade.

With one shaking hand, I grab the poster of my bed. "It's sort of grandiose and stunning."

He grins. I bite my cheek.

"People would kill for the view."

"Yeah?" he asks. "But everyone isn't granted that opportunity, are they? To kill for something they want?"

He's a tease in the best kind of way. I'm so wet he could go swimming in my vagina and get lost in the current. His muscles flex and bunch as he talks, and he doesn't even realize he's doing it. He's so cocky. He's an asshole. A mean guy. The definition of sex encapsulated in a package so divine I can't control myself while he's in my proximity. No woman can. That's why he is the way he is. Women are to blame for this. And I still want him.

"They aren't granted opportunity. It's an exclusive building," I reply. I can keep this charade up as long as he can. It's distracting me from the fact a perfectly comfortable bed resides mere feet away from this man's body.

Leaning up, he tucks his chin to his chest. He crosses to me in two large steps. "The thing with me is I'm privy to all exclusive things. People don't tell me no. Ever."

"Women don't tell you no, you mean?" I amend his obviously untrue statement.

He shakes his head, puts his forefinger under my chin, and lifts my head to look up at him. "Sweetheart, you won't tell me no. I can have you any which way I want."

He could. I lose my breath looking at his face. The darkness enhances his perfect features. Shadows cut across the planes of his masculine physique.

"You couldn't." I hear my own lie. So does he.

He grins. "Yeah?"

"Yeah," I reply, tone breathy.

He leans down. His breath is warm and it makes me delirious with lust. I'm about to combust. I can't take it anymore. My body calls out to his. Goose bumps rise on my skin the second a shiver racks my body. My nipples are tiny peaks of excitement. They're straining against the fabric of my dress. I'm asking to be fucked tonight, and I'm surprised he hasn't called me on it yet. He's not a gentleman. Grabbing the back of his neck, I bring my mouth up to meet with his. I catch a glimpse of his fucking smirk a second before I kiss the ever-loving shit out him. He pulls my body to him so I can finally feel the steel-hard erection against my stomach.

It's heaven. It's hell. His kiss is poison and pleasure wrapped into one. I know it's a mistake, and I want to make it. I want every single inch of this mistake. His tongue snakes in my mouth as he tilts my head back by a quick tug of my hair. The rough gesture makes me moan out. I don't like a man taking control of my body by using another body part. It takes away from the moment. Usually. Nothing is usual or normal about Macs and his lips and this kiss.

You know the rush of adrenaline that comes when you're doing something scary or new, or something you merely know damn well is wrong? It's whirring in my bones so profusely that my head is swimming. He's picked me up, the black stretchy cotton high on my hips, and my legs are wrapped around his waist. It only takes a few moments before he's walking me back to the fucking window. *The fucking window.* That's what I'll call it. He's holding me up using one arm. The other one is busy fondling my breast. I arch my back because more than anything I want his mouth sucking on my nipple while his cock dives deep inside my body. The warmth of his large hands melts through the fabric and sends tingles spreading throughout my belly and neck.

More. *More*. It's the solitary word traveling through my mind. If I weren't wearing a thong, I'd be sliding him inside me. Macs halts his lips on my mouth and travels down to my neck. I hear him groan as he drives his hard cock into me, wishing we weren't wearing any clothing. He's wild. Out of control, only wanting one thing. *He wants to take.*

I want to give. He raises my weight with ease and yanks my dress down so one breast breaks free.

"Fucking perfect," he mutters.

He looks at it for a second or two, just breathing heavily, almost like he's forgotten that body part is attached to a live human, and then he takes my nipple between his teeth. I grind myself against him while the coolness of the window presses against my back. I hear the traffic below us, a honk of a car horn punctuated by the wet laps of his lips sliding around on my skin.

I'm almost there. My thighs tingle, and the ball of pleasure is right at the cusp of spiraling out of control. I'm about to have a dry fucking orgasm. I've never been this worked up without penetration or oral sex before in my life. I know it's this insane crackling chemistry between us. He feels it too. I sense it in every harried, frenzied touch. Every time his lips glide over mine, in every sound or begged plea of release. What does it mean? I don't ponder long because his lips are back on my mouth, teeth clashing, moans synching in a ballad of ecstasy. My core clenches one final time before I cry out, eyes closed, orgasm tilting the room sideways, my arms wrapped around his chiseled neck tightly. I inhale the scent of the perfect male specimen while I come apart in the cradle of his arms.

Macs places his lips right below my ear. He doesn't

kiss. He merely leaves them there, letting the wetness and his presence in the moment be known. "I can do whatever I want to you, can't I?" he asks. His words ricochet to my core.

Breathing heavy, I wait to come down from the high, but it's not happening. Not while his dick is pressing against me. Not with his sweaty skin so close and his words laced with so much promise for more.

"Can't I?" he says again. "I wanted to hear you come. I wanted to see you come. I wanted to kiss you until you came. I do what I want." Macs keeps his lips against my neck as he speaks.

"Yes. You can do whatever the fuck you want as long as you give me orgasms like that."

His throaty chuckle rumbles against my chest. "You aren't filtered when you're satisfied. Noted."

I shiver at his words. "You're not filtered when you have blue balls, are you?"

He lets me slide down his body, sinfully, slowly, his hooded eyes concentrating on my face. My eyelids flutter closed as the rippling wall of his muscles slides against my body. I watch his face. He doesn't respond, but I can see he wants to say something. His mouth is already open as he pants out long, drawn-out breaths of longing.

"I don't know," he whispers. "I've never had blue balls before." He smiles.

It's all teeth and seduction. In the same breath, he drops me and backs away, his hands balled in fists by his sides. When he reaches my bed, he bends over and places his palms flat on the mattress and lowers his head.

"Kissing's over?" I ask. I've nearly caught my breath, but everything else is on fire. "I can help you with the problem, you know. There's no need to be scared." I giggle. It sounds so petulant given the type of man in my bedroom, but I can't do anything to stop it. He causes me to giggle, and I think I hate that fact. I can't be sure.

My stomach flips when he turns his focus back to me.

"I have twenty-two cents riding on this. I can't be sure, but I think what you did against that window probably doesn't count as just kissing. I know for a fact you helping my aching stomach and balls is off-limits. Second date, remember? I want to fuck you. No amount of time with your mouth spent on my cock is going to fix the problem," he says. He runs the palm of his hand down his erection and cringes a little. "Fucking you is the only thing that will put this thing to bed. Do you understand?"

"You're underestimating my blow jobs, Macs. Just saying," I reply, pushing my lips to one side. He is well and truly underestimating me. "Three minutes tops."

His eyes widen as he interlocks his hands over his head, and I can't help but look at his shorts and the huge, hard cock that lies just below the surface. I want to drown in his naked body like cum in a bukkake porno. My heart races along in anticipation even though the words coming out of his mouth make perfect sense. My friends don't matter right now. Neither does Vegas, or the bet, or even my goddamn self-worth.

"I want you," I say.

I step in his direction, but he moves away briskly. It's like a game of cat and mouse. His grin transforms into a laugh as he walks backward out of my room and into the living area. I follow him.

"You may have escaped my dungeon, but you'll be back." They always want back. Even men like Macs.

"That's a promise," he says.

I lick my lips. "Another drink then?"

He's already shaking his head before the full question leaves my lips.

"Water? An ice pack? Something for the pain?"

He flops down on the white linen sofa. I try not to make a face. It's not really a sofa for sitting. More for admiring. It took me several weeks to locate the throw that's perfectly draping over the left arm. I saw it on Pinterest and located it using reverse image searches and a lot of phone calls to random home décor stores. Macs leans down and puts his head on it.

I sit on the opposite end, the one where there aren't any expensive, clean blankets, and drop his bare feet on my lap. "Okay, what next then?" I ask.

"Give me a few. I'm still trying to erase the image of you writhing against me while moaning from my mind."

I bite my lip as my core clenches again. Tightly this time. It wants sex. Macs's sex. "After you do the impossible, what then?"

My cell phone buzzes on the countertop. He turns his head. I'm not sure if he's wondering if it's his or if the sight of my cell phone reminds him of something, but he stands up. Pacing back to the window, he looks down again. I fluff the blanket and go to stand next to him.

"I should go," he whispers. When he looks at me, his face is changed. It's weird having him here and not naked in my bedroom, so it's hard for me to not agree.

I nudge him from the side. "We're doing such a good job, though."

He laughs. It's a joke. We're seconds from having sex on every surface in my house.

"I understand if you want to take off."

He needs to get off.

He tells me he has a work trip and probably won't see me for a while. I try, and probably fail, to hide my disappointment. I tell him I'm busy at the studio anyway. He gets nervous, turning his head as if to stretch his neck.

"Spit it out," I prompt him.

"So we," he says, motioning between our bodies, "we're exclusive?" He grimaces, and it's over exaggerated, so it clues me into a couple of things. He's uncomfortable asking, so he's using humor, and he's also testing the waters with regard to our fake dating deal. It seems less fake every second we're together. There's no way I'd tell him that.

"You're not banging dudes?"

I raise one brow and suck in a long breath. "You're not banging chicks?"

He turns away. My cell buzzes on the counter again. It draws his attention immediately. I know why.

"You can do whatever you want to do, Macs. I'm not your girlfriend. Or your mom. Just go."

He smiles. It hurts my stomach. It's what he wants to hear. "You're my dream come true, you know that?" he exclaims.

The pain in my stomach turns solid and sinks even further. I can't and won't go on any dates with anyone else. Crossing my legs at the ankle, I try to squelch the desire coursing through every nerve ending. "Yeah, yeah. I get that a lot. So, next date?"

Macs senses the change. He turns my face using one finger on my chin. He can't see disappointment. I won't let him. The shield is confidently in place.

"Third base date?" He studies my face, ostensibly looking for any sort of deceit. He won't find it.

"You won't leave with blue balls?" I try a joke.

He laughs, but his smile doesn't reach his eyes. He holds my chin in his hand, like I'm a petulant, disobedient child.

Instead of saying something meant to reassure me, he leans down and kisses me, his tongue diving in my mouth. He's careful to keep his body away from mine. It's just a kiss. Something I can't say I've ever had. A kiss with desire and moans, one that doesn't lead to anything else. No blow jobs or finger banging, just a meeting of mouths because we both enjoy the way it feels. I think, anyway. I can't get a true read of him. Both of his hands are on either side of my face. He holds me reverently, gently.

He pulls away and looks at me through eyes that aren't hiding anything for the moment. My kiss has disarmed him, if only for a second or two. He's just as intrigued by our chemistry as I am. "I'm not going to be with any other women, Tay-la," he growls.

"Oh," I say.

It doesn't make any sense. Men don't look one way and then act another. They always behave in a predictable way. Men like Macs take what they want from whoever they please.

"I don't want to have sex with anyone else. Just to clear that up," I explain.

"You don't say?" He smiles.

I roll my eyes. "You're so cocky. I should, just to spite you."

Shaking his head, he says, "Never do anything to spite me. That would mean I care, and I don't. I'm not doing anything to ruin our science experiment. Now I'm curious as to how this will play out." The smile fades from his face. He doesn't like the idea of me having sex with another man. It's something, I guess.

"I'm not a science experiment," I deadpan.

He backs away from me, toward my large, ornate front door. "I don't fuck experiments, babe." He's not fucking anything tonight. Or, according to him, he's not. I'm not sure I believe him. "And I'm definitely fucking you. Your body is going to haunt my damn dreams," he says, very obviously running his eyes up and down my body. A jolt of energy spikes in my system, like electricity taking the place of blood in my veins. "Not tonight. Call your friends back and tell them about the first kiss with a side of orgasm."

I can almost feel his tongue on my neck from remembering it. I shiver. He watches. Forgetting his keys on my counter, he leans forward to grab them. I notice he glances at my phone.

Placing my hands on my hips, I say, "I'll walk you out."

Clutching his keys, he chuckles. "No, you won't. Not unless you want to fuck in my back seat?" Macs tilts his head to the side in the direction of his car. When I don't respond, he says, "Thought so. Good night. I'd kiss you, but I can't."

My heart skips along this furious pace I'm not familiar with. I get a little lightheaded. It has to be lust. I need to have sex or engage in a long date with my vibrator. He flashes his dimples, and he's out of my door and heading down the hallway to the elevator. One of my neighbors is unlocking her door, her little barky dog in her arms. She gapes as Macs walks by, and as if I'm a second thought, she turns her huge brown eyes my way. I wave my hand and then put a finger under my chin and bring my lower jaw up to meet the top with a click of teeth. She scurries into her apartment with an embarrassed scowl on her face. I laugh but can't tear my gaze from his retreating back.

The way you move says a lot about a person. I see it in yoga, through the poses and the fluidity of movement. I can decipher their skill level, determine things about their personalities. The way Macs moves is something else entirely. Something predatory lies in the depths of his stride. It drips with confidence and danger. He has a sway in his walk, his muscles preventing him from looking ordinary, even though he's not even trying for extraordinary. It's something that comes naturally to him. He doesn't look back before he gets on the elevator.

Not even a quick backward glance in my direction. I hear my heartbeat in my ears, a cacophony reminding me I'm in dangerous territory, and feel the wetness between my legs. He doesn't just walk like a predator. He is the goddamn king of those motherfuckers.

CHAPTER TEN

Macs

THE ELEVATOR DOORS CLOSE, and I take a huge, deep breath. *Fuck. Fuck. Fuck.* Walking away from her was the hardest thing I've done in a while. My dick is rock-hard and dripping in anticipation. I don't think that fucker has been this drooly in his entire life. I couldn't think straight with her in front of me. I know it's because I need to fuck. It had nothing to do with her personally. I'm sure of it.

I'm sure of it.

Her neighbor was hot. I could easily get in her pants. What if Teala heard? Why do I care if Teala heard? I rush out of her small lobby and make a right-hand turn to exit into the parking garage. I'm still catching my breath when I slam my car door and start the engine. It's like I just did the obstacle course. I feel crazy. Out of control. My phone is still glowing in the cup holder, the messages pouring out of it like my favorite song. I turn up my music to drown out everything else. My head is too full right now. My cock is too full right now. It should be considered a dangerous weapon.

I told her I wouldn't sleep with other women. I thought it was a lie when I said it, but now I'm not so

98

sure. It's as if a part of me, the good part of me, spoke, and now I have to obey him because my pride won't let me lie. I'm good at my core. It's everything else that's fucked up. I need sex. It's akin to denying me oxygen. Surely she wouldn't fault me if I picked up my phone and hooked up with one woman tonight. She knows what she did to me. What did John call Jessica? Sexual Napalm? Yes, that. Teala is that to me. It is partly because I can't have her whole body up front, but also partly because of something else.

I like her.

I like her personality. She's funny. I find myself enjoying her company the most when we're just talking. I liked telling her things about myself. I like kissing her. I like the way she smells. I like the way her body presses against me. I lift the neck of my shirt and take in a breath. It smells like her. It's sweet. It's sex. It's forbidden. I slam my steering wheel with the palm of my hand with a groan. "Fuck!"

My voice is loud and angry even though it's not anger I feel. It's something I don't recognize. My phone chimes, and I'm so irritated that I look at it. As I suspect, they are messages from my app. Women who could fix me right now if I let them. I scroll through the messages, and one pops up while I'm scrolling. It's a text message from Teala—a photo.

I click it open. It's the sloth photo in her bathroom, no message attached. I laugh. How stupid and asinine. I take a deep breath. I don't reply, but I'm not so frustrated anymore, and the sloth made my hard-on recede a touch. It's enough. I put my car into gear and drive home.

I think about Teala all the way home, our kisses on replay in my mind. I'm dissecting every move and every word spoken between us. Does it help decipher what is happening between us? Not one bit. I'm not certain there's anything there but pent-up lust and the promise of mind-blowing sex. Also, I'm not sure what compels me, but when I pull into my drive, I ignore all the notifications from my matches and head into my phone settings to change my background to that stupid fucking sloth.

I can't look at it without smiling. She's right.

Repacking a parachute after it safely guides you to land from twelve thousand feet is the bane of my existence. It doesn't matter how good you are at repacking, it still takes fucking forever. You have to do it right, perfectly, or you'll die on your next jump. Perhaps that sounds a tad melodramatic, but it is truthful all the same. Tahoe is in the space next to me, rolling and packing with extreme precision. A lot of times we have people do this for us, but not today. Everyone is busy doing other shit.

The drop zone is a large open field with a few ratty structures and an airfield for takeoff and landing. Airplanes buzz overhead and parachutes litter the sky above the drop zone. My team goes up in waves. Today we're doing HALO jumps, high altitude, low opening. It's just an average day at the office. I have my phone silenced so it doesn't interrupt me at inopportune times. After I finish packing my chute, I take out my phone to check the time and see I missed a call from my mom. She left a voicemail. She's in the generation of answering machines, so she always leaves a godforsaken message even though my voicemail greeting says, "Are you sure you can't text me?"

My stomach grumbles, reminding me I haven't had

lunch. I walk to the trailer in the corner to find my cooler of food and listen to my mother's voice as I go.

"Sweetie, are you okay? The news is saying awful things. Have you watched it? I know you're busy, but you really should turn on the television every once in a while. That's silly, though. I'm sure you know what's going on. What's that?" she asks someone in the room. My father. "Your father wants you to call him tonight. He has a theory."

Raising my brows, I let out a long, annoyed breath. I love talking to my parents mostly, but my dad has some real theories about the state of our world. Let's just put them into the conspiracy category for lack of a better word.

I sit down at a tattered table in the corner and nod at a teammate named Mason. He grins at me and tosses an obscene gesture my way. I'd send one back if I wasn't listening to my mother prattle on about the terror attacks happening.

"Okay, Gem," she says, because I'm the crown jewel. "I'll let you get back to work now. Call us later. We miss you. Are you coming home for a visit soon? We'd love to see you. Please be safe," she says.

My father's beard scruff rubs against the phone, and then his voice says, "I love you, son. Kick some ass. Come home soon, though, okay?"

It takes a lot to make me feel guilt. They just had a full-on, one-sided conversation, and guilt is all I feel. I'll have to go home soon to visit them. Especially before I deploy. I'm not so naïve as to assume it won't be the last time. My job is one of the most dangerous in the world. Imminent danger is evident in every facet of my life. Take today, for example. I'm jumping out of airplanes over and over. The odds will stack against me one of these days.

I compare it to cats. How many lives do they have? Nine? How many life-sucking hobbies and adventures can one person practice before they catch up to their given amount of allotted lives? You can never anticipate how you'll go down. Personally, I hope I go down in a blaze of fire and glory, doing something to help my country. Most people want to fall asleep peacefully and never wake up. Not me. I want to know I'm alive when I go. I want to feel every nerve ending as they click off for the final time. I want to feel it all.

My morbid thoughts are broken when Mason throws a wadded-up napkin. "Where are you at right now?" he asks.

My sub sandwich is half gone. My friends know not to fuck with me when I'm eating. It's a sacred time of day. I love food.

"Fuck off, Mason. I'm trying to eat a peaceful lunch."

"Chute packing got your panties in a bunch? You prima donna," he says.

He's wearing the smirk that lets me know he's trying to bait me. It's no secret that I'm different than my friends. Where they could give two shits about their clothing, hair, or their appearance, I'm in the opposite camp.

I once told a group of them that I pay forty dollars for my haircut every three and half weeks. Combine that with my collection of designer T-shirts, and it was a recipe for a slew of nicknames. If I have to wear T-shirts, why shouldn't they feel soft and nice against my skin? Most men don't care about stuff like that. I get it. It doesn't change me, though. My money is copious because I don't have a family. All of my bonuses are saved for the most part or are poured, like water, into my house.

"I like nice things," I say, shrugging and chucking the napkin back at his head. It's a direct hit. "Just because you're fine wearing Batman boxer shorts doesn't mean that you should. Standards, fucker. Get some." I'm joking, but I see the competitive glint in his eye. We're all type A personalities. It's a constant battle to best each other. At work and at home. If you can drink five beers and act rationally, I can drink six. Target practice is a pissing match. How hot our chicks are, too. Though that's mostly an unspoken rule if we're talking about wives.

Chicks and fucking are fair game in discussions so long as they're only girlfriends or sidepieces. The second they turn into wives, you forget they have a vagina. It's odd because you know sordid details about Mold-A-Dildo kits and fingers in asses and what sounds they make while they have orgasms, but when your buddy marries that same hot girlfriend, you are supposed to forget it all.

Mason changes the subject to our next jump, and I listen to him prattle on and nod in appropriate places, and because I'm still eating, he doesn't expect me to respond verbally. My phone flashes a text message. It's another photo from Teala. Of some green fucking plant in the lobby of her yoga studio. Where are the tit pics? She doesn't send me actual text messages very frequently. It's usually photos without captions. I turned off all the notifications for my fucking apps. Deletion wasn't an option. Not yet. I'm not ready. And what happens after I fuck Teala and return to my old carousing ways? I don't have time to reinstate my profiles. It's freed me in a way I didn't know I craved. The tether to my phone disappeared.

I'm not sure what she expects me to reply with. I'm staring at the photo when Mason makes his way to my table. I'm finished eating.

"Who are you swiping at?" he asks.

No one has noticed I'm not my normal self. I've realized I wanted this challenge. Needed it, even. It's not about Teala even if it seems that way. It's about determining how much control I actually have over my body and emotions. I control things. Nothing else does. Not even my dick. I snap a photo of the trash from my lunch in front of me and send it to her. If she wants a game of random, I'll give her that.

"Ahh, you know, just the usual," I reply.

Mason scrunches up his face.

"What the fuck are you doing? Did you just take a picture of the water bottle?"

This is where I could come clean, but Mason has a big mouth, and everyone will know within hours that I'm not swiping any pussy on this trip, and it will be more of a spectacle than I want. Typically, I've got at least three chicks waiting in whatever city we're traveling to. It's a game. See how much of a whore Macs can be. My need for sex almost affected a start time once, and I got in trouble. Not real trouble, but it was enough to force a chick cap. I meet Mason's eyes.

"Texting my friend. How's your girlfriend?"

A trick everyone should know. People love to talk about themselves. They prefer it to almost any other sort of conversation. Even if it's bitching about their horrible lives, it still means more than if I was talking about my awesome life. He takes the bait.

"I broke up with her. It got stale."

Picking up my trash, I wad it using one hand. "Too many missionary trips?"

He shrugs. "She was awful at head, too."

I nod like I know exactly what he's talking about.

"Joining the dark side now?"

Mason squirms. "No one is as dark as you." Little does he know. "It's hard to find anything stable with all the trips. It's okay, though. Being single works right now anyway. Maybe after deployment."

I agree with him and tell him it's a great idea. I tell him about a few of the apps I use, and he seems interested, if only for the reason to switch the conversation back to me and my life.

"Hey, I gotta get back at it. I want to get on the next lift," I say, hiking my thumb at the door. I palm my phone when Teala texts back and slide it into my pocket. My dirty little secret isn't so dirty.

He's looking at his own phone, searching the app store for the ones I just mentioned. Mason is a good guy. I wonder if I can turn him into a baby me. The thought makes me smile and cringe. Giddy with power, but sorry for the corruption.

Mason mumbles his goodbye, and I amble out the door into the cool breeze. I take the phone out of my pocket to find a photo of her bare foot against a solid, dark, wooden floor. Just one foot, and I wonder where the other foot is. Is it in some yoga pose pulled over her head? What position is that? Could I fuck her in that pose? My mind wanders away from me for a second, and I tamp down on my testosterone coursing straight to my dick.

Her toenails are light blue, like an Easter egg. I think it's an unusual color choice for nails. Red and pink are what I'm used to. One of my favorite sights is of pretty pink nails on fingers wrapped around my cock. Yes, that's a sight I like, one I'm accustomed to. I resist the urge to ask if her fingernails are blue and send a photo of Tahoe floating to the ground in the distance, his large, lumbering legs dangling like useless strings. She won't be able to recognize him, nor has she even met Tahoe before. That's a meeting I'll avoid at all costs.

That is amazing! You must love that. What do you love? Give me a list, is the text message Teala sends back.

Ah, something worthy of her words. A few moments later, Tahoe lands safely. Landings are always sketchy depending on the winds. Knees get blown pretty easily. We're big men, and unless conditions are for us, landings are against us. I watch as he unhooks his chute and bends down to start retrieving the nylon fabric that spreads across the ground around him.

Your foot was so beautiful. I wasn't sure what could compete with it, I reply back to her quickly.

The gray bubble pops up instantly. She's into our conversation, or she's bored, perhaps in between classes or already off for the day. She told me her schedule, but I've already forgotten it.

I wouldn't be disappointed if you wanted to send me photos of other body parts. I send it before I think twice.

My heart hammers, but I try to distract myself by watching landings as I type out a list of the things in life worthy of my love. There are a lot. It's not as if boobs and pussies aren't something I typically get in messages, but they aren't from people I've met before. They're strangers I'll meet up with later. This is somehow different. Everything about Teala and me is different. The gray bubble disappears, and her message comes through. A photo of her hand. Red nails. I laugh, and then another message.

Your list is longer than War and Peace. I just rattled off the first things I could think of. I pocket my phone.

Making my way to the plane, I pick up my chutes— the main and the backup. With a stomach bordering on too full, I get on the small aircraft and ready myself to deal with nerves. Believe it or not, the worst part of skydiving is the ride in the plane. They pack us in too tightly. What if someone bumps my gear in a way that makes it defective? The smell of fucking farts is also foul and nerve-racking. Ascension causes gases in the body to exit. I still curse out Moose and scowl at the shit-eating, or better yet, shit-stinking grin on his face. There are two benches lining each side of this metal tube of death. Lights that the pilot turns on let us know when it's time to start falling out into the sky. I stare at the red light above the hatch with disdain and will it to turn green.

My heart thumps a little jaggedly, and I have more adrenaline in this moment than I will when they finally let me out into the vacant atmosphere, plummeting toward the ground. Because I control that. It's all on me. I'm not relying on pilots or worried about the dickhole sitting behind me accidentally screwing with something. I play well with others when it's in my best interest.

I stare at the red light while I let my mind fill with everything that needs to happen next. Plan A and then plan B and everything after that and in between. It's mostly autopilot at this point in my career. I've skydived hundreds upon hundreds of times. I've jumped out of an airplane at night when it's pitch-dark, when it's raining, when we're so high we have to wear oxygen, and it almost feels like we're in outer space. Someone lets a fart rip, and it's so loud I hear it over the goddamn roar of the engine.

The light turns green. Just in time. I was about to add another name to my hit list. The hatch is opened, and the sound of the wind overtakes the small space. I stand immediately, holding on to the bars overhead. Sweat beads on my forehead as I watch a few of my teammates exit the plane. They drop like rocks the second they leave the hatch. We only have a certain amount of time, and it's with precise accuracy that everything is measured. A few moments later I'm freefalling, finally able to take a deep breath. I have my altimeter on my right wrist, and I glance at it every few seconds so the ground doesn't creep up too quickly.

The world looks round up here. If Christopher Columbus had this view, there would be no doubt the earth is just one spinning dome. The sky is the place where I feel smallest. There's no way I can change anything significant in something so large. I'm a fleck. A minuscule thread woven into a tapestry so vast you can't even tell what the pattern is. My altimeter says I'm at three thousand feet, so I pull the ball on the right side of my parachute strapped to my back. I look up and over my shoulder to make sure it's deploying properly and grab onto the handles as they rise over my head.

I see my friends who jumped out before and after, everyone a perfect distance away, forming an octagon of sorts. I steer, pulling one handle and then the other to close a gap. Under parachute is the longest part of a jump. After falling at what feels like warp speed, cruising to my landing seems to be at a snail's pace. Studying my surroundings and the tiny buildings on the ground, I find my way to the landing zone. Minutes pass, as does the agonizing thump as I hit the rough grassy patch of field.

I look at my left wrist and calculate the time. *I did it.*

I went a whole thirty-six minutes without thinking about Teala. I snap a photo of my parachute behind me and send it off without another word.

I did it. Why does this make me so happy? I start cutting away so I can drag my rig over to begin the packing once again. She doesn't respond right away, but when she does, it simply says, *Take me next time.*

I raise my brows. That definitely has potential for a date. "Why do I care about a date?" I chastise myself under my breath.

Tahoe grunts from behind me. A place I didn't realize he was. "You're acting like a straight fool today, man.

What's going on?" His voice is cavalier. He doesn't really care, he's just asking because he's my friend. That's the way it is with dudes.

"I hate this shit," I mutter. I turn to glance his way, and he nods, his piercing blue eyes assessing. He'll think I mean packing my chute.

He grunts again. "Leave your phone in the car. You're a little bitch with it today. Checking it constantly. What's the problem? Is the pussy well dry here?"

I could lie. He wouldn't have a clue if I was being truthful. I think back to the voicemail. "Nah. Family issues," I reply, doing my best to avoid his acid gaze.

"What's wrong with Shirley and Robert?" he asks. "They doing okay?"

I should have known better. I'm digging a deeper hole. SEALs pride themselves on honor, and I adhere to that ethos. I'm shit at deceit.

I nod. "They're fine. Ma wants me to go for a visit. I'm trying to hash out the details. We've got a lot going on the next few weeks." All truths.

He spits, a huge, brown, hued pile behind him. "You're a cagey motherfucker. It has to do with a chick. Check that shit, bro. Check it," Tahoe says.

I could argue, but I want his help this weekend. And his tools.

I sigh. "Don't spit that nasty shit near me," I snap back. A lot of the guys dip or chew. I find it repulsive. I tried it a time or two when I had to. You'd be surprised at the things SEALs have to do to blend in. The long-ass beards and mustaches while deployed are just the tip of the iceberg, what we want you to associate with us. I can be another person entirely. That's true for me more than other guys. Because I do care about clothing and my hair and vain things most don't think twice about. I can also go without showering for weeks while rotating two outfits that stay filled with sand, dirt, and sweat.

Tahoe laughs, spits again, farther away this time, and shakes his head. He knows. I'm failing at keeping Teala and our arrangement hidden, and it pisses me off. My skin prickles with heat as my hands work. I won't look at my phone again today. Maybe not even tomorrow either.

I decide I'm done for the day and check the fuck out. I head back to my hotel, a five-star resort that carries Pappy at the penthouse bar. I dial my mom as I drive the shitty rental car down the long road. When she answers, I put her on Bluetooth. I tell her I'll be home for a visit the following weekend. She's so joyful and her voice is so soothing that I go a step further. "I'm going to bring someone home I want you to meet," I say. I don't think I've heard her that happy in a long time.

She squeals, screams the news to my father, and then tells me she has to go so she can prepare. What she really means is she needs to go so she can call all her friends and spread the good news faster than burning chlamydia. Teala will agree. She has to.

What's that saying? It's easier to ask for forgiveness than it is to ask permission?

I hang up the phone and concentrate on the road. It's not until I get back to the hotel parking garage that I realize I haven't stopped smiling.

CHAPTER ELEVEN
Teala

I'M DRIPPING SWEAT, pacing the lobby of the studio, a watering can in the shape of a flamingo in one hand and a spray bottle in the other. I love my plants. I keep them alive. I'm not an animal person yet. Give me a complicated houseplant, and I'll crush that shit every single time. I spray one large flowering plant and water the soil of the one next to it.

Charlotte rushes in and halts when she sees my appearance. "I knew where I was picking you up from, but I didn't think you'd be fresh from a class, Teala," she scolds.

I look down and shrug. It'll dry fast.

I stow my watering items once I splash the orchid on a low shelf. "I'll throw on my sweater and I'll be good. It's lunch. Not tea with the queen," I reply.

She blows me off and makes a beeline to my computer behind the counter. My friends have been my friends for so long that a lot of the normal lines are blurred when it comes to boundaries. Most of the time I don't care, but since my new relationship sham, I'm finding that I notice things I never did before.

"I have to see if the package is delivered yet. I'm

trying to intercept before Tim comes over," she explains. She knows the password to unlock the computer.

"Your cell phone not working?"

She doesn't respond right away. "It's in the car, and I just thought about it. Why?" She leans to the left to peek at me from behind the large Mac screen. "You don't want me on the computer?"

I lick my lips. "I don't care what you do. It was just a question."

My mom rounds the corner. She's fresh from the shower and has on a cute maxi dress. She hands me my sweater with a megawatt smile. Charlotte beams at my mother and hops off the stool to give her a hug.

"Oh, sweetie, you look amazing! Teala told me about your promotion. Congratulations!" My mother coos at my friend. "You couldn't make the class? It was so good. Teala really did a fantastic job!"

Ah, my mother. She compliments my friend, but then feels guilty, so she works in a compliment for me, too. It stems from my self-conscious teenage days. I like hearing nice things about myself too much to tell her she doesn't have to do it anymore.

Charlotte brushes down the sides of her sundress. "Thank you, Viola," she says, looking down at the floor. My mother's beauty makes most people uncomfortable. "You look just as beautiful as ever. Teala always runs great practices. I'm hoping to catch one next week."

My mother and Charlotte dive into a full-on conversation, so I disappear to straighten myself using the makeup bag I leave under the counter for times like these.

A little powder, some mascara, a brush pulled through my hair a few times, and I'm ready. I wonder if people view me like they view my mother. I know I don't affect people in the same manner she does. The truth of the matter is I would have attracted a different man, a good man by now, if I did. It reminds me how absurdly stupid my father is, and a rush of rage enters my system. He's a man who doesn't place value on things that matter, one who doesn't appreciate what he has until it's gone.

Macs hasn't called or texted in a couple of days. Not since he'd sent the skydiving photo. It's taken everything in me not to send him a random photo. My stomach turns when I think what he must be doing while on his work trip. I wonder how many women he's been with, how many lips he's kissed like he kissed mine. Not that a kiss can change anything. That type of fairy tale doesn't exist in my world, but kissing Macs was a devastating blow to my ego. His lips on mine cause a palpable weakness. I would have bought anything he was selling. I get angry thinking about it.

He's a forbidden fruit. As soon as I have sex with him, I'll be able to leave him and never look back. That's what I tell myself anyway. I know he's getting back from his trip sometime today, but I didn't tell my mom in case him showing up to meet her didn't work out. I'm glad I didn't count my damn chickens before they hatched. The blush and lip gloss is applied, and I look halfway decent. Prettier than most women, I'd fathom a guess. It's not conceit if you know it as a truth.

From the locker room in the back of the studio, I hear the rumble of a male voice in the lobby. My heart skips a beat and then another. Charlotte laughs. My mother isn't as obvious as my friend, so I can't hear her voice. She's too ladylike.

Laying a hand over my chest, I gather my wits. It has to be him. If it's not, I will not be upset. *I will not be upset.* If it is him, why wouldn't he text me? What type of man shows up at a woman's work without a complimentary call or message? It's plain rude.

I grab my bag and swing the door open in an exaggerated huff. I play at nonchalance as I round the corner. It's twenty degrees cooler up here where the heaters aren't pumping. My skin prickles at the cool blast, and I stop short when I see Macs Newstead.

He's talking animatedly to my mother while Charlotte stands off to the side biting her lip, ravaging his body with her gaze. I stay still, undetected for the moment. The man takes my breath away. In jeans and a T-shirt, he does casual better than any man I've ever met. I smell his cologne—a mellow musk with a hint of sweetness...like brown sugar. His gaze finds mine over the top of my mother's head. I swallow down the lump of hesitance and smile.

"What are you doing here?" I try for annoyance, but it comes out more Elle Woods than anything else.

Macs presses his lips into a firm line as he lets his gaze dip to my body. He doesn't even hide it in front of my mother. She turns to look at me but immediately looks back at Macs. She's deciphering body language, my face. She's picking apart this moment so fully I know I'll hear an earful later. I can't care, or take my eyes off him. He's looking through the surface—it's as if he's seeing inside,my every thought entering his own.

"I wanted to surprise you," he says.

My mother faces me again. That draws my focus, and I clear my throat.

"I invited him to lunch with us. I hope you don't mind, honey," Mom says. She already knows I don't mind. Viola Sebrof just planned our wedding. She blinks, her smile widening. She just picked out my wedding dress. Another smile. She clamps her hand over her mouth, like that has the ability to hide her excitement. "Are you ready to go?" she asks, finally gaining the good sense to live in the now instead of in her dream world.

I nod at her and roll my eyes. She smiles again, the grin melting all annoyance.

"Macs, I see you've met my mother."

"Did I ever," he replies, waggling his eyebrows.

She didn't catch it, but Charlotte did, and my friend laughs.

"What's funny?" Mom asks. "Charlotte introduced me to your friend. Why didn't you tell me he was so—" she stutters.

This is going downhill fast. I have to nip it in the bud.

"Out of contact?" I supply for her.

Macs steps out of the circle they've made around him and approaches me. He's doing it again. Moving like he owns the world. I close my eyes for a second or two.

He lays a hand on my shoulder. The warmth sends shockwaves to every part of my body. The butterflies in my belly turn to vultures, with long wings and big, pecking beaks.

"I'm sorry. I got busy at work," Macs whispers.

I know they heard.

"Do you want me to come to lunch with you?" At the sincerity of his voice, I glance up at his face. Dimples greet me.

"Don't use those things to get what you want. Of course I don't mind if you have lunch with us. I mean, you might regret it in the end, but this is what we're doing, right?" I ask, speaking so he is the only one who hears. "I wasn't sure what was going on. You kind of dropped off the map there."

The smile falls off his face. He has this stoic super-model face. Blue Steel without trying and no duck lips. I make a mental note to use this as a teasing arsenal for later. He knows how good-looking he is, but I'm not sure he knows how everyone else sees his beauty.

"I apologized already," he says. It's the only explanation I'll receive.

I nod. He doesn't even owe me that. The lines with this thing are blurring too. The lines of my whole life are one big fuzzy mindfuck. "I'm starving. Let's go," I remark, grasping for control.

He takes my hand in his, and I don't miss how tightly he's holding on.

Charlotte and my mom ask Macs a million questions. He answers some, is cheeky with others that he can't answer, but he's completely disarming. I find myself smiling at him while he talks, and my mother notices. She is beaming like a lighthouse after lunch is finished. She tells Macs stories about me from when I was small. This is when I realize she's planned more than my wedding today. She might have her grandkids named as well.

It's my fault for not giving her anything of substance all of these years. No boyfriends. No reason to believe I was ever ready to take the next step with a man. She sees a man like Macs and my interest in such a man, and it's all over. Maybe that's my problem too. Even if it's fake, for the first time I'm letting myself wonder what is normal in a relationship. What I realize is that it's not that bad. Other than my heart being on the line and the severity of what that could lead to.

Macs holds me against him as we walk out of the café. It's now starting to get busy, and I'm glad we chose the time we did. "I'm going to take a walk around the Gaslamp, Tay," my mother explains when we exit to the street. My apartment is only a few blocks over, and she has a key.

Charlotte says she has to go stalk the mailman, but

not before waggling her brow, and Macs and I are left staring at each other on a sidewalk filled with people.

"What now?" I ask. A car horn blares, startling me. Macs is unaffected. I wonder if his hearing is messed up from being around gunfire and explosions. I bet he has psychic powers and predicted the horn would go off. Oddly enough, that's a more rational hypothesis.

He clears his throat and looks over my head. Flicking his gaze back to me, he asks, "It's the third date?"

I grin. "Do you know what that means?"

Eyes narrowed, he pulls me against his body, cradling the side of my face in his large hand. Macs has fire in his eyes, desire so wild and feral it causes me to lose my breath.

"Where?"

"Not the sidewalk, please," I reply, widening my eyes. I have to say it. I can't read him right now, and if he really wanted to take me on the sidewalk, I'm not sure I could stop him.

After kissing me on the lips long and hard, he leans to my ear. "I need you. I'm desperate for you."

I want him too. "My apartment? I mean, I can't promise my mom and Charlotte won't meander in at some point, but we can be quick." I hike my thumb behind my shoulder. "I feel like I'm propositioning you right now."

He shakes his head. "I want you for longer than that. It's third base. I need to take my time." He looks up at the tall buildings surrounding us, his gaze feverish. "A hotel?"

I step out of his arms. "A hotel? Seriously? I'm not a prostitute, Macs. I was just making a joke about propositioning. Ha. Ha. You know?"

He can't be serious with a hotel.

"I never said you were. Normal people go to hotels,

too. You don't have to be a lady of the night to frequent the fine establishments."

I shake my head. "I'd rather be quick at my house. Or...we could go to your house?"

Macs looks at me in a way he hasn't done before. You'd think I'd suggested a visit to a proctologist. He's met my mother. I assumed we were past this. I understand his need to keep his private life private, but this is a normal occurrence in a real relationship. Why can't we have it in our fake relationship?

"I brought you into my home," I add on.

He shakes his head. "That's different. You bring all of your...men there."

I scoff, pulling out of his arms. "I have to go, Macs. Call me later?"

He grabs my bicep, his grip loose. "No, no, no. Are you sure we can't go to a hotel? I know there's one several blocks over. I can drive us."

Do I give in? I want his body, but I want his respect more.

"Call me," I repeat. My voice wavers, but he's too wound up to realize I'm on the fence. I'm seconds away from being his call girl. He's a complete one-eighty compared to how he was in front of my mom and Charlotte. "Yeah?" I ask, prompting him to make up his mind or just freaking agree to call me later so we can get on with our lives.

He's still staring at me, like I'm a freak on display. I have nothing to be self-conscious about, and I still find myself running my hand through my hair and smoothing my lips together, back and forth.

"Fine," he growls. "I'll drive."

"Fine, what? You'll call me?" I smile at him.

His scowl doesn't budge. His eyes narrow even further through his irritation. Macs bites his bottom lip.

"We can go to my house. My living room," he explains. "Not my bedroom."

I jump up once and clap my hands together. "I'm so excited!"

He grunts and furrows his brow. Stepping back into his space, I lean up on my toes and put my lips against his. I've wanted to kiss him since he sucked his full pink lip into his mouth. His lips move against mine, and he takes me against his solid body immediately. His hard length presses against my stomach, and the anticipation is almost too much.

"No sex," I say. It's more of a question, even though I know we've played by the rules this far and he won't mess it up now.

Looking around, he makes sure no one is looking before he readjusts his bulge, then he takes my hand and leads me to his car.

I text my mom and let her know that Macs and I are grabbing some dessert and I'll see her at the apartment later. Charlotte texts me thirty seconds later. She's obviously still with my mom. *Third date, Tay. You know what that means?* She follows up with a smiley face. I should be a real bitch and ask her to explain, in detail, what it is I'm allowed to do.

Instead, I text back, *Everything but sex?*

Macs is busy driving. He doesn't take his eyes off the road. He's zoned into it like I'm not even sitting next to him. I watch him while he's busy with traffic. I try to remember the last time I was with a man as beautiful as Macs. It's been a while. I'd have to break it down by sections. A body as perfect as Macs's? That one is easy. Moose. A face as attractive? I'm not sure I've ever been with a man with a face quite like Macs's, but maybe one other. He was a bronzed professional surfer. He had blue eyes and the most defined, sculpted chin I'd ever seen.

He was an awful lay. He called me "dude" after he came on my bedsheets. Now that I'm thinking about it, that makes him sort of awful. I decide he shouldn't make any of my *best lists* for that reason alone, his Adonis chin be damned.

Everything goes. NO penetration by penis. Because you're so prolific, I'll add, no penetration by penis in ANY holes. Charlotte's text is more graphic than I expected.

Don't call it that. It's a cock. I reply to her message right away, making a noise of disgust. *Any holes would imply he can't put his cock in my mouth hole. Allowed, right?* I smirk.

"What are you groaning about over there?" Macs asks.

I jump in my seat a little bit. I looked away for four seconds, and he's already tuned into me.

"Penis. It's such a horrible word," I tell him.

He laughs, but his smile doesn't reach his eyes. He's frustrated.

"When is the last time you've had sex, Macs?" I ask, letting my curiosity get the better of me.

He swallows and then works his jaw.

"It's been a while?" I ask. This realization makes me giddy even though I shouldn't be. I don't want to be excited he hasn't banged any other chicks recently, but I already know I will be.

Charlotte texts back that blow jobs are permitted, even though she's sure my mouth is on it right now.

He releases a drawn-out sigh. "Before you," he whispers.

"You're such a liar," I clap back.

"I don't lie about sex, Teala. I committed to this."

My heart skips a beat. I let my mind replace the word *this* with *you*.

"It's the longest I've gone without sex since age sixteen."

Silence fills the car as I weigh my response. "I get the commitment to holding up our charade, but why not have sex on the side?"

We're on a long stretch of road without any other cars around, so he glances over at me. "That would be too easy. I thought you knew me at least a little bit by this point. Challenges are sort of my thing. I committed to our pseudo-relationship, and maybe part of me was curious about how it would be if it were real. Not that it is real," he explains. "Make no mistake of that." His voice doesn't sound so sure.

"Of course it's not. I mean, you did just have lunch with my mom and give me an orgasm by dry humping me against my bedroom window. What's real about that?" I retort. I watch his face. The corner of his lip quirks. It feels real. He knows it. I know it.

"I need a distraction for the next five minutes," he says. "That's how long until we get to my house. I might explode," he says, wincing as he readjusts his hard-on.

I giggle. "Do you trust me?" I bite my lip.

Macs furrows his brow as I lick my lips and circle my mouth with my pointer finger. His eyes pop open wide. "If you're talking about what I think you're talking about, the question should be, do I trust myself?" He rubs his hands on the leather steering wheel up and down. "Go. Do it," he says—the quickest decision that ever came to fruition. He leans his seat back using the buttons on the side panel of his door.

I unfasten my seat belt and bend over to start working on his button and zipper. His shaft is pressing against his jeans uncomfortably. I pull it through the fly of his boxer briefs. It's just as large as it feels through his pants. It's silky, with veins and a robust head. I do have a good comparison, so when I say his dick is beautiful, it is. Wrapping my hand around his girth, I watch his face. It's a mask of determination and lust. His fists flex around the steering wheel, causing a cracking sound.

"Suck my dick," he says. "Suck my fucking dick," he repeats. Everything below my belly button turns to mush.

Typically I'd object to his order, but I'm so turned on. He's waiting for me. I'm the only one. Right now, at least. Even if it's just for now, he is a monster of desire, and I can't wait to see exactly what he can do with every part of his body. I lick the tip, swirling my tongue in small circles. At first contact, Macs groans, a guttural noise piercing the air in the cab of the car. My core clenches in response to the primal noise.

I let my mouth work down the shaft a bit before I start pumping my hand at the same time. I pull away to look at him while I keep working my hand up and down. The corner of the center console digs into my stomach, and I readjust my positioning.

"I'm sort of good at this. I figure I should warn you in case you think you'll be the hero here," I say.

He smirks, his eyes now so hooded I think I may combust from the desire I see there.

"I'm always the hero. Now suck my dick. I'll tell you if you're too good." He's playing. He has no clue how dangerous I am. Not in this regard.

I shrug, sliding my hand up around the head of his cock and all the way back down. My spit is lubricating and it's running dry, so I bend over and, using precise aim, I let a mouthful of spit fall on the tip of his dick. He moans. I suck and use my hand at the perfect speed. My lips shield his softness from my teeth, and I work him into a complete and utter frenzy. When I sense he's getting too close, I back off with my hands and lick the underside up and down in long strokes. Macs is bucking his hips, trying to get me to swallow him whole. I wonder how long it will be until he releases his grip from ten and two and pushes my head with one hand. It's only been a couple of minutes, and Macs is tapping out. Not tapping my shoulder to let me know he's coming, actually moaning that I need to stop before he blows his load all over the Italian leather interior.

He's breathing in huffs and puffs blown out of his mouth at an erratic pace. I lean up, wipe the string of spit from the corner of my mouth with the back of my hand, and retreat to my seat.

"FUCK!" Macs yells, a huge smile on his face. He slams his palm on the steering wheel. His eyes widen. "You suck dick like a goddamn professional. We were joking about it before, but fuck. Can I lock you in my closet?"

I laugh. "I should take offense to that, but I'll run with the compliment. You're not locking me anywhere." I shake my head.

His grin is wide and confusing. When he looks over at me it's like he's viewing me for the first time. "What the hell are you, Teala Smart?"

I grin. "I'm a lot of things, but I'm mostly your worst nightmare." I tilt my head in the direction of his cock, still ramrod straight and begging for more attention. "Want more?"

"Fuck!" he yells again. He shakes his head, still grinning like a lunatic. "We're almost home," he says, readjusting his dick so I can't see it anymore. My face must fall, because he responds, "Baby, you can have so much more of that. However much you want. All of it. Anytime you want. Let me park the car. If I thought I could safely get us there and come down your hot fucking throat, I would have let you continue. I think my whole body was buzzing." His eyebrows are raised, and his dimples are on full display. "Jesus, your mouth."

He rubs a palm down the front of his unzipped jeans.

"And we better do it fast before I get blue balls again. God, I want to come in you so badly," he says, shaking his head.

"I'm more than a mouth, you know?" I should have downplayed my skills. This always happens.

His dimples disappear. "I know." It's a simple response, but it insinuates so much more. "Trust me, I know." He pulls into a long driveway.

His house is beautiful. It's a ranch-style home with landscaping and lots of tools and sawdust out on the front patio. He parks in front of the two-car garage and explains that he has so many projects going on this weekend with some friend named Tahoe, he had to use his garage to prep. He usually parks his vehicle in there otherwise.

His sexual excitement turns into something else as we approach his front door. He starts talking faster, explaining why certain things are the way they are even though I never asked. He avoids looking at me as he pulls out his key. It hangs from a Louis Vuitton keychain and holds nothing else but the fob that starts his car. He pushes the door open and motions for me to walk in first. You can taste the hesitance in the air. I feel like he's going to push me out of his world at any moment, decide it's a horrible idea to have me in his life now that coming down my throat isn't at the forefront of his mind. Because that's all I'm truly good for. I'm almost sorry it's the third date because after this he'll be less and less enthralled until we have sex, and then he'll be done with me.

"I want you to know how much this means to me. I don't let people in my world," he admits.

I hear his keys hit the table in the entryway as I look around. It's beautiful. Even in the dismantled state it's in, I'm able to see his vision. The ceilings are high, and everything is open. The walls are a crisp white, and the furniture he does have is tasteful, expensive. The scent of sawdust and new paint is overwhelming. I wrinkle my nose.

Macs is watching my face. "What? What is it?" He cranes his neck to see my line of vision.

I see a door down the hallway. It's closed. "It's beautiful. I love the entrance." I point to the glass doors that open to the beautiful California view. "The eau de construction is strong, that's all." Facing him, I place my hands on his strong shoulders. "You're pretty awesome with your hands," I say, hoping the compliment will lighten the mood. It doesn't.

His eyes dart to the closed door and then back to me, and he swallows. "Want something to drink? I have beer or water."

I raise one brow. "It's the middle of the day. Beer?"

"I'm feeling real squirrely right now, so I hope you don't mind if I have one."

He leaves me for the fridge, pops the top off a brown bottle, and downs it in several gulps, his head tilted toward the ceiling. When he finishes it, he stares at me, unblinking. I press my lips together, and wait for him to say something.

"Maybe I'll have one more," he finally says. He does. Then he looks at me again, like my face holds the answer of what comes next.

I laugh. "This is ludicrous. If you have to get drunk, I shouldn't even be here."

He shakes his head. "I'm not getting drunk because you're here, Teala. I'm getting drunk because of what it means. Still want to have our third date?" he asks, pulling his T-shirt up to expose his abs. He bites the dark, cotton fabric, like men in fashion magazines do. With his abs flexed, he poses so casually, so fucking drool-worthy, so over-the-top, and he gets away with it. He tosses the shirt onto the counter, with his tongue caught between his teeth.

I blow out a breath. It's as hot as a Channing Tatum movie. More so, actually, because I can touch this body, can do whatever I want with it. "How am I supposed to say anything but yes when you don't play fair? You're over there with your goddamn abs and dimples and precision stripping skills." I motion to his body.

"Babe, you played dirty first. Your mouth is like a fucking dirty poker game. One you'll win every single time."

I wrinkle my forehead. "Thanks, I guess. Third date?" I ask, tilting my head to the side.

"Let's go to my bedroom." He rushes me then—all muscles and stolen breaths in between teeth and kisses. "It does smell like work out here."

CHAPTER TWELVE

Macs

MY HEART MIGHT EXPLODE out of my chest. It's pounding with so much adrenaline I'm not sure how to control it. Honestly, I don't want to control it. She's in my arms and her lips are on mine, and I'm opening the door to my bedroom. It's like I'm Indiana fucking Jones, and I'm opening the door to the room filled with riches beyond my wildest dreams. Teala is in my space. She doesn't look around when I let her feet touch the floor, though. Not like I would. I'd need to study every single detail first. She doesn't know what this means, has no clue of the magnitude of what's happening. Hell, what's already happened.

She's warm against my body, and I can't tear my gaze from her mouth. Her perfect fucking mouth that does things I never knew were possible. I kiss her. Just once. Hard and furious because I want to taste her now that she's in my bedroom. Does it feel differently? It doesn't. It feels just as surreal.

She sucks in air and looks at me with this "fuck me" smile and eyes only for me. I'm not sure what made me take her here. I could have talked her into a hotel room by her apartment. I saw it on her face. I could have bent her to my will. She wants this as much as I do.

I want her here in my space. In my world. In my fucking bed. I want her. Not because I haven't fucked in a while either.

Because sometime while we were playing pretend something shifted.

"Can I use your bathroom?" she asks, eyes wide and cheeks blushed.

I point to the side of my room where a set of white double doors leads through to my bathroom.

She waggles her brows, then spins on her toe. "I'll be right back."

I watch her walk, her workout pants leaving little to the imagination. The curve of her ass is exceptional.

She kicks off her sneakers. "Just a quick shower," she explains.

I tell her where I keep my extra towels, and with a shark-like smile, she closes the door behind her. The lock doesn't click.

"No clothes on when you come out," I yell, cupping one hand beside my mouth.

She doesn't respond, but she laughs. She rolls with anything.

I pace the floor, running a hand across the side of my bed to smooth the covers. I scratch my head and lay a wide palm across my stomach. I do twenty push-ups as quickly as I can. The shower turns on, and I close my eyes.

I unbutton my pants and step out of the uncomfortable jeans. The splashing of water forces my attention to the bathroom door. No one else has been in here before. I wonder what products she's using. The assortment of gels and facial products is pretty extensive. The shelving in my shower is larger than average, customized for all of the shit I use. She's singing now. It's not the screeching warble of the customary shower singer. It sounds…nice. I don't recognize the melody or the words. Teala's voice echoing in my space sends a pit of dread directly to my midsection. This won't end well. How can this possibly end any other way except with destruction?

Dropping to the floor, I do more push-ups, not even counting as I brush my chest against the cool wooden floor. This helps check my dick, and it burns out the thoughts I'm not ready to face. Sweat beads at my hair-line, and I know I need to stop before I go from a sweet, muscular pump to a stinky, inconsiderate fucker. I'm not showering. The water turns off, and with that action, her singing halts as well. I imagine what she looks like as she steps out of the shower onto my white bath mat.

Does she dry off before she gets out, or does she step out sopping wet and get water all over the floor? There are two kinds of people in the world, and they fall into either of those categories.

"Can you bring me my bag?" she asks.

I confirm I can, because I'd do anything she asks right now.

Craving distraction, I pick up the leather bag sitting on a console table in my living room and walk back to my room, holding it by the straps at the end of my pointer finger. How does one carry a woman's purse? I sling it over my shoulder, but that feels odd, so I hold it by the top handles before I knock on the door.

Teala peeks out, hair wet. "Thanks. I'll just be another minute or so." She smiles, my dick twitches, and she closes the door. "I feel like we need to establish some ground rules before we begin."

She's mad. Absolutely raving mad if she thinks I'm going to let anything dictate what I'm going to do with her and to her.

"What does that mean, exactly?" I raise my voice so she can hear through the door.

Instead of responding right away, she pushes the bathroom door open, naked but for the smile on her face. Hissing a breath, I clench my jaw as I let my gaze flick from one perfect body part to the next. Her workout clothes leave little to the imagination, yet I'm still a bit shell-shocked with her nakedness so close. Bringing a fist to my mouth, I bite down on my knuckles. Teala laughs.

"I'm clean. Want to get dirty?" she asks.

I suck in a breath. Her confident gaze doesn't waver. There's no hiding the desire I see reflecting in her eyes. Her lips slide together, and her tongue flicks out to wet her bottom lip. Every move we make, the other notices. It's obvious our chemistry is off the charts, but we're not just synched. We're on the same page.

"I can't fuck you, and that's the dirtiest," I reply, sliding my hand down the front of my underwear to shift my dick.

Her body is smooth all over and lithe, her pert breasts standing up unnaturally, with pink nipples hardened. If I were to take pieces and parts of other women—my favorite parts—and mash them together to form my ideal woman, Teala would be it. She wins the prize.

She walks up to me slowly, the steam from the bathroom pushing the scent of my body wash into my awareness. I groan. She smells like me. I never would have understood what a turn-on having my scent on a woman is unless this happened. My mouth waters a bit. When she's close enough to touch, the heat clinging to her body rushes to my chest. She's on fire, and she smells delectable. Fists clenched by my sides, I wait for her to make the first move.

She tilts her head to the side and narrows her eyes. "Rules," she says, holding up one finger.

I shake my head.

Pointing at my dick, she says, "You can't put that inside my vagina or ass."

I grin. Her mouth is deliciously filthy. "But you can put it inside yourself?" I think about what that would look like, and my cock throbs in agreement as it looks pretty awesome. "I'm joking. I know." Seeing her bare body lets me know I'm in for a real nice challenge. "But looking at you makes me realize how wonderfully we'll fuck. Just so you know. Fucking is going to be amazing."

She nods. "It will be masterful. The most awesome fucking two individuals ever encountered." She's joking, but I'm buying it. There's this buzzing in my body I've never felt before. I've never felt so much...want. "With that said, let the games begin."

I grab her by the waist and pull her against me. "I don't play games, Tay-la," I whisper into her ear. Goose bumps prickle her skin on her neck and shoulder blade.

Her hands immediately go to my cock, and I have to close my eyes and find some sort of inner strength to pull her delicate little cum usurpers away.

She raises her brow in question.

"I have a head start, remember? Your dick-sucking skills about made me blow my top in record time. I want to touch you first. Taste you. Fuck you with my fingers," I growl, leaning into the crook of her neck. I take the soft skin between my teeth and gently bite her. "You'll beg for my cock. Beg me to fill you, fuck you, stretch you until you think you'll break."

"I'll beg for it now," she says, voice meek.

I've won her over already. Her hands are tracing my abs, my biceps, the hollow of my neck, my pecs. She's everywhere except the one place I want her to be.

"Where do you want me?"

I can't bring myself to tell her to get into my bed.

She's already in my room. Fuck, she's showered in my bathroom. The most OCD zone in my world, but the words don't come, and I won't force them. I kiss her, fisting her tight ass in my palms as she writhes against me. My fucking underwear will be my saving grace, the only thing keeping me from falling into her pussy on semi-accident. These bitches have to stay on for as long as possible. I repeat that a few more times in my head while I lose the rest of my brain, focusing on her kiss.

"Your lips are so sweet," I say, caressing the side of her face. Taking her bottom lip in between my teeth, I bite down. "I want to eat you."

We both smile at my double entendre.

I lean back to see her face better. "Close your eyes and don't move," I rasp.

Closing her eyes, she lets out a breath. Her face, free of makeup, looks like she fell out of my personal wet dream.

I hit my knees in front of her. Like a good girl, she keeps her eyes closed and lets me do as I please. I lift her left leg over my shoulder. It's not a cumbersome move. It's fluid and graceful, like a yoga pose. I'd considered the benefits of having a flexible bedmate but never took fore-play into consideration.

With my left hand I grab her ass cheek and push her pussy into my mouth.

Sweet. Wet. Ready. I lap at her using my tongue, while moving her exactly where I want by steering her ass. She's pliant, going with whatever I desire. Flicking my gaze up, I watch her face as I dip my tongue in and out. She's moaning, her fingers laced through my hair, and her perfect, fucking pink lips forming a subtle O shape. Her body is sturdy, but she's still a lightweight. Lifting her weight, even with one hand, is easy. She's riding the waves of pleasure, and I don't stop until I see her base leg buckle a little bit. There's not another option. I ease her gently up into my arms and bring her over to my bed.

"You're not finished," she squeals, her legs splayed wide, knees bent up into a W shape. Teala moves her hips up and down to show me exactly what she wants. "Hurry," she whimpers.

I'm trying to, but the sight of her on my bed, hair fanning around her head like a halo, is enough to cause more than a pause in both my libido and my brain. *What am I doing?*

"Macs," Teala whispers. Her voice draws me from my thoughts. She's slid her hand in between her legs, and she's working her clit with both her middle and her pointer finger—small, fast circles. "Come finish me off." Her voice is pleading now.

I lick my lips and taste her. *That's what I'm doing.*

"I'd say let's sixty-nine, but I really want your undivided attention," I say, crawling up between her thighs, kissing the inside of one and then the other before setting back to work. I halt her hand, and she gets the message straight away. "You taste so fucking good," I growl. I need a straw. I suck her clit and slip a finger in to feel her tightness. I'm lightheaded. All of the blood in my body has traveled to my dick.

"Another finger. Fuck me with two fingers," Teala orders.

Her back is arching off the bed as I bring her closer to the brink. It's a turn-on being with a woman who knows exactly what she needs to come. It makes my job easier. Gets us to the good stuff quicker. Except I want more time with her. I could stretch this on all night long if I had my way.

"Please," she begs.

Her eyes are focused like lasers on me, and I give her what she wants. I fuck her with two of my fingers while sucking her clit at the same tempo. It doesn't take her long once I'm double-teaming her tight pussy. She comes, and it's loud and powerful. Curse words mixed with praise and incoherent sentences escape from tired lips connected to a limp, well-pleasured body.

Leaving one finger inside her, I release my mouth. "You're beautiful, Teala Smart." *And captivating, stunning, and mine.* "How was that for you?" I ask, smiling at her through her legs.

Finally she tilts her head up to see me, grabs the pillow next to her, and puts it under her head. Through labored breaths she says, "I've been waiting for that for weeks. Mmm, that felt so good."

I quirk a brow and slide my finger inside her a few times. She squirms, a happy, sated grin on her face.

"Weeks? You haven't been with anyone else either?" My hard-on is waiting and ready and even more excited at this revelation. While I was skydiving, I came to the realization that part of the reason I was so upset with my behavior was that we didn't really set any rules. We've let this thing breathe on its own. There's no one controlling it.

"You knew that," she says, twirling the long parts of my hair in her fingers.

I like the way it feels. I swallow hard, remove my finger reluctantly, and kiss up her hard stomach, over her perfect tits, her neck, behind her ear, and finally, with the scent of her filling my senses, I kiss her lips. She squeaks out a sigh, and my heart leaps.

I can't breathe for a second or two. I want to fuck her. My god, I don't think I've wanted anything more. She sits up on her knees but is able to keep our lips connected.

"I'm going to finish what I started in the car now."

A proclamation I won't argue with.

Taking a mental step back from the edge, I exhale. Yes.

This will work. I can deal with this crazed feeling if she's making me come with one wet hole on her body. It may not be the one I crave, but it will do. For tonight.

"Suck. My. Dick," I command, flashing my dimples her way.

"Like I have a choice when you ask me so nicely," she replies, mock irritation lacing her words.

In response, I brush some of her hair back and twist the long, wet strands around my hand. She knows what comes next because she wets her lips. *Good girl.* I pull her head down and push her face onto my dick.

It won't take long. Not that it would have taken that long earlier in the car, but now I have the taste of her pussy on my tongue and her ass in the air as she works those pretty fucking lips and tongue like a Jedi Master. I'd usually try to hold myself back, try to impress a woman with my ability to hang on awhile, and try to convince her my stamina is the best of them.

"Fuck!" I hiss when she starts pumping her hand. It's wet and warm, and her mouth is nirvana. I don't care about holding out. I let myself think about everything that's happening. I don't mute the moment. I turn the volume up. I live in it so fully I can't tell where I stop and her mouth begins.

She's humming now, her hands cupping my balls gently. It's a well-oiled process, and she stays steady because that's the one thing men need to come. It's pace. And hers is slamming. Teala has showmanship while she's sucking cock. She doesn't hate it.

I don't even have to push the back of her head. She swallows me all the way down in her furious pursuit of taking my pleasure. She wants it for herself, and fuck, do I want to give it to her. The sloshing noise of spit and fury surrounds me as her hand pumps, and I lose it. With her hands on my balls, she pulls my length all the way to the back of her throat, and I let go, exploding down her throat in several hard, hot thrusts.

Eyes watering, she lets her gaze flick up to meet mine. I don't say anything. I just breathe, or rather try to catch my breath. Slurping, Teala slides my dick out of her mouth. It feels cold and bereft. She doesn't take her eyes off mine as she licks her lips, swallows hard, and wipes the spit off her lips with her wet hand. It's an intimate moment that some could construe as awkward, but nothing about watching her is odd. It's something else entirely. I want to see more of her like this. Vulnerable.

"I don't even know what to say after that." My voice breaks. I swallow to correct it.

She shrugs, doesn't smile, and heads to the bathroom, saying she needs to wash her hands. When she returns, I'm still kneeling in the same fucking spot, trying to figure out my next move. Our next move.

"You don't have to look at me like that. There's nothing wrong with you. My blow jobs are always the crowd pleaser." She walks to her bag, still naked. She tries not to meet my eyes.

I frown. "I don't want to think about you sucking some other dude's dick right now," I reply, grimacing. "You only suck my dick now."

"Oh," she says, turning her head to look at me. Her pretty face looks startled. "I guess I didn't think about it that way."

She wouldn't. I wouldn't either if I wasn't going through some weird fucking hang-up over here. She obviously has her head on straight. For the first time since she entered, I catch her looking around, her gaze landing on certain things in my room. I approach her because I want her lips on mine. She has other ideas because she walks up to one of my bags packed for our next trip.

"It's huge," she says. "Where are you going next?"

"It's a dead hooker," I reply.

Teala scrunches up her nose.

"That's what the bag is called because you can fit a person in there."

She laughs, but I can tell she's waiting for an answer to her other question. "Why a hooker?"

I shrug. "We love sex?"

"Ah. I see." She runs her hand over the dusty bag in the corner of my room and makes her way to the window.

"I deploy shortly to somewhere in the Middle East. These bags are for CQB," I say and then decide to amend for the military newbie. "It's where we practice clearing rooms using our guns and gear and stuff."

She nods.

"It's one of our longer, more important trips. Usually it's two to three weeks."

She asks another question about training and deployment, and I answer her honestly. We're both naked, uninhibited by bare skin. It feels personal, and while I'm giving her all of these details about my real life, it almost feels like a violation.

She gets in my bed and pulls back the covers. "At least I don't have to worry about your sheets being vagina juiced." She laughs.

"They're probably covered in more cu than the *Playboy* I had under my mattress as a teenager," I retort.

She sighs in a contented whisper, calls me a liar, and lies down. I can't help it. I get in next to her and prop my head on my hand while staring at her. She is this weird, new prop in my fucking bed.

"I hope you realize our date isn't over yet. I need to assess your finger-fucking skills. No mouth," she quips.

I'd almost say she was joking, but for the carnal appetite shining in her eyes.

"Ah, we're just getting started," I say. Just to make sure she knows I'm good on my word, I slip my hand in between her thighs and find her clit.

She opens for me, grinning.

With a quiet moan, she closes her eyes. "This has to be the best no-sex date I've ever had."

It is the best date I've ever been on. I make her come again while watching her face. She likes when I stroke her G-spot and pinch her nipples. I like her hands and mouth more than I've ever liked anything else.

I excuse myself from my own bedroom to grab a couple of bottles of water from the fridge in the kitchen. I drink another beer instead, taking a moment to myself.

The newly painted walls seem to close in on me a touch. I'm rattled, terrified by whatever the fuck is happening between us. She calls my name in her sweet singsong voice and then asks if I can eat her out again— her nasty, perfect words ricocheting down the hallway.

And I forget to be scared about anything except the fact that I may not be able to come a third time in one afternoon.

Oh, the fucking horror.

CHAPTER THIRTEEN
Teala

I'VE NEVER FELT AS WELL FUCKED as I did when Macs dropped me off at my apartment that night. He offered to let me spend the night, but I had to get home to my mom. I knew she wouldn't care if I left her alone for a night, but I'd have to answer more questions than I'm ready to. Questions I'm not even sure I know how to answer. Macs was a different person today.

I'm lying in my bed, staring at the black ceiling, wondering what in the ever-loving fuck I'm going to do about the problem at hand. He asked me to *spend the night*. I'm in deep water, or deep something.

I'm falling for him, and if I'm not mistaken, he's definitely warming up to me. Or at least the idea of a relationship with me. He asked me to accompany him to visit his parents. We leave this weekend. It's a little bit of a drive, and I'm already giddy at the prospect of being trapped in his car with him for any length of time. The unfortunate part is that this is officially a date we can mess around again, and we'll be at his parents' house. The date after that, Charlotte and Jasmine said, is officially deemed the sex date.

If they only knew what we've already done is the

equivalent of sex in so many ways. He finger fucked me so well that my eyes rolled back in my head. The man knows how to work a clit. The man knows how to work a woman's body. He sees no reason to pretend he's something he's not. Macs has been around the block and knows exactly what he's doing. We are a match in that department, and if I had to guess, I'd say my skills at sucking dick are what enamored him most. It's why I was sort of sad after I blew him.

He looked at me like I was an alien, his eyes wide with wonder and his lips forming a beatific smile. My phone alerts me to a text from Macs.

Still thinking about your blowjobs.

I sigh. Instead of replying with text, I snap a photo of my black ceiling and hit send. I should be happy I attracted his attention, but I'm not stupid. I know his interest will wane and I'll just be another woman on his long list.

I roll over to sleep, but my phone rings. It's Macs. I hit the green button quickly, not wanting to wake up my mom in the room next door. She's been asleep for a while, but I'm unable to force my brain to turn off. "Hello," I say, whispering even though I know there's no way she can hear me talking through the thick wall.

"Why don't you ever reply to my texts?" he asks without any sort of greeting first.

"I do," I tell him, rolling over to my back to look at the ceiling again. "I sent you my ceiling."

"While I appreciate the view of your ceiling, I'd rather see it while you're riding my cock. You know that's not what I mean," Macs growls.

My core clenches with desire. I have no control over it anymore. Any talk of Macs and sex, and I'm as horny as a teenager. I want anything he'll give me.

"I think photos say more than words can," I say.

I hear his deep breathing for several long moments. It's the only indication he hasn't hung up the phone.

"Sometimes I want your words. It helps me understand what's inside your head."

Ha! What's inside my head would make a smart man run in the opposite direction. When my father left my mother, he bashed her so unmercifully I remember overhearing her talking on the phone to a friend. She said words like useless and inept weak-willed...words like clinging, gullible, obsessive, and overemotional. My father broke her with these words.

"I want to know you better, Teala. Do you understand?"

His words are a punch in the stomach. He cares far more than I gave him credit for, and I'm not sure how to reply. I've never been in the business of accepting feelings. I do everything in my power to reject them. Their feelings and mine both.

I click on my bedside lamp because I want to be able to see. Not that seeing makes a difference, but the darkness feels as if it's closing in, and my stomach is flipping with unease.

"Are you there?" he asks.

I clear my throat. "I'm here. I'm trying to figure out how to respond. Sorry," I explain.

Macs lets out a groan that sounds more like a growl. "Listen, forget I said anything."

Shit. "No. No. I understand what you're saying. It surprised me. I thought we were on the same page," I lie. "I want you to know me better." I chose my words carefully by flipping his statement.

"It would be helpful for when you meet my parents," he says. The butterflies that were in my stomach sink faster than the *Titanic*. "Especially my mother. She's in the business of asking too many questions."

"Oh. For the game." I click the light back off and roll over, keeping the phone by my ear.

"Of course," he says. "Unless…"

"Unless what?" I ask. "Don't pretend you care. I'll respond to texts with words from now on. What do you want to know about me? What would be prudent to understand for your parents?"

"Are you mad?"

I sigh. "What do you think?"

"I have no clue. It's why I'm asking."

Sometimes men can be so dense. I don't have anything to compare this to, though. "Why don't you sleep with other women? If it's just a game, then why act differently?"

Macs clears his throat, and I can tell he's moving, the phone scratching against his stubble. "I don't want any other women."

"That doesn't sound like a game to me," I reply.

"It doesn't."

"You go back and forth between it being a game and actually giving a damn about whatever is going on between us. I'm trying to figure out what's real and what's not. That is what's wrong with me."

He stays silent on the other end, so I bluster on.

"Which is it?"

"I want to understand you," he whispers.

I let out a pent-up breath. "I want to know about you too."

"Good. So what's the moral of this story? We kind of lost our way," he says. I hear the smile in his voice. He's blaming me for detouring the conversation.

"We're on the same page then. It's a game, but we care enough to know about each other?"

"No," he replies, zero hesitation.

"The moral of the story is you want me to use words

to text back. I've agreed, but now you're saying we're not on the same page, so you're going to have to enlighten me."

"No. It's not a game."

My heart leaps again. I roll out of bed and sit on the edge. When I steady myself, I walk over to the huge window and throw the drapes open. I'm giving him a few more moments to explain before I pepper him with questions.

"I care," he mumbles, so low I barely hear him.

A car races by on the street below me, and a few office lights are on in the building across the way. "What was that?" I ask, letting a smile slip.

"Seriously? You heard me."

"I didn't," I say. I bite my lip.

"I said I care," he growls.

"Was that so hard?"

"Yes," he replies. "I'm not in the business of telling people things I'm not comfortable sharing."

"We shared our bodies with each other all afternoon, Macs."

"That's different. I'm used to sharing that with other women, and don't pretend you aren't used to sharing yours with other men. It's to us as a coffee date is to most other people. Agreed?"

I think about it for a few moments. He's both right and wrong. "A fucking awesome coffee date, though," I agree. "This afternoon felt different than other times." If we're playing the honesty game, I'm going to dive right the fuck in.

"I know," he says simply.

"Because we care."

"So you care, too?"

I narrow my eyes. "How can you possibly wonder that?" I mean, we're both sort of at a disadvantage where emotions are concerned, but surely he's able to tell that I feel for him more than my average date. "Of course I care. Every time we're together, I find myself trying to keep my mouth shut before I say something that scares you off. Intimacy is an easy place to hide. For me, anyway. Everything else is what's difficult."

"I couldn't be sure. I've never done this before."

"Did this just turn into a real relationship?" I have the express desire to call my friends and squeal like a pig, then I remember they think this relationship has been real for weeks. It's a killjoy.

"Somewhere in between car head and you screaming profanities at my ceiling while you came a half dozen times, it happened without our permission."

I can tell he doesn't like admitting that, like perhaps it makes him a lesser individual for not being able to control his feelings. Doesn't he know I feel the same way?

"It wasn't because of the, well, the messing around, right? I established rules about men spending the night for this very reason. You know this probably won't end well?" My stupid insecurities force me to ask questions that embarrass me.

Macs laughs and swallows hard. "No, Teala, it's not because you have the mouth of an angel, though I'm sure that helped things along. I like you. And you're right, it will end with fire and venom, I'm sure." He says it with a serious voice, and I can't help but laugh.

"If you haven't noticed, I'm sort of easy-going. I'm not the kind to hold a grudge and promise destruction of your life if it doesn't work out. I'm good by myself," I remind him. "I like you, too." I imagine his face right now, and I sigh.

"See how much was accomplished with words?" he asks. "I'll see you in the morning."

He clicks off the phone, and I'm so fucking giddy I scream out loud and stand to jump around on my bed.

My mom flies into the room and throws the light on. "What's wrong?" she asks, her eyes wild, her head looking left and right for a threat. The gesture reminds me of when I was a little girl and she'd save me from my nightmares. Her gaze finally lands on me, standing in the middle of my bed with a grin on my face, and her face softens. She smiles, shaking her head in confusion.

"It's official!" I yell out, jumping once more just for good measure. I sit on the edge of my unmade bed and hug my cell phone to my chest.

"You're officially something," she says, walking toward me, her sleepy smile warming me. She sits next to me and pats a hand on my bare thigh. "What's official, honey?"

She wouldn't know the truth, either. She's in the same category as my friends. I want to tell her how Macs was a womanizer, how he hasn't slept with anyone else since he met me. I want to tell her how we haven't even had sex yet, even though we probably would have on our very first date. I want to tell her how it all started off as pretending, and then things turned into something real and visceral. I can't tell her any of those things, though, because I'm messed up and I don't want to put it on display.

"Macs and I," I state. It's as simple and as complicated as that.

"Was it not before?"

"It was," I say quickly. "We just kind of solidified it. That's all."

She smiles at me again, her white teeth gleaming. "I could have told you that earlier. Don't you see the way he looks at you?"

I don't, and it makes my stomach roll in disbelief.

Viola is an expert at reading people. After my father broke her, she spent a lot of her time studying those around her. I think she was trying to figure out how she didn't see the blow coming. She trusted too much. Loved too much and got destroyed because of it. Now she sees things the normal human can't possibly understand. It's a gift that only those who have been tortured in a very specific way can claim. She pats my back.

"He's crazy about you," she says.

I'm lost in thought—in revelation. Could she be wrong? Or am I that unseeing? Just like Viola was before she was crushed? Tears prick the corners of my eyes. "Why did he do that to you?"

She takes my shoulders and faces me head-on. "Don't compare the past to your future."

"Only idiots don't learn from mistakes, Mom," I say. A traitorous tear cuts down my cheek. "Why did he do that to you? You're perfect. Look at you!" If she can't hold onto an awful man, how am I supposed to keep Macs Newstead? It's hopeless.

"Because it was a lesson I needed. That's it. You deserve to be happy. You're already successful. What makes you think you can't have a successful relationship? You think I don't know about your commitment issues, Teala? Anyone can see them from a mile away. That man watches you like you alone shift the earth on its axis. I'm not wrong about these things." She hugs me, and I go willingly into the crook of her neck and inhale the sweet scent of her facial lotion. It smells like flowers and honey. It reminds me of so much.

Closing my eyes, I breathe. I'm an adult woman seeking solace in my mother's embrace. What must she think of me? How weak can one person be? "I'm scared," I admit.

"If you weren't scared, it wouldn't be worth it," she

says, smoothing my hair down like she did when I was a little girl. "Macs is probably just as scared, honey. Love is funny like that. It pushes you up to the edge of a really steep cliff and gives you an option to jump and fly or jump and fall."

I pull away to look at her face. "That's utterly morbid, Mom." I narrow my eyes, letting my tears stay where they are.

She smiles and wipes at my face with her thumbs. "All you have to do is remember to flap your wings. A little falling is inevitable." She pats my head, turns off the light, and walks out of my room without a backward glance. She doesn't shut the door, and I hear the television in her room. She has the news on.

I close my door against more bad news about the state of our world. Retreating to my bed, I throw myself back and slip under my covers, feeling like a small child.

I think about a lot of things while I'm trying to fall asleep. Like, does my mom adhere to her own advice? Is Macs scared too? What happens to us when he deploys? Do I even want a relationship? Will it affect my studio? No, I won't let it. What happens if it doesn't work out between us?

What happens if it does? I need to talk to Carina. She's in the same boat I am. She'll know what to tell me.

I fall asleep eventually, my thoughts on one very masculine, dimpled smile and the words he said that changed everything.

CHAPTER FOURTEEN

Macs

TEALA IS SITTING on the porch swing next to my mother. I'm watching them through the kitchen window while my father fixes lunch. My hands are twitching by my sides, and my heart is thumping jaggedly—a reminder I'm not myself. I have no clue how the fuck to control my emotions, or my own body, or my thoughts. Wild doesn't even describe how I'm feeling. She sucked my dick on the drive here. I had to pull over a few seconds after she started because my eyes started rolling back in my damn head.

See? No control over my body. She's good, but it's more than that. She swallowed my hot load without spilling a drop, leaned back into her seat, and smiled at me. She reminded me of a tiger hunting prey. Eventually I regained enough composure to pull back into traffic and finish the drive. It helped for a little while, but I'm having withdrawals again. Not just for her mouth. I want to be close enough to touch her body, smell the skin on her neck that's been swept by fragrant hair.

It didn't happen gradually. Falling for her happened like a landslide. A light was switch thrown, and in its wake lies a mess of emotions I have no fucking clue what to do with. My dad is prattling on about the football game and how he lost a bet with Murray from down the street. He's cursing under his breath, and I'm offering a few words here and there. He has no idea how wrapped up I am in my staring. It's not often I get to glimpse her when she is unaware.

My mother can't stop looking at her either. Teala's beauty is truly something to behold. You can't really appreciate it fully unless you do stare rudely for a while. That's how you notice the freckle on her cheek, or the flecks of color in her eyes, or the way her slender neck curves so perfectly before her chin begins. It's all too much to take in at the same time. So, I stare now—I practice being enamored by her even though I hate the essence of it to the core.

My father clears his throat from right behind me. "Sure is a looker, Son," he says. "I said that a few times, but it seems you were too busy thinking the same thing to hear your old pops."

My rudeness knows no bounds today, obviously. "Yeah, she is, isn't she?" I turn to face him, as politeness dictates. "Mom looks well," I say, trying to change the subject.

He claps me on the shoulder and offers the trademark grin he passed down to me. "She's well and fine now that you're home. Seems she's takin' a liking to your new bird, huh?"

He turns it around again. "Seems so," I reply. "Need any help?" I nod over to the counter where he's spreading cold cuts and cheeses for sandwiches.

He shakes his head. "Nah, I'd rather have a chat with my boy. It's been too long, Son. You're taking off again now, aren't ya?"

I sigh, relieved he's asked about work. Work is safe. Work is a known entity I can talk about for as long as he wants. My job is foreign to him. He's worked a white-collar job his whole life. The military isn't some handed-down tradition in my home. It's my thing and my thing only. With my penchant for hair products and designer jeans, one of the only things he's interested in is my career. I tell him what I can, but I don't tell him where I'm deploying. He asks me about the terrorist attacks that are cropping up all over the world and if I know who is fully responsible. He's happy with the answers I give him even if they're veiled truths.

I glance out the window every once in a while and catch sight of Teala. She's talking with her hands and smiling a lot, and a pang of envy strikes me square in the chest. It's too new to share her with anyone else.

My father asks about my training trip coming up. The one where we shoot each other.

"It's paintballs this time, Dad. Don't worry," I say.

His eyes still turn down in the corner, and I'm reminded that he'll always worry about me whether I tell him to or not. He nods and turns his gaze to the porch swing.

I clear my throat. "Lunch?" I ask.

Distraction. That's what I need. Before, when I didn't know any better, I thought I needed space away from Teala. I didn't want to see texts from her or hear her voice on the phone and only see her for bits and pieces of time. Now, I realize the only way I can fix myself is if I give myself over to this completely and hope I can fuck her out of my system.

He goes out to the porch and tells my mother it's time for lunch. Both of the women look up at him and smile their acknowledgments. He sits back down in front of me. "You still thinking of moving to Virginia Beach?" he asks.

As a SEAL, I only have a few options for duty

stations. It's San Diego, Virginia Beach, or Hawaii. The pipe dream has always been to end up in Virginia Beach. That's where the elite SEALs work. Better known as SEAL Team Six. The selection process is severe and long, and only the best of the best are chosen for a spot.

My heart thunders out a staccato as I watch Teala stand from the swing and make her way to the house. "No, no. Not now anyway," I admit. It's a lie, but I don't want that conversation anywhere near her ears yet.

"Oh, no?" he asks, busying himself with the condiments and drinks. "What changed?"

Teala and my mother walk into the kitchen. They walk so close their arms brush together, and their smiles are effortless.

"The house, you know? I want to give that some time. Get everything together and fixed. Get a couple more deployments under my belt." Initially I set out for it to be a quick flip of a job, but I've grown attached to it over the months. "Maybe down the road," I tell him, honestly.

Everyone is listening to our conversation at this point, and all I can do is hope Teala doesn't ask questions.

I smile in her direction. "You two seemed to be having quite the conversation," I tell her.

The smile worked. Her attraction to it is unflinching. I almost feel guilty for using it against her, but I can't. I'm not ready to have this conversation with her. She wouldn't want to hear it anyway.

"What were you talking about?" I edge.

"You," they both say at the same time.

"I was afraid of that. Mom, I told you this was a new…arrangement. She doesn't want to hear that kind of stuff." I have no idea what they were talking about, but I can only imagine.

My mom drawls out a warning for me to hush then says, "It's only fair this beautiful woman knows what she's getting herself into. Someone needs to warn her off." My mother and father laugh, but Teala's face drops, and she looks like she's going to be violently sick. My mom's joke hit a little too close to home.

Dating wasn't something I was ever interested in when I lived in my parents' house. Oh, I fucked all right. Under the bleachers, in the locker room at the high school, the playground equipment at the local park in the dark of night, but they never saw girls in my world. I went stag to all of the mandatory dances like prom and homecoming and took advantage of opportunities to get off in between. I was a dog. I am a dog. My parents don't know that. What could my mother possibly caution her against? My schedule?

I force a laugh. "Everyone can see the caution tape around my body, Mom. Teala doesn't need any warnings."

Teala nods and stands next to me. I notice she doesn't brush against me. She keeps her distance. We eat lunch and drink fruit punch and try not to eye fuck each other. She excuses herself to use the restroom, and I tell her I'll show her where it is even though she's already been once right when we arrived. I follow her into the upstairs bathroom and close the door behind us.

"Your parents know we're in here together," she says dryly.

I waggle my brows. "As much as I'd love to fuck you in the bathroom where I was potty trained, I merely wanted to ask if anything was wrong. What did my mom tell you?" I feel a little panicked. I'm worried about something small and insignificant. That's not my way. It's never been my way. Give me a large problem and let me give you ten ways to solve it effectively.

Teala smiles. "She was joking about warning me, Macs. She regaled me with funny tales from your childhood and asked a whole bunch of questions about my studio. I think she wants to take a class." She looks down at her nails and starts smoothing her nail beds with her thumb. "What she said about the warning merely brought me back into reality." She looks at the wall. A photo of a beach stares back at her.

I sigh. I can deal with this. "The reality is I'm away much of the time. Even when I'm home, I'm not fully here, and I've never had to worry what that means for someone else. She was joking, but it should be a warning," I deadpan.

Her eyes meet mine, and for the first time I see a vulnerability there. Something that isn't inherent to her, a guard down and an open heart begging for something I can't give. "It's worth trying?" she asks.

I think about our chemistry and remember what it feels like to have her skin burning against mine. "Yes." Closing the distance with one step, I take her in my arms. I don't want to remember what she feels like. I want it right now. "I have no idea what that means."

"I don't either," she admits, pressing her face into my chest. "I should ask my friends." Teala laughs, and her shaking body gives me a hard-on. She stiffens when she feels it.

"If you ask them, they'll give you the dictionary version. We're doing this our way. No rules. No preconceived notions about right or wrong." A little definition would be nice, but it's too late for that.

Clutching the sides of my T-shirt, she looks up. "It's wrong we're hiding in a bathroom," Teala whispers, her hand sliding down to cup my cock.

"What's wrong is that your hand isn't inside my jeans," I counter.

"I have a valid question about something first," she says, pulling her hand away.

Sighing, I nod.

"What happens after we have sex and you lose interest?"

I shake my head. "What if you lose interest after I fuck your brains out?" Turn it around if you can't answer honestly.

"There are hundreds, maybe thousands, of women lining up to take my place. It's a lot of pressure. I don't have that draw."

She always seems confident, so much so it never occurred to me to reassure her of anything. She's beautiful. I've never wanted a relationship with anyone but her, or even that her business's success is extremely impressive for someone her age. Surely she knows these things.

I kiss her instead. Her arms twine around my neck the way they always do when I kiss her. She presses against my body so our every curve and muscle are pressed together. Her tongue slides inside my mouth as the kiss deepens into something a little more—something that shouldn't be happening in this bathroom. I pick her up and set her on the edge of the counter and reach behind her to turn the water on.

Handwashing seems a suitable activity in here if my mother has any questions. I realize how ludicrous it seems moments later when Teala lets out a moan against my lips. She pulls my lip with her teeth and lets it slap back into place.

"We should go," she whispers.

"Conversations in bathrooms always mean more than any place else. No rules?" I remind her.

Sliding her hands under my shirt, she lets her fingertips glaze over my abs, one by one. "Agreed." A shiver runs up my spine from the coolness of her fingers. Slowly, she scoots off the counter and picks up her cell phone. She snaps a photo of the framed beach on the wall. "This is proof," she explains.

And I sort of get it. Why she thinks photos mean more than words can. She summed up our relationship discussion with one low-quality image stored in her phone that will reside there for God knows how long. We enter the living room looking guilty, but it doesn't matter. Neither of my parents even knows we exist. They're transfixed with the news and the horror scrolling across their screens quicker than the news anchor can speak. Another terror attack happened overseas.

"It's so awful. You won't be dealing with those people on your next deployment, will you?" my mother asks, turning to face me with wide, terrified eyes. Is that a joke question?

I speak so little of my actual job that I force her to hang on to every word I do give her. "Mom. You know I'm always safe. You don't have anything to worry about."

Distractedly, I brush a piece of lint off my jeans. Teala watches me and not the television when my gaze finally wanders back to find hers. The questions in her eyes mirror my mother's sentiment, but she's not taking the Kool-Aid I'm offering.

I shrug. My mother has already turned back to the TV, my statement all but forgotten or written off as a harmless lie told to placate a scared parent.

"I'm being terribly rude. I'm so sorry, dear," Mom says.

Teala turns her focus away. "Don't be silly. You're not being rude at all." The questions in her eyes don't go away. If anything, the can of worms is open and airing to be ready for later. I swallow down the unease I feel with that realization. I don't owe anyone anything. I don't want to explain myself or have someone worry over me unnecessarily.

My mother explains that my aunt called and that's why she turned on the television. They aren't usually in the habit of watching the dumb box. It's the truth. When I was growing up, they didn't let me watch anything fun. MTV was banned, and anything not considered educational was blacklisted. When I got old enough, sports were allowed. Mostly because my dad watched them and she couldn't say anything about that.

"It's so rare, or rather, never have we met any of Macallister's friends. I'm sorry to be so caught up in this." She motions to the TV but turns around to face us, several throw pillows toppling onto the floor.

"Macallister?" Teala says, voice loud and incredulous.

I grin. "Guess you didn't get all the details when you had a little chat outside?"

She shakes her head. Mom tells her it's a fine, Scottish name, and Teala agrees even though her face is still contorted in confusion.

Taking my pointer finger, I tap the bottom of her chin. "Close your mouth. It's not the time nor place for that." Lies. There's always a loophole for her blow jobs.

Her expression morphs into mortification, but she ends with a chuckle. My sick humor is appreciated in this instance. I've also successfully turned her attention away from the television. Eventually they turn off the news, because even if it bothers them, no one wants to listen to it all day long. People want to mask atrocities, push them to the corner where they won't ruin their lives. It's true. Most people dislike change and will do everything in their power to avoid it. Move their sofa around the living room, sure. Think about a world changing by the hands of terror? Nope. Blinders in place. It's just as well. The average human can do nothing to stop it.

Teala sends glares my way in between banter and baked goods, and I have no fucking clue what they mean. She seems to be having an okay time with my parents, even if it's making me fucking sweat. If I wasn't confused about our situation, I am most certainly now. Our conversation in the bathroom did nothing to quell my own insecurities about letting another person into my life. A compassionate bone doesn't reside in my body. Taking on another's worries is tantamount to compassion.

What do I know about her? Truly? That doesn't have to do with her tight body or sex appeal? She loves her mother, and Viola is the most important person in her world. She scowled when her mother mentioned her father at lunch. She's unlike her friends when it comes to most things, but that seems to work to her benefit. She likes vodka and laughing more than she likes dessert and serious conversations. A large bookshelf lined a wall of her apartment and contained various authors and genres, so she must enjoy reading. Sloths. That's a given. She's enamored by my looks, but not my career, which is always a plus. Men gravitate toward her like she's the fucking sun and they've been trapped in a nuclear winter. Are those facts enough to establish any sense of a person? Who. The. Fuck. Knows.

"She's rickrolling me in sugar, Macallister. You have to get me out of here," Teala says, breaking me from my trance.

She has this tiny little beauty mark on her face. It rises when she smiles. I don't object to my full name, but I can tell she says it with ill intent—meant as a jab.

She licks her lips because she thinks that's where I'm looking.

"You can tell her no," I reply.

"I did. Several times. She doesn't care if I'm full." Her eyes widen, and she presses her palm against her tight

157

stomach. "We should get going anyway." Teala looks at her wrist and taps her watch a few times. "I have a million messages to reply to. My studio is hosting a yoga retreat. People are having problems signing up." Her face contorts as she excuses herself to grab her cell phone to make a few calls.

She told me about the retreat, but it was before I cared what she had planned in the future. Now, these are things I'll be expected to remember.

My phone vibrates in my pocket, and I pull it out. It's the team's group text. It usually isn't active in the middle of the day. At night, in the middle of the night to be exact, is when the porn memes and inappropriate photos start flooding the feed. If the average human glimpsed our texts, we'd be judged harshly.

I laugh at the image Tahoe texted and click out of my messages lest anyone see the travesty of our collective, sadistic humor. Teala is pacing back and forth in the back room, her phone pressed to her ear and her free arm swinging wildly.

My mother presses a glass of lemonade into my hand. "Thanks for letting us meet her. I do hope you'll care for that one. She's a keeper," Mom says.

"As opposed to what?" I ask, smirking. I find the word "tosser" on the tip of my tongue but chuckle instead.

She clucks her tongue. "You know the type. The ones who roll around with any manly beast."

My chuckle turns into full-blown laughter that draws Teala's gaze.

My mother has no clue. Or Teala is that good at acting. She runs her fingers over her lips as she continues speaking into her phone. I can't hear her words, but I can read her eyes. She likes my laugh as much as she likes my appearance, and we'll need to do something about that soon.

Gently I place my hands on Mom's shoulders. "As funny as that was, I don't think you should talk about manly beasts and rolling with them." I glance at my dad.

He smiles and shrugs. Must be genetics.

"Oh, stop it. I'm old. Not dead!" she fires back. The light is back in her eyes now that we've had the television off for a while. "Promise me you won't mess it up. A woman is the only commodity you can't work for."

Ah, she knows my personality well. My hands fall from her shoulders, and I shove them in my pockets. I haven't even slept with Teala yet. *I'm working, all right. I'm working fucking hard.*

Mom hugs me. "Stop and smell the roses every once in a while. It won't kill you."

It fucking just may. Teala appears behind me and changes the subject to yoga. Dad pretends to be interested, but I know he's envisioning lewd poses. It's a guy thing. My phone vibrates in my pocket again, but I don't dare take it out with everyone around. Teala hears it and makes a show of staring at my pocket and then flicking her gaze back to my face. I pretend I have no clue what she's insinuating.

Teala has a Tupperware full of cakes, muffins, and brownies sitting on her lap on the drive back to her apartment. She stays pretty silent as I drive, texting every so often. She answers when I ask her if she had a good time, and it's not an open hostility, but I feel it simmering just below the surface.

I park in the parking garage, in the same spot as before, and trail behind as she makes her way to the elevator. I'm basically staring a hole in the side of her head by the time we make it to her front door. Her effort at ignoring me completely is commendable. I tell her so.

"I'm not ignoring you, Macs," she says, unlocking her door and pushing it open.

I walk in behind her and close it. I clear my throat. In favor of ignoring me some more, she takes the confections into her kitchen and starts piling them on a serving tray.

"I was thinking about leaving these at the studio, but then again most of my clients don't really frequent the sugar," she explains to thin air.

Making my way to the sofa, I rumple the throw blanket casually tossed across the arm. Her head turns quicker than the exorcist, her gaze like daggers, aimed at the blanket.

Smirking, I say, "I leave tomorrow, Teala. Can we spend some time together? Alone?" Patting the seat next to me, I cock my head to the side in question.

The plate lands on the counter with a loud clank as she puts it on the serving bar. I wince. Irritation unlike anything I've ever dealt with courses my veins.

"If you're mad about something, say it. Whatever this is," I say, waving my hand in her direction, "isn't getting your point across."

Her mouth puckers in a scowl. "I'm not in the habit of telling anyone anything," she replies, folding her arms across her chest.

I stand. "And I'm not in the habit of prodding, so I'll go ahead and head out?" I point at the door with a dramatic flair.

"You were on your phone all day, Macs," she says. Breathlessly, she sighs and hangs her head, like I've punched her. That's how much it takes for her to admit this to me. "We talked about trying to start something real, and then I see you on your phone all day. It makes me think it's all bullshit and you're toying with me. I hate feeling self-conscious. I hate feeling like I have to ask you.

I hate that you were on the phone and that I gave a shit. Do you see what's happening already? This is awful. Who am I?" She pulls her hands through her hair and avoids looking anywhere near me.

She picks up a brownie and walks to the window. I watch as she looks at the chocolate like it may bite her and then shoves a bite into her mouth.

"A couple things. If this is jealousy, then this isn't going to work. Jealousy breeds mistrust, and if we don't have trust between us, we have nothing. I'm gone constantly, Teala. You have to trust me. I was texting with my friends, or rather they were texting and I was watching the group message unravel into complete depravity. I'm not toying with you." I stand next to her, nudging her shoulder with my side.

She swallows her mouthful. "Exhibit A. This is madness, and I've concocted it out of thin air. Fuck. I'm so sorry. I'm not a jealous person. I swear it," she says, groaning.

She's not, but our chemistry is changing both of us. I pull her tightly to my chest and lean down to kiss her. She's still cocoa sweet. I moan into her mouth when she runs her hands up my arms and clutches onto my biceps, her grip firm and cool. Her tongue lashes out to meet mine as her body goes limp in my arms. I pull away and can still taste her on my lips. I lick them. "I'd say I won't be jealous, but what's mine is mine," I admit.

Teala grins—this unabashed show of undeniable happiness. "You have no idea what that means to me. I've always wanted to be cavemanned."

I shake my head, my bottom lip between my teeth. "I'll drag you by your hair and club you into submission if that's your thing."

She laughs, leaning back to get a better view of my

face. "If anyone else heard you joke like, that you'd die by hot pokers."

Raising my brow, I shake my head again. "If anyone saw my group text, I would be sent to prison and then flogged to death."

That forces her smile to disappear.

"I'm joking, Teala." Somewhat. I palm the side of her face with both hands. "What?" I see questions in her eyes. "What's on your mind?"

"I was just thinking about what you said at your parents' house. What do you do during deployments? Consider me a military virgin. I know nothing." A fact that's both alluring and frustrating.

I sigh. "I liked where things were headed when you were jealous," I exclaim.

She slides her hands down my biceps, over my chest, and down to the button on my jeans. With a grin, she cocks her head in question.

"Yes. That jealousy," I encourage. Closing my eyes, I wait.

"You'll have to tell me things eventually, you know?" She unbuttons and unzips my pants and then stills.

I peek at her through one lowered lid.

"We're not pretending anymore," she says.

"When I'm deployed I do what you…assume I do."

"*Call of Duty*?" she asks innocently. She wants real answers. My stomach rolls.

I smile. "No. Not *Call of Duty* at all. Although I think they've replicated our uniforms pretty spot-on by my last account."

She stares at me.

"There are missions and bad guys."

She stares some more.

"It's dangerous sometimes and boring at other times. I

use weapons and eat shitty food." More staring. Fuck. "I'll be able to call you while I'm away."

Her eyebrows rise. Finally.

"Connectivity is pretty good on the larger bases, which is where I'm usually at. The smaller outstations have spotty connection, but I'll always be able to get in touch." Or so I've seen with my friends who have spouses to report back to.

"That doesn't sound too bad, although I have nothing to compare it to. What if it's harder than I anticipate?"

I wave my palms in front of me. "Wait, wait, wait. We haven't even fucked yet. We could be completely incompatible and never see each other again after this."

"This?" she says, pointing to the floor. "Like, we're going to do it now? Shouldn't we make it special? We did the prison sentence of four dates."

I love that she ignores my barb. It was such a lie it wasn't even worth her responding. The second my dick sinks home, I know it will feel like home—the opposite of incompatible.

She stares out the window again.

"You're overthinking it again," I say.

"Can we do it at your house?" she asks, slinging her hands on her hips.

"We aren't teenagers, Teala. Stop saying we're going to do it." I chastise.

She laughs.

"I'm going to love you all dowwn," I croon, grabbing her by the waist. Pressing my groin into her, I hump her a few times for good measure. Teala gags and leans over to fake retch. I pull her ass against my cock because the urge is too hard to resist.

"That was a record," she says, shaking her head, glancing up over her shoulder. "You haven't rapped during a conversation in, like, twelve hours."

I think I have, but she just didn't recognize the song. It's criminal. I tighten my hold on her waist.

I shrug. "What can I say? Sometimes I don't have the greatest material to work with. You should give me some better lines."

She spins in my grasp. "Quite the opposite," she says. "I like the challenge. I should walk around quoting Shakespeare. You'd never be able to rap anything ever again."

I kiss her to shut her up. "You don't give me enough credit," I growl into her mouth. "You really want to wait until tonight? At my house?"

She moves her lips against mine, and it's a whisper of carnal pleasure. She's not kissing, just brushing, and my dick responds immediately.

"I'd like that," she says.

And that seals the deal. I would have gone to town right now against this glass, on the floor, sofa, or her bed would have worked as well, but if she's asking this of me, I'll make it happen. Not because I think it's what I'm supposed to do, I realize. I want to.

I nod and gently push her to arm's length. "I'm leaving right now. I hope you don't find it in bad taste. I want to fuck you, you understand? Also, I'm technically allowed to fuck you. You're in my arms with your hands wandering my body. You want it to be special, something I don't understand but will relent, but I have to go before I trip and fall and my cock ends up buried inside your pussy, you understand?"

She bites her lip. "You understand I want that?"

Blowing out a breath, I let her words hit me square in the dick. "Come over later. We'll have dinner." The doorknob in my hand, I peer at her over my shoulder. She hasn't moved. I'd fathom she hasn't taken a breath since I last spoke.

"And we'll do it?" she asks, eyes wide.

I chuckle. "Oh, we'll do it all right."

I shut her apartment door and suck in a deep breath. The rules are exhausting. Relationships are exhausting. Not only am I worried about what I want and feel, but I almost have to anticipate what she is feeling as well. If I don't want to come off as a dick, that is. I have too many other dick tendencies to not give this my best effort.

As I drive to Tahoe's house, I find myself hoping Teala is in fact an awful lay.

CHAPTER FIFTEEN
Teala

BECAUSE NEITHER OF us has any clue what we're doing, there's a lot of gray area and awkward questions. Against my better judgment, I'm at Charlotte's house, and my girlfriends are all staring at me like I'm a marmoset at the zoo. Eyes squinted, like maybe I'm a figment of their imagination. Let's be honest, they're also in complete shock.

"One more time. No sex? You haven't had sex with him?" Jasmine asks. She's the one who called the emergency meeting. Jasmine shakes her head while Charlotte laughs. "It's unbelievable. We thought for sure you've been screwing that man the entire time."

"I didn't think she was," Carina interjects, her voice soft and soothing.

I fake mock outrage. "Thank you, Care. Someone who doesn't think me a liar!" I am, but not about what they're suggesting. No need to correct that minor oversight. "I've followed your advice implicitly. It's the fifth date tonight, and we have plans," I explain. Normally I'd wax poetic about dicks and sex just to jar my friends and shake things up, but talking about having sex with Macs is different. The thought makes me shiver. "It's hot in here,

Charlotte," I add. I fan myself with my hand. I'm turning a bright shade of chartreuse.

Carina lays a hand on my back. "It's going to be okay. I know what you're feeling right now."

I look at her like she's mad. She's living with a SEAL whom she hasn't fucked yet. I saw her boyfriend, Smith, from afar once, and afar is how I want to keep him. He's scary and beautiful, but by Carina's accounts, he's also the nicest man on the damn planet. I didn't get one of those. I probably wouldn't want one of those either. "Things have a way of working out whether you think they're good ideas or not."

Shaking my head, I say, "Don't do that, Care. That thing when you're trying to make it seem like you're wise and all-knowing, when you just know how to throw words together to make the biggest impact."

Carina smiles and looks down at her lap. "I can't help it." She laughs then, and I'm relieved I didn't hurt her feelings with my jest. "It's a good sentiment, though. Regardless of my...talents."

Charlotte clears her throat. She bumped the thermostat down and grabbed a veggie tray from the kitchen. "It's leftover from my leggings party last week. I wouldn't eat the ranch, but the veggies should be good," she explains. Charlotte works from home as a web designer, so a leggings party sounds like something she'd embrace fully and truly.

Carina crunches a carrot like a little rabbit.

Jasmine thanks her with a snide remark about cleaning out her fridge once in a blue moon, then she turns to me again to pepper me with questions. Vegas is brought up, and they've hailed me the winner—Charlotte, begrudgingly. "There's really no way to prove she isn't lying. I saw the way that man looked at you, Teala," Charlotte squalls.

Jasmine chimes in, and they get lost in a conversation about Macs's looks. I'm not even mad because they don't over exaggerate any one detail more than another.

My watch pings a message, and I glance down. *Photo from Macs* is displayed on my wrist. The three words make my heart pound. I try to be casual as I bring my arm to my lap and tap the message to bring up the photo. It's a photo of his neatly made bed. My insides turn to molten lava, and Charlotte could crank the AC down to arctic level and I'd still feel hot. I click it off quickly.

The urge to tell him that photos *are* equipped to say more than words arises, but I squash it. It would ruin the moment, and what a moment it is. My friends are dissecting my love life as they compare it to their own. Carina is lost in a text message, smiling like a lunatic, but she chimes in when they start a conversation about kissing.

"Carina knows how to kiss. She writes it like she lives it. I bet she's super good in the sack," Jasmine says, forcing Carina's cheeks to turn scarlet. Jasmine isn't just Carina's best friend, she's also the literary agent for her alter ego, Greenleigh. They have a relationship so intertwined that no one questions it anymore. I'd imagine the edges blur when you write about something you also live.

I pull my hair into a ponytail. The only reason I left it down is because I thought it would be more alluring, but I can't deal with the extra heat right now. The anticipation is making me nauseous. "Enough. No more talk about my sex life or the lack thereof."

"Here, here!" Carina injects, flipping her cell phone face down in her lap. "Can we just eat Charlotte's leftovers and talk about shoes or something?"

"This is where you guys should give me advice about sex in relationships," I say. "How is it different? What's expected after? Cuddling?" Cringing, I shake my head. "Never mind, don't tell me," I affirm. "I'll do what I feel is best and hope it's not weird."

"It's going to be weird. Sex is messy," Charlotte says.

She tells us a story about the first time she had sex with her last boyfriend. I'm left gaping, wishing I never had to look her in the face again. Carina is covering her mouth, eyes wide. Jasmine is laughing, and Charlotte ends the story with a smug, closed-lip grin.

Standing from the couch, I tell them I'm going to be sick and rush into the bathroom, slamming the door. I hear their raucous laughter through the thick wood and smile. I pull my phone out of the pocket of my workout jacket and look at the photo Macs sent one more time. I should send him a photo—something scandalous and lewd—something that would make Charlotte's story sound like child's play.

There's a soft knock on the door. "Are you okay?" Carina's voice floats through.

I open the door and make sure my smile is in place. "I'm fine. I was joking. Charlotte is so gross sometimes. My stories are way worse anyway. It takes more than a dripping wet panty hamster to make me vomit."

Carina laughs and then agrees, but her smile fades. "I'm having sex with Smith soon, too. I get it. I'm already in love with him."

Her declaration sets my teeth on edge. It makes me question my feelings for Macs and ask myself what the hell is love? Carina exited a relationship prior to Smith— not that long ago either. How can she possibly know she loves him?

If there ever was a person to explain it, she's standing in front of me. I reach behind her and shut the bathroom door with a soft click. "What is love? Explain it."

Carina laughs. "You're having an existential crisis,

aren't you?" Her eyebrows rise, and her shoulders shake. "Do you not want to have sex with him?" It's a stupid question, but given the circumstances, it's warranted.

"Of course I do," I reply, letting my hands rise up and slap against my legs. "Sex is my thing. I never know those men, though. It's just...sex," I explain. "This is," I say, pausing.

"This is more?" Carina supplies for me.

Coughing, I try to hide my emotion. "When you say it like that, it makes it sound like I'm goo-goo-eyed in love with him, and I'm not sure that's the case. It's the chemistry between us."

She nods. "I saw it." She sees everything. Then she turns around and writes about it. I wish I had that skill. I'd be less messed up, I bet.

Charlotte has fifteen bottles of perfume sitting on a mirrored tray by her vanity. I pick one up absentmindedly and spritz the air.

"I'm worried he's going to bail after sex," I admit. Waving my hand in the air, I try to disperse the flowery scent. "That's what always happens, and I don't think this is any different. I'm not sure if it's going to be different, and I'm preparing myself mentally for a few different outcomes."

"That's just because it's all you know, Tay. It's different, and you know it. It scares you. Have you talked to him about this?"

I laugh out loud—a sardonic cackle. "Macs doesn't do emotions. If I had this conversation with him, he'd head for the hills so fast, my head would be left spinning."

"You should probably try. I bet he'd be receptive. He's only dating you, correct? No other women?"

I wince. "I think it's just me." How can I be sure? I feel like he's always on his cell phone. I explain how wrapped up in the app dating culture he was before me, and now she's the one wincing.

"Then he may be feeling the same way if he's given that lifestyle up. Big changes are hard and scary. Even for men who aren't afraid of anything."

I pick up another bottle of perfume and sniff the top.

"Don't spray that one. It already smells like a French whore on a Saturday night in here," Carina snaps.

It doesn't. Not really. Charlotte is into things like perfume and makeup. I have a couple of bottles to my name, but nothing like what she has. Exquisite bottles in deep hues and clear bottles that look like diamonds. Maybe I'll buy another bottle the next time I'm at the mall.

I set the bottle back down. "You never answered me."

She sighs. "What is love?"

I widen my eyes. *Duh.*

"It's different for everyone," she says, turning her eyes away from me. "It never feels the same twice."

Bullshit. Absolute bullshit. There has to be some singular quality that resides in love for each and every person. "I don't believe that." Though I've never experienced it.

Carina silences me with a look. "I thought I was in love, but when I met Smith, I realized the error of my ways. Sometimes love placates. Sometimes it washes over you like small waves coming and going. Sometimes it's so deep you drown in it."

I nod. I understand that. "Drowning. Death. Sounds about right."

She laughs. "You'll know. I think you already know."

"I don't know him well enough to say that for sure."

"You miss him?" Carina asks. "You get excited to see him? You rearrange your life to fit him in it?" Even now,

I'm jonesing to text him back. I miss him when we're not together.

In favor of answering her questions, I tell her I'll talk to him. She likes that answer better anyway. I can tell she doesn't like being peppered with questions about love when she's contemplating her own feelings in a new relationship. Does Smith love her? I wonder.

"How do you know if he loves you?" I ask quickly.

The bathroom door is open now. "He gave up an entire life for me." Sadness replaces her former smile, and my stomach turns. What must it feel like to live with that guilt?

"He got the better end of the deal," I reassure her.

Her smile in response doesn't meet her eyes. After she leaves, I snap a photo of a perfume bottle and send it to Smith. *Love and perfume*, I think. He'll never get that one.

I walk back out to my friend's gray living room and announce my departure.

"Don't do anything I wouldn't do," Jasmine whoops.

Charlotte hugs me briefly and pushes me back toward the door.

"I have to get ready for my own date. It's number two, though, so I won't get to have as much fun as you," Jasmine adds.

Stupid, stupid rules. I can't fault them that much because I'm in a completely different place now that I followed along with their guidelines. I'd admit defeat before I admit they might hold some merit.

"You guys do realize I've banged a guy before, right?" I ask.

Carina smiles.

"Not one like him." Charlotte cackles. "That man is intimidatingly beautiful."

I shrug. "Not everyone can be as lucky as us," I say, nodding at Carina.

She blushes. I close the door behind me and exit into the warm SoCal breeze. It will get colder by the minute at this point.

I text Macs a photo of my steering wheel, the German emblem barely visible in the low light. It doesn't take long to get to his house using the freeway. Less than ten minutes later, I'm pulling into his driveway with shaking hands and a roiling stomach. Did I eat acid-tinged lettuce for lunch? Silently I give myself a pep talk as I pull my hair elastic out.

I flip down my mirror and fix my face using the few items I keep in my handbag. Mascara needs another coat. Blush for color I surely won't need in T-minus five minutes, ChapStick instead of gloss. Gloss gets messy on dicks and lips. I'm comforted by the fact I'm going through the motions. This is what I would do before any normal date. Nothing is odd about my appearance or preparation. It's comforting.

It's everything inside me that is strange. He won't see that part, though. "Breathe, Teala," I whisper.

Locking my car using the fob, I sling my leather bag over my shoulder and head for his front door. Many of the tools and construction equipment that were here the first time I came over are now gone, and I'm able to see how truly beautiful his house is.

Macs is leaning against the doorframe when I round the corner. I startle.

"Hi."

"Hi back," Macs replies.

He's shirtless, with a pair of lounge pants riding low on his chiseled, narrow hips. Even with a quick glance, I see the outline of his cock hanging against his leg. I don't let my gaze stray anywhere too long, and when I meet his eyes, he's still studying me through narrow, hungry eyes.

"That was fast. Did you speed?"

I take a few more steps until I'm standing in the light shining in front of his door. "I never break the law."

One brow rises in surprise. "I'd like to agree to disagree on that one. I'm pretty sure that body is illegal in every continent." He runs his gaze up and down my height one more time, but it's like he's undressing me with his eyes this time. There's nothing subtle, and he doesn't care if I know what he's doing. With his lip still tucked into his mouth, he motions for me to come in.

I'm still shaking my head at his bad pick-up line as I brush against him and into his house. It's clean. Immaculately so. There's no sawdust scent or unfinished pieces of random projects in sight. He must sense me judging the space because he clears his throat from behind me. I'm startled back into reality.

"You cleaned?"

"You noticed," he says.

A white candle is burning softly in the corner of the room on a polished wooden table. There's a shaggy rug beneath his coffee table now, and the kitchen is finished.

"Figured if we were making it special, we shouldn't fuck in a construction site." There's laughter in his voice, but I hear the seriousness too.

This means a lot to him. More than he thinks tonight is worth. I'm not even sure the proper level of enthusiasm that should be shown. He stands next to me, and I take his large, hard hand in mine.

"It looks beautiful. You're right. If it were a construction zone, I'd demand you get out the GoPro and film us for a pay-to-play porn site. Construction babe gets drilled. Think of the possibilities. The tools," I say, raising one brow.

When I meet his gaze, I can tell I made the right call by using humor. His shoulders relax, and he kisses the top of my head. He calls me some sexual pet name, but

I don't respond in favor of surveying the rest of the space.

"I got most of it finished with Tahoe, but the cleaning was all me," he explains, puffing out his chest. "Make yourself comfortable. Wine?"

I nod and smile in what I think is a reassuring gesture and take a seat on the couch. Suddenly the bow-chicka-wow-wow phase has arrived, and I'm uncomfortable. Because this is how all my normal dates start out. There's nothing different. The wine. The effort. Everything. He just wants into my pants.

"Do you know me?" I blurt out frantically. "Truly know me?"

He picks his gaze up from a shining wineglass to meet my eyes. He's unsurprised by my line of questioning, like maybe he anticipated my crazy, and he's ready to defuse it.

"Know you in what regard? I'm trying to remedy the only way in which I'm not familiar with you right now." Macs holds up the wineglass.

"Because I know you're a SEAL, and now I know your real name and that you don't do relationships. Sure, there are other things I know about you, but I don't know what makes you you."

Now he looks a little stunned. He swallows a sip of wine and brings me my glass. I drink it down in four large gulps and brush a drip off my chin with the sleeve of my sweater.

"What makes me me?" I ask.

He's looking at me with wide eyes.

"I know. I'm a little nuts. Get over it."

"That was a nice bottle of wine. What did you think of it?"

I look down at the empty glass and feel mortified.

"Want another glass?" he asks, dimples popping.

"Please."

He sets his glass down and returns with another glass and hands it to me. His hand shakes a little as he extends the cup, and that ratchets my anxiety to another level. Why is he nervous?

I take a small sip and actually taste the Chardonnay this time. It's perfect. The finish is fucking perfect. "Oh my god, this is so good. What is it?" I swirl it around in my glass a few times and take another sip. I moan.

He tells me the name, and finally I relax back against the sofa.

"Better?" he asks, sipping his own.

He tells me the blend and year and how he has a few other bottles. He says he loves white wine but feels like he can't drink it unless he's with a woman. I tell him white wine isn't just for chicks, and he tells me it's akin to a piña colada. Another girly drink he loves to imbibe. I'm laughing in no time. And he's effectively flipped the mood in the room to something more bearable.

He clears his throat and meets my gaze. "You grew up in a family where your mom was everything and then some. Your dad was important until he broke your trust. It's why you don't trust yourself enough to trust. You're trying to keep plants alive, which tells me you'd like to have a pet eventually." He pauses to gauge my reaction.

I smile, urging him to continue.

"You're a nice person. It's why I'm having a hard time with this." The smile vanishes from his face.

"What does that mean?"

"It means I don't usually care enough to do any of this. You know that. And, well, I can't explain it, but whatever is between us is," he replies, looking at the ceiling and bringing a thick hand through his gorgeous hair.

"This is more," I say.

Carina is so wise.

His gaze flicks back to mine. It dips to my chest and back up. "Yes. I don't know what that means. I don't want to go on my apps. I don't want to date other women because all I can think about is you. It started off as a challenge, and I want you to know that. My intention was to fuck you and forget you, Teala. I never wanted things to get this far. I still don't even know how we got here," he says, waving a muscled arm around the room. "You are sitting there like some fucking illusion, and I'm sitting here wondering how you got there, and I know damn well how you got there." His voice is loud, angrier than I think it should be.

I understand everything he's saying.

"I put you there because you deserve to be there."

"I feel the same way." Reaching out, I take his hand in mine. He closes his fist around my fingers, and I flinch.

His eyes are a little frantic as he looks at my hand. "You're not a fucking illusion. And you mean more than I want you to."

This is Macs doing emotions. I didn't even have to ask him. Carina was right about everything. He's just as fucking scared as I am.

"I'm scared too. I've never done this either." Suddenly the only desire I have is to take my clothes off and give myself to him. The elephant in the room might disappear when we're both in our element.

He can't get to me quick enough. Macs takes my head in his hands and presses his lips against mine. His grip is firm on my head, and he tilts my head back. Peeling the sweater off my shoulders, he kisses every inch of exposed skin on each arm as he goes. "I want you so bad. I can't believe I finally get to call you mine," he growls before placing a wet kiss on my collarbone.

When my sweater hits the floor, I stand and push him

back into a seated position and straddle him. His eyes are wide in surprise and excitement.

"I've been yours," I correct him.

His cock flexes against my core once and then again.

"I've been yours," I say again just to see if I can get the same reaction twice.

The smile he responds with is the most earth-shattering, beautiful thing I've ever seen. I kiss him passionately. It's madness and depravity. His lips slant against mine like they were made to mold against my mouth. His teeth pull my lip anytime I moan out in pleasure.

"Are we taking this into the bedroom?" I ask. My breaths are frantic, and I couldn't control them if I tried. This is beyond cardio. This is my heart hammering out a furious pace in warning.

With both hands under my bottom, he picks me up and carries me down the hallway and into his dimly lit bedroom. Our kiss stays fierce and tangled as he walks, and I don't even wonder if he'll drop me. He's multitasking like a boss, and I'm sure if I asked, he'd be able to carry out a few other tasks at the same time. Grinning against his mouth, I tell him how hot he's making me.

He pulls away when we're at the foot of his bed. One glance and I'm certain his space looks exactly the same as it did before. There's not a thing out of place. The big pieces of luggage are gone. There is another candle burning on a low dresser that draws my eye.

"I wanted it to smell nice," he explains and inhales against my neck. "I didn't realize you'd smell so delicious on your own."

I need to ask Charlotte the name of that perfume. Mental note made.

"I would've fucked you even if it smelled like sawdust. That was kind of hot, too," I say, then bite his lip and tease it with my tongue.

Macs's eyes flutter closed. His eyelashes are thick and fan against the top of his cheeks. This man is so fucking exquisite I know I'll never tire of looking at him. His hands squeeze my ass a little harder as he lowers my body down his stomach and then presses me against his erection.

He's hard. He's ready. Our kiss ends abruptly when he sets me on the edge of his bed and backs up a step or two. He's watching me, and I know exactly what he wants. This is familiar territory. I strip out of my shirt and bra and stand to peel my pants and thong off. I turn around and bend over the bed to give him a perfect view of what he finally gets to take for his own. I look over my shoulder, and he's staying put. Maybe he wants me to dance. I sway a little bit, creating a song in my head.

"My entire bed smelled like you. Even after I washed everything twice," he says, voice gruff.

"Did you like that?"

"No," he replies.

I turn to face him then. "Oh?"

"I woke with a hard-on in the middle of the night thinking you were in bed with me. I had to jerk it out to get back to sleep. Everything about you makes me hungry for more. To answer honestly, yes, I did like it. More than I should."

At his remark, I make a show of crawling on his bed, and with my knees spread, I sit down on the top of his comforter. When I rise up, it leaves a wet smudge.

He's watching me with a side grin now.

"Oops. Looks like I got a little of me on your bed." I put my hand over my mouth and widen my eyes.

Macs moves then. Straight for me.

CHAPTER SIXTEEN

Macs

SHE'S KNEELING in the middle of my bed, bare but for a wide smile. I've dreamed about this moment on repeat, and now that it's here, I want to savor it. Teala separates her knees and slides down so her pussy rubs my bed. I have to remind myself to take breaths.

She leans up. "Oops. Looks like I got a little of *me* on your bed." She covers her mouth with a delicate hand.

My dick is unbearably hard, and she's extraordinarily beautiful, and like a heat-seeking missile, I decide to take what's mine regardless of cost. Costs don't matter when you're out of control and starving.

I'm on top of her in less than a second. She's laughing, and she smells like sex and perfume and shampoo, and I'm delirious with want, lust, and fuck if I know what else. My mind is twisted and foggy with anything else except what I want.

"I can't wait to know you," I growl into her ear.

She responds by pulling my head in for a kiss and pushing my weight on top of her. Her mouth is frantic, a plea for more. A decadent cry for everything.

"Know me well. Know me real good," she says.

I roll off her because I need to touch her. Trailing my

fingertips from the tip of her chin down her neck, across her breasts and down her stomach, she writhes beneath the sensation, her abs flexing and releasing as she tenses. Her eyes are closed, her face soft, her body pliant—fully in my control. In past experiences, I've noticed some of the women I've been with have been shy or uneasy at my forward approach. Teala takes my approach and turns it on its head. Her body is a familiar instrument, and I know exactly where to touch and what to do to get a response. We've practiced. I know her. This has a multitude of benefits.

My hand drifts between her thighs, and she opens her knees wider to give me access. She's already soaking wet, and my finger slips before I make the decision to dive in.

"Like before?" she says.

"Yes. I'll do it the same way," I reply, leaning over to suck one of her nipples in my mouth.

Teala laughs, a throaty, turned-on noise that ricochets directly to my cock.

"Although I'm not sure how long I can pretend I don't want to be inside you instead."

Teala brings my hand up to her mouth and licks the finger that was just inside her. "I'm ready. Let's get you ready."

Thank God for fast miracles. She warms up in seconds. There's no time spent making sure she's comfortable and wet. I'd wager she was dripping for me the second she walked through the door. It's not even because of me—I don't give myself that much credit—it's because she hasn't been fucked in weeks and she's wild for it.

She pushes my hand away and rolls toward me, then mounts my stomach when I'm flat on my back. I keep my hands on her. She might think she's in control, but I want my presence known. Then she begins her slow descent, licking, tasting, kissing a trail down to my boxer briefs. When she gets there, she doesn't hesitate. With her narrowed eyes on mine, she removes them and lets them fall to the floor.

"He looks ready," she exclaims, raising one brow.

I nod furiously. "Understatement of the year," I deadpan.

It sounds desperate. She doesn't notice. She smiles and takes me into her mouth like she owns my mother-fucking dick. I hiss out a breath and try to think about my grandma on a cold, wet day. It doesn't work. I don't think that ever works, but I put my hand on her head and try not to think about how wet and warm her mouth is. I look down when she slides slowly up my shaft and sucks the tip lightly. She's whale eyeing me. Fuck.

"You keep looking at me like that, I'm going to come down your throat instead of on your tits. How do you want it?"

She watches me as she slides my dick all the way down her throat one more time.

"Fuck," I growl.

Teala finally relents and comes away. She keeps my shaft in her hand. "I like doggy style, but I want every-thing. All of it. Give it to me in every single way. We have lost time to make up for," she says, eyes burning a hole in my willpower.

Leaning up to the sitting position, I grab her by the waist and pull her back on top of me. The rush of skin on skin sets my teeth on edge. I lean over to my nightstand and pull a condom out of the box in the drawer. The wise and practical part of my brain applauds this decision, while the rest of my fucking body is saying, "Plunge into her and spray your fucking cum into every orifice of her body." *Congrats, wise section of brain. You win. Tennis claps for you.*

Teala takes over, rolling the condom down my dick, and I watch her hands work with a stomach roiling in anticipation. The scent of the latex switches me into a mode so carnal and barbaric I won't come back until it's over—until she's sated, and my hot load is dripping somewhere on her perfect fucking body.

"I'm going to ride you first. I need to get used to you," Teala explains, gripping the base of my shaft.

I merely nod because talking would require more brain cells than I have available at the moment.

She shimmies up my body on her knees one at a time until her pussy is close enough for me to touch. I stroke her, and my fingers glide around in her wetness with ease. I sigh and close my eyes for a moment or two, reveling in her tightness. It's finally fucking happening. She sighs, and I meet her gaze. There's a crinkle between her brows that usually isn't there.

"What's wrong?" Panic sets in. This isn't a face you want to see when the condom is on.

"Will you want me after?" she asks.

Leaning over, she kisses my mouth—her lips cool and wet—trying to distract me from her asinine question. I don't close my eyes, though. I keep them open to watch her, to examine her every move. Her body language tells me the answer to my question is important to her.

"You're irrational." I smile against her lips.

Throughout this exchange I haven't stopped circling her clit with two fingers. Teala is grinding her hips against my hand, and she's still capable of trying to have a serious conversation. I'm not doing something right. I work harder to make every nerve ending stand on end. She opens her eyes.

"Of course I'll want you after," I tell her. "Sex won't change anything."

She seems to accept my answer as truth, because for once, it is.

The vulnerability in her expression forces the alpha to the surface. "Now sit down on my cock before *I* go fucking crazy."

She smiles and moans when I move my hand away from where she wants it. Finally, she obeys me in something. She's sinking down slowly, and my eyes roll back in my head. I let out a loud groan. I have nothing to compare it to, but I think when you first enter a woman, the pleasure is so overpowering it's like a drug hitting your system and morphing your sense of awareness completely. Her pussy is tight, and it grips me as she inches herself down, slowly.

My hands are on her hips, firmly. I'm letting her do the work because I'm trying to be a gentleman, but she only has a few more seconds before I take over. She knows it. She's watching my face, anticipation twisting her features. Teala bites her lip in this beautiful fucking porno-style move and takes my dick all the way in.

"Go. Go," I urge, teeth clenched.

"You're so big. I'm getting used to you," she explains.

I know she's toying with my emotions. Her hips rise up and lower again, faster this time. My fingers are a vice on her muscular hips. I have to make the conscious effort to not crush her bones with fucking desire.

"Compliments are nice, but I need you to fuck me like you mean it. Now, Teala. I'm not playing around anymore."

Her neck works to swallow, and she leans over to kiss me again. I don't take my hands off her hips even though part of me wants to touch her face, her clit, her tits—my need for control dominates those urges easily.

She rides me hard then, up and down, her pink nipples hard, and her perfect tits bouncing to my favorite rhythm. *Fucking*. I blow out a breath and try to maintain some type of composure.

"Like this?" Teala asks through gasps and moans. She runs a hand through her long hair as she arches her back.

It's a view unlike any other in the world.

"Just like that," I say.

She works my cock too good from this position, so when she leans over to put her hands on my shoulders, I flip her onto her back and pin her to my mattress. She lets her hands fall crossed over her head because she knows exactly what I want. Control. I thrust into her slowly at first and relish the new sensation from this angle. Teala kisses my neck but keeps her arms away.

Kissing her neck in return, I say, "Good girl. Just like that."

I plunge into her harder, trying to keep most of my weight on my elbows. She's hooked her legs around my ass and is meeting me thrust for thrust.

"Fuck, Teala. Just like that. This feels too good," I admit. I thrust hard, as far in as I can. "Fucking," I say, sliding out slowly, "you"—I jut my hips back in—"is my new"—I glide out again, feeling her clench me in protest—"favorite," I growl, plunging back in again, "obsession."

My statement makes her crazed. She reaches between our bodies and starts stroking herself in time with my thrusts. I don't like it. I want all her pleasure. Removing her hand is easy. Keeping my weight off her body as I stroke her clit is the challenge. It gives me something to focus on besides coming. I know it will be quick if we don't switch it up. Teala moans loudly, her face a mix of ecstasy and orgasm. I pull out at once.

"Don't stop," she rasps.

I have to, I think. I grab under her and flip her onto all fours. I won't have to look at her face, and it might slow things down for me. It's not lost on me that I've never had this problem before, and even the thought is enough to cause pause. I don't waste any time once her ass and pussy are on display just for me. With the base of my cock in my hand, holding the condom in place, I slide into her. She growls like a motherfucking panther and starts bucking her hips back to get me in further. With a firm grip on her hipbones, I slam into her so hard that the sound of skin slapping skin fills the air. She lets her head fall down into my pillows. I watch my dick slide in and out until I can't watch anymore. Her pussy grabs it like it doesn't want to let it go.

Teala tells me she's coming, so I reach around and stroke her clit until she screams my name and braces herself on her elbows. My dick starts throbbing with need when the waves of her orgasm massage my dick. A little stiffness leaves her body as she tries to catch her breath.

"Flip over. Let me see your face," I pant out.

She obeys even though my dick has to slide out so she can do so. She's on her back, her hair a tangled mess of sex, and her face serene. God, her lips. Her fucking lips. I take them in between my teeth and pull. I could bite them off and keep them in a jar. Look at them for the rest of my life.

I slide into her and still. "I'm about to come," I whisper against her mouth.

"Please do," she says. "I'm impressed with your control."

The funny thing is I have no control right now.

A few more pumps and my balls are tight, and I'm tingling with the coming blast of pleasure. I lean back on my knees, tear off the condom, and stroke until hot bursts are flowing onto Teala's tits. My face is turned to the ceiling to hide the twisted look of pure desire. My body juts a final time, and with a sigh, I look down at the beautiful mess I created.

"My god, I didn't think it would ever end," Teala says, a laugh in her voice.

I sink back on my knees, totally spent. "I didn't either."

She sits up. Her tits don't budge at the movement, but my cum does.

"Shower?" I ask.

Bringing up her hands, she cups underneath the dripping mess and makes a joke about how she just got one. She rubs the cum into her chest and explains it won't drip that way. I raise my brow, impressed with her cunning. I'm lightheaded when I stand from the bed and make my way to the shower. I turn it on so the water can warm and look over my shoulder when I hear her approaching. She's coated with me, walking in my room, stepping into my shower, with me.

I smile.

CHAPTER SEVENTEEN
Teala

HIS SHOWER PRODUCTS are nicer than mine. He spends a fortune on personal grooming, a fact that surprised me the first time I showered here. We're drying off in his bathroom, grinning at each other. He has a goofy look on his face, and I'm not sure what that means. His hair is tousled and wet, and his thick eyelashes are clumped together with water. His body is insane. Not that I haven't seen it in all its glory and know exactly what it's capable of, but with a towel slung low on his hips and his gaze fixated on me, I'm noticing things I haven't before. Maybe he hasn't worn that smile before. Maybe he wasn't lying when he told me nothing would change after we had sex. I didn't believe him. How could I?

I drop my towel and sort through my bag for the black pair of thongs I threw in there for this exact situation. I slide them on, and he watches my every move with a feral gleam in his eye. The wide, dimpled smile is still in place.

"What? Spit it out. What's on your mind?" I ask. Even half naked, I'm going to command authority.

He shakes his head, laughing now. "Nothing. I was

just thinking we can call showering together done," he says, facing me. He turns toward the mirror and slides a comb through his hair. "Check that zoo life experience off the list," he mutters quietly.

I cock my head. "What do you mean by zoo life?"

He presses his lips into a firm line to stifle his laughter. I urge him on with a blazing look, my arms crossed underneath my breasts.

"You peed in front of me. In the shower. It kind of creeped me out," he says, chancing a side eye glance in the mirror.

I sigh. "You peed in front of me first, Macs. Don't be so weird."

He slams an open palm down on the warm-colored granite, again, the smile working its way across his face. He doesn't meet my eyes when he responds. "My pee is a perfect straight stream."

"And mine is what?" My face heats.

Now he has the good sense to turn his dimples down the counter. "Something out of *National Geographic*," he whispers. "Like a zebra or a reindeer. When they pee at the zoo, you know? It looks all wild and wide and sloppy. No aim whatsoever. Like a dam being unclogged or a pipe bursting."

I throw a hand over my mouth. I'm too amused and shocked to take offense. "How long were you thinking about that?"

He does this often. Has the perfect formulated response to stupid things most people don't even register. Most times he keeps them to himself. He probably would have kept this whole comparison locked away in his twisted brain had I not asked for an explanation. He continues smiling.

"How long?" I ask again.

"Since the moment you opened stream in my presence," he admits.

I shake my head, keeping my gaze locked on his guilty-looking face. He peeks up at me through his envy-worthy lashes, eyes slanted with happiness. He gives me a look that says, *Hey, you wanted to know.*

I nod, wiping the amusement from my face. "I suppose you wish I had a dick then? I'd be able to pee in a nice straight line. We could sword fight next time."

Macs is holding his stomach, bent over, roaring with laughter.

"Better yet, we could pee at the same time and make it a game. Who can pee the farthest with the most accuracy?"

With happy tears streaming down his face, he wraps his arms around me and pulls me against his warm, bare chest. "No. No. I like your zoo display. I do. I've never seen something so...wild before. That's all."

I'll admit. I was peeing before I even realized what I was doing because it's a habit.

I keep my arms pinned by my sides, still refusing to reciprocate his hug, but it gets harder and harder as every second passes. His skin is so hot and tinged with the musky-scented body wash it makes my mouth water. My cheek is pressed against his hard chest muscle, right on top of his solitary tattoo. It's a dark blue inked portrait of a skeleton frog. It spans an entire pectoral muscle. He told me most SEALs have the tattoo, and it means a lot to him. I bring up one hand to trace the outline with my finger.

"You hurt my feelings," I say, smiling because he can't see it. Inside I'm wildly happy to see how happy he is right now. It's a carefree nature I've never seen before. "Are you this nice every time you have sex?"

His body stiffens under my fingertips. I feel his chin

come down to rest on the top of my head. "No," he says, grudgingly.

"Was that a hard question or something?" I ask, confused.

He shakes his head on top of mine and clears his throat. "A simple question. A hard answer," he replies.

I try to pull away to glimpse his face. My heart is thumping at a rapid pace. I try to bury the excitement at his confession because I'm not sure exactly what it means. "Explain," I reply, knowing I could avoid this messy conversation by simply moving my hand lower and releasing the white, damp towel around his waist. I could make him forget everything in a matter of seconds. I could use all my skills, everything I've learned about pleasing a man, and he would be as good as putty in my hands, but selfishly, I want him to tell me what's going through his mind right now.

"How was sex for you?" he asks.

"Amazing," I reply. Perhaps it's the way I'm going about asking. I'll take his lead. "How was it for you?"

"Worth the wait," he says. Finally, he leans away from me. "Fucking amazing. I want to fuck you again. And again. And I'm thinking about it right now even though you violated my shower."

I huff. "You violated it first," I say. "So we're clear, I like your cock very much too. And the fact you know what you're doing. I want to fuck you multiple times as well." *And I'm falling in love with you.*

I tuck my fingers into the waistband of his towel. His dimples pop. Just one side, though. "Why was answering that question hard, Macs?" I use his name in hopes of getting his attention.

He sighs. "I thought I could fuck you out of my system."

"I'm in your system?" I ask, grinning.

He shrugs. "And it looks like you're staying there for the foreseeable future." He shifts uncomfortably. I see the cost it takes to admit this to me. "If you want to be there." There's a question in his gaze. He's asking, even though he stated it as fact.

I put him out of his misery right away. "I want to be in your system. In fact, wait here," I say, holding up one finger. I retrieve my cell phone from my bag, open the camera, and hand it to him. "Take a photo of me," I command.

Macs quirks a brow and looks at me like I'm crazy.

"Just do it. Take a photo of me right now."

He raises the phone up and focuses with a tap of the screen. I try to look innocent while topless but sexy because I am wearing a black fucking thong. I smile softly, no teeth. He smiles at the screen as he watches me fidget to find a proper pose. He clicks the button a few times.

"Send the photo to yourself," I say.

He doesn't reply, but I can tell he's going through the motions to send the photos, plural, to himself because his grin doesn't fade a smidge. He hands me the phone back. I snap a quick photo of him, and he makes a move to duck out of the frame but ends up smiling wider than he was before. I click the drool-worthy photo and toss my phone in my bag.

"What was that about?" he asks, stroking my nipples in between his large fingers.

My body has become his. I can tell by the way he touches me. No one else has ever touched me with such reverence, with such appreciation.

"You've realized by now that photos mean different things," I say, watching the muscles ripple in his arms. "That one you just took of me was the moment I knew I was falling for you." I swallow. The words tasted dangerous, villainous—traitorous. I don't back down from them. I face him head-on, bare of any pretenses.

His hands still on my chest, and I chance a glance up. His eyes are on my mouth. "Say that again. But look at me," he whispers.

"I'm falling for you. Not because you're an amazing fuck, either." Adding humor to soften the emotional blow is a tactic I'm going to always use with Macs. He responds to that.

His face is stoic, completely unreadable. He doesn't respond or reply to my sentiment. He leans down and kisses me so passionately, there's no question he feels the same way. He holds me tenderly, like I'm a fragile doll expected to break any second if he doesn't show me how he feels using his lips and his tongue. I see stars and fireworks, and my stomach turns as my hands wander up his chest.

It's not falling. In this moment I know it's not. It's love. And everyone is right. It feels like nothing else. Goose bumps prickle my skin, and I'm aware of him and nothing else. The world vanishes around us and whatever our chemistry has transformed into. He picks me up and backs me into the wall. I lock my hands around his neck and meet his kiss head-on, telling him I know what he's trying to explain without words. I'm hot and chilled to the bone. I'm terrified. He has all the power, and I'm helpless to surrender. I clutch his hair in my hands now to intensify the kiss and to try for some control.

It's a tugging match of power. He wants it. I want it. The common denominator is we both want it for the same reason. We know what power means. What it can destroy.

Everything.

Somewhere during our kiss, he lost his towel, and he's fumbling in the bathroom drawer and comes away with a condom. He tears the package open with his mouth and has it rolled down his erection in mere seconds. I realize that's a skill well practiced. My back is against the bathroom wall again as he fills me. He fucks me so hard he leaves his hands on either side of my shoulders flat against the wall and pins me and my weight with only his hips and dick.

It's a quick, blissful pace, but he's kissing me with the same passion as before. He chants my name like a prayer in between stealing my breath.

This time it's quick, and my orgasm takes me fast and hard. I slump over his shoulder when he comes, his cock buried as deep inside me as it will go. Minutes pass, and we stay connected that way. Him holding me while I'm tangled around him. We end up back in his bed, under the covers.

I'm rolled onto my side, looking at him as he gazes back at me. He looks like he's trying to figure me out. The feeling is mutual because from this angle, lying in bed with him, I want to know what it is about him, too. I trace the planes of his face with my fingers. He doesn't take his hand off my hip and the side of my stomach.

"I'm glad you told me," he says. His voice is creaky. Neither of us has spoken for what seems like forever.

My nail brushes over his bottom lip. It's so full. "I didn't know how you would respond. If I knew it would be with orgasms, I would have told you sooner."

He offers a soft smile. "Consider me felled, Teala."

I flick my gaze up to meet his. "Yeah?"

"I don't say things without knowing for certain I meant them. Especially ones as significant as those. Let's not label our feelings, though. Don't call it something. Then it won't be the same."

Love. He won't say it. And I'm so in shock right now, there's no way I want to hear it anyway. This is what he's saying without using the word. Isn't that exactly what Carina told me? This indescribable feeling that's different for everyone?

"I feel the same way," I admit.

I've regained my composure enough to scoot toward him for a small kiss. Macs crushes me to his chest and kisses every place on my face he can fit his lips.

"You just became everything."

"I can't *become* something, Macs," I say into the crook of his neck. "Especially *everything*."

He sighs. "Tell that to my heart."

My own heart leaps out of my chest. There's no harried panic in his admission, just truth, and it puts me at ease, and I think this is the happiest I've ever felt. I relax against a man, in his bed, for the first time in my life. He falls asleep before I do, and he does call it something, because Macs sleep talks. He tells me he loves me four times before I fall asleep, wondering how many more times he can take my breath away with three simple words.

"I do a lot of things well, but cooking isn't one of them," Macs exclaims, standing in front of his new range with his hands on his hips.

It's early. So early the sun hasn't risen, and the coolness of night still warps the air. I'm wearing one of his T-shirts that hits mid-thigh and no panties. We made love this morning. And I finally realized there was definitely a distinction between the two. Fucking is hard and selfish. It's about orgasms and carnal desires—about slick openings and hard, throbbing cocks that taste like salted caramel. Making love is a completely different animal.

It's slow and thoughtful. Perhaps it's best described as giving what you think you don't own and taking what you don't think you deserve.

I ask him if he has plain oatmeal, and he looks pleased he does and sets off on his task to not fuck up oats for our breakfast. He tells me, sort of surprised, that oatmeal is his breakfast of choice too.

"I'm going to look around," I tell his wide, muscular back.

He grunts his approval, and I take my mug of steaming coffee and wander down the hallway on the opposite side of the house. The guest bedrooms are over this way.

"Careful in the back room. I'm building a bookshelf, and there's some equipment in there," he calls out.

It truly is a marvel what this space looks like now compared to what it did when I first came over. He turned it into a home. I can imagine myself spending time here. My stomach starts spinning, but I don't let it control me. I open a door and see a large, disassembled bookcase. Books are neatly stacked in piles, lining the bare walls. Some titles I recognize as the classics. The thick tomes that you have to be in just the right mood to tackle, he also has an equal number of non-fiction works. The types of books you read when you want to read, but you also want to learn. I've never really understood that practice, but I can appreciate it.

I walk in and head for the back window. It's long and rectangular. The view is just as stunning as my view at home, yet completely different. The sun is rising, and the colors are magnificent. Buildings block my view of the sunrise. The pinks create a halo around the burnt oranges and reds. It's silent still. The time of morning I usually spend by myself, flipping through social media on my phone, huddled over oatmeal before

I head in to teach the early class. I swallow at the reminder of change. Not all change is bad, or even that life-altering, I remind myself. Some change happens without disturbing anything else. It's possible. It has to be.

"Your gourmet oatmeal is ready. I sweetened it with honey and raisins. Figured it was a morning to celebrate," Macs says, his voice commanding the small room. His bare feet make a firm noise as he approaches from behind. "Some view, huh?"

"I was just making a pros and cons list. This might top my view, and I never thought it possible." Because I never considered any other options. The dark of night is giving way to the dark royal blues of morning, the sky lighting the surrounding area.

Macs pulls me against him, my back against his chest. My head tilts back automatically. "What time do you have to go into work?" he asks, his lips already skirting the edge of my neck. It's a whisper of a kiss.

Tilting my head to the left so he can continue his assault, I close my eyes and grin. "My thighs are still sticky from sex less than an hour ago, Macs," I breathe.

There's no conviction in my statement. He knows it. My appetite for him is probably even larger than his for me. My core clenches a few times at the thought of having him inside me again.

"Let's go eat, and then we can take another shower," he rasps into my ear.

I make a joke about the zoo, and he holds my hand all the way to the high bar in his kitchen. He goes to switch on the news, but then turns the television off again. He's not used to having company in the morning. Old habits die hard. I understand completely.

"Should we talk about last night?" I ask in between bites.

The oatmeal is a little firm. I make a face when I crunch on a bite. He apologizes with a cute grimace.

Macs has a way of masking any emotions he may not want to show. The thing is I now know when he's doing it, so I'm able to see when he's trying to hide something. It's just as telling. He does it now. I clear my throat.

"I'm not sure what to say. Can we let last night speak for itself?" he asks, taking a bite.

I take a sip of coffee. "The thing is I'm going to have to answer to people, and I'm not sure what to say, and it seems crazy I even have to ask. But assuming makes an ass out of you and me." Humor. Again.

He shrugs. "Call it what you want."

Macs doesn't comment on the fact that all of my friends know about us, but his friends don't even know what the hell is going on. He's like me. A master at evasive techniques. We decided not to label it, so I decide we'll be together. That's good enough for me.

We finish our breakfast and our coffee. The conversation is light and breezy as we discuss the facets of his kitchen. I don't have to pretend to be interested. I truly am. I tell him I want to redo my kitchen, and his eyes light up at the prospect of another project. He takes our bowls and mugs to the sink and disappears down the hall to the bathroom. It's where my stuff is, so I can't get ready yet. Approaching the sink, I wash the dishes myself.

I startle when someone pounds on the front door. My heartbeat leaps into my chest as I peek around the corner to peer out the window. His driveway is hidden by the garage, but I see the uniform right away. I've never seen Macs wear it, but I know merely by sight this is one of his teammates. The severity of the slamming on the door forces me over. I unlock the deadbolt and pull the door open as quickly as my fumbling hands allow. This man, this beast of a man, looms over me like a goddamn nightmare. Where Macs is beautiful, this man is...rugged. His eyes flare the second the door opens and he sees me.

"Oh," I say, pulling at the hem of my shirt. "I'm sorry. You didn't seem very patient," I explain. "I'll go get Macs." For a second I think I should introduce myself, but then I decide against it. Macs should do that.

He shakes his head, closing his eyes. "I knew it. I fucking knew it," he says under his breath.

Macs rounds the corner with his towel slung over his shoulder, wearing only his boxer briefs.

His whole demeanor changes when Macs sees this man. "Tahoe. What the fuck?"

"Time to stop playing fucking house. Grab your shit. We need to leave. Like now. Like fucking yesterday," the man named Tahoe explains using a gruff, emotionless voice.

I step to the side and take a few steps back.

I've never seen this side of Macs, and I watch his face change as he processes the vague information given to him. His brow furrows, and his lips turn down in the corners. No dimples or smiles or warm eyes. His face is made of stone and ice. You could carve a fucking swan out of it and set it on display on a cruise ship. This is work Macs, and I don't know him.

"What's the matter?" I ask. No one looks at me. "Macs," I say, my voice pleading. I look between the men, and it's only been a matter of seconds since Tahoe spoke, but it feels like years.

Macs is heading back into the bedroom, and I'm left standing in this beautiful room with a man who looks like he deals out death for a living.

"What happened?" I ask, trying to swallow the lump in my throat. It matches the pit in my stomach that sinks further and further every second.

The beast named Tahoe flicks his gaze to me instead of the hall Macs disappeared down. "Stay here today. Don't go out," he says.

My brow crinkles in confusion. Tahoe doesn't notice, though. He's eyeing my bare legs up and down, wearing a smile that looks like it belongs in Shark Week. The dread is so deep I don't even give him a zing or readjust the tee. I stare at his uniform. The camouflage-printed fabric that looks starched to death, the seams, his boots, the collar, and the trident emblazoned over his heart. It's weird to see it, but I know what it means. I can't look at it another second. I retreat to the bedroom. The first thing I notice is the bed. It's still in a disarray, the covers and sheets a tangled mess from our morning sexual escapade, then I see Macs. He has the bags out of their hiding place, and he's tucking his white shirt into his twin camouflage pants.

"Macs," I whisper.

He glances over his shoulder, and his face looks pained. "I'm sorry I have to go. I keep a spare key under the doormat. Take it. Okay?" He approaches quickly, his pants still unbuttoned. His hands embrace my cheeks. "I'll call you."

"Is everything all right?" I ask.

His face closes down. "I'm sure it is. I'll call you," he says again. "I missed a bunch of calls this morning." Macs shakes his head, irritated.

I frown.

"It's my fault. For being so into you." He tries on a smile, but it fails. No dimples or happiness. He kisses me slowly, lips and tongue and the desire that always simmers when our lips are joined is there, but he's not. He's already the other person. He releases me. "Stay put for a second."

I sit down in the middle of the bed. I hear him talking

to Tahoe in hushed whispers, and when he comes back to collect his bags, he's a different person.

"Will you be gone for a long time?" I ask quickly.

He shakes his head. "I have no idea. I need to get in to work and figure this out. Bye, Teala." He leans over, putting his palms flat on the bed to reach me for another kiss.

I lean up on my knees to wrap my arms around his neck.

"Be safe," he whispers.

"Text me."

A small grin starts to appear on his lips but disappears just as quickly. He tells me the same thing Tahoe did about staying home, and then he's gone. Trusting in someone other than myself might be the hardest thing I'll ever do. I don't know what the hell is happening, and I've never had to accept half-truths before. I grab another cup of coffee and open the sliding glass doors in his living room. The sun is a burning ball in the sky now. Somewhere in between him holding me and Tahoe banging down the door, I know something huge changed.

I won't heed their instructions to stay home. I shower and dress quickly and pull my wet hair into a bun on the top of my head. On a whim I take a photo of the messy bed before I make it and send it to Macs. He doesn't reply right away, and I know he won't. I grab the key from under his welcome mat, lock the door, return the key to its hiding spot, and head for the yoga studio. I call my mom on the way, but it goes straight to voicemail. I narrow my eyes at my phone and try it a dozen more times. My Bluetooth must be glitching, so I turn it off completely. The radio automatically picks up where my morning playlist left off. It's not Adele blasting through my speakers anymore. It's a frantic radio host screaming about a terror attack.

"Tone it down, buddy," I say, grimacing.

I mute the mayhem with a shake of my head and try my mom again by doing it the ancient way, with my phone pressed to my ear. It's still going straight to voicemail. "Where are you?" I ask the air. "Call me back, Mom. Where are you? Why is your phone going straight to voicemail? I have news I need to talk to you about ASAP. Call me back. Your phone never goes straight to voicemail. What is going on?" I hang up the call, and my fingers twitch on my steering wheel, tapping out a furious rhythm of annoyance. I park my car in the empty parking lot and check my watch to find it's ten minutes before nine. I unlock the mirrored door to the studio.

The business phone is ringing off the hook. I run over and answer it by leaning over the counter. I answer with the standard greeting.

"I'm going to the mall," Carina rushes. "What was the name of that tea you made the other day? I want to grab some while I'm there."

We talk for a few more minutes, and she's happy, and I'm happy. I forget I can't reach my mom, and I'm worried about tea and everything being right in the world.

And then it's not.

CHAPTER EIGHTEEN

Macs

HERE'S THE THING: when you have something you care about, you want to keep that thing next to you at all moments. You want to protect it. You want to shrink it and put it in your pocket encased in a steel bubble. And any time you want, you can put your hand in your pocket and feel it there. It's reassuring. When the thing you care about is a person, you can't keep them in your pocket. You can't keep them at home either. The key is under my doormat, but Teala's car is gone. I curse at the top of my fucking lungs.

A woman is the very last thing I need to worry about right now, but wouldn't you know, she's the fucking first —the only thing I can think of after the fucking terrorist attacks erupted. It's war. We're going to war. Not the kind of war you see on the news in far-off deserts with a definitive line between good and bad, either.

When we got to work, we were introduced to intel that warned of terror attacks that would span the whole fucking planet. By the time the intel reached us, the first attacks were already happening. Widespread. Death. Destruction. Life-altering, world-changing attacks on humanity. They aren't concepts that are unfamiliar to me.

IED explosives, car bombs, suicide vests, M4-wielding bad guys spraying metal into crowds of innocents, but the spotty footage of the terror was something I will carry with me until the day I die. I watched it happen on US soil. I heard the screams of civilians crying for help. They were confused, and rightly so.

There were multiple bombs in San Diego alone. Two at shopping malls affected so many of the guys that after the reports came in, everyone dispersed. It's fucking melee. Cell towers are down, and traffic is unlike anything I've ever seen. I wanted to take a motherfucking chopper to my house, but those were all being used, go figure. They sent us to check on our loved ones, because even in my line of work, family comes first, but I know we'll be shipping out to spots around the United States to protect our citizens from the monster that lurks within.

That's the worst part. The terrorists weren't obvious. They were neighbors, friends, unsuspecting men and women who planned this for God knows how long and by what means. For them to skirt our intel and pull off a feat at this scale means there were some big financiers behind this. People who pose as our friends. The death toll was in the hundreds of thousands when I left our compound to find Teala. Tahoe and a few of the other single guys stayed back to formulate plans and get everything ready. The confusion isn't something I'm used to. No one ever thought it would happen here. In the land of the free and the home of the brave. Tactics will have to change. Everything we knew about being SEALs will be turned on its head.

I listen to the scratchy radio in my car as I speed toward her yoga studio using back roads. I dial her at least five times as I go. Her cell is going straight to voicemail, and the studio line beeps back at me in a busy signal. The news anchor has replaced the radio DJs, and they're reporting on the attacks. They list the US cities first, and I match them to the corresponding states and realize I don't think any states were left untouched. They move on to the international attacks, and I find myself gritting my teeth and surrendering to the pure rage coursing through my veins.

Some get scared. Hell, I saw fucking terror on several of my brothers' faces. Others process things of this magnitude in a more ambiguous manner. They're methodical. Tell them what to do, and they'll do it.

The news anchor does a recap that's meant to be swift, but it's anything but. *"Sixteen elementary schools, fifty-five shopping malls, four theme parks, one hundred multi-level parking garages, three cruise ships, eight beaches, two hundred and still counting restaurants, commuter trains, airports, and tourist destinations."*

I have to switch it off. It's all information I know, and hearing it twice gives me the equivalent of rage goose bumps. I swerve in and out of traffic, and cars are stopped, lining the highway. They're either afraid to continue or they're so absorbed in the news anchor's words they can't focus on driving as well. It makes for a trip longer than it should be.

When I finally pull into the parking lot, my satellite phone rings on my passenger seat. Thank God for technology. I answer with a swift, "Newstead," and listen to Moose rattle on about our plans. He's calling me from his car and tells me that Smith's girlfriend was likely affected by the attack at the mall here in San Diego. My stomach goes sour, and I find it hard to reply to that. It's my biggest concern.

I reached my parents earlier, and they reassured me that our family was safe. Logically I know Teala is only at one of three places, but not knowing is driving me fucking batty. Hearing about Smith's girlfriend only adds to that anxiety. I ask if our hospital was affected, and he confirms it hasn't been hit, but it will be overloaded and understaffed. I rattle off a few things I need from my cage to complete my go-bag, and he agrees to get them for me if he gets back to base before I do. He asks if I'm going to Teala's, and he knows because everyone fucking knows without me saying a thing. I'm in love with her, and I never told another soul. I didn't even tell Teala. I roar out a string of swear words that would make my grand-mother roll in her grave and wish him luck. I don't answer his question about where I'm going. There's no need.

The door to her studio is locked when I get there, but I spotted her car in the parking lot from the street. She's here. Teala is somewhere, and all of a sudden this fucking plaza doesn't feel safe. It feels like a trap. Real life feels like a trap. My gaze scans the parking lot as I'm comforted by the weight of my weapons on my hips. People are erratic. There's no way to judge a person when the state of panic is so severe that no one is thinking clearly.

It's hysteria, and the fact it isn't just confined to one shopping plaza makes it all the worse. This is happening all over the world. It's only a matter of time before the president hands down the order for martial law. Our entire country has already been declared in a state of emergency. I shiver. I won't be here by then. My steel ball in my pocket will be rolling around all on her own. I bang on the glass of her window, peering in. She has to be inside there. She wouldn't be dumb enough to go anywhere else. The attacks hadn't stopped when I left work. The larger attacks were fading, but the smaller ones in grocery stores and gyms were gaining momentum.

I see Teala's terrified face peek from the corner of the

yoga room. My heart hammers out a staccato similar to when I'm getting ready to kill someone. It feels the same. It confuses me even further. I can forget everything else for the moment by the sheer look of relief that washes over her face when she sees it's me.

She unlocks the door and pulls me inside, and she's folded around me in her next breath. I lock the door because she failed to and relish the weight of her in my arms.

"You're okay," I whisper into her hair.

Teala pulls away to look at me. "What's happening, Macs? What the fuck is happening out there? It's not real, right?"

Tears streak down her cheeks, and her eyes are wild. Like a wild animal trapped in a cage. That's what she reminds me of, and I feel guilty for thinking it, but I'm too glad she's unharmed to worry about the train of my thoughts.

I swallow down my vanity and prepare to be the person who tells her it's real life and everything she's hearing is truth. "Teala, I'm going to find the people who did this." That's a truth I can give her.

"Oh my gosh. I can't believe this is real. I can't get ahold of my mom, Macs. I have no idea if she's okay. The mall. Carina went to the mall. I don't know if my friends are okay. The phones aren't working!"

Her lips are trembling, and that's all I need in the way of an invitation. I kiss her, pulling her to me and slanting my mouth over hers. She responds immediately, and this is a place where we're okay. Nothing else matters for the seconds or minutes when we live inside this show of emotion. An emotion that isn't anger or rage or fear. It's the purest thing I've ever experienced.

"It's going to be okay. Everyone is okay," I whisper against her breaths.

There's so much death in the air that a body count won't be readily available for weeks, maybe even months. Smith's girlfriend is Carina. Fuck. I slide the satellite phone out of my pocket.

"Call your mom," I say, extending it to her.

Her eyes light up. "I need to go to her," she wails.

I shake my head. "You can't drive out there, Teala. It's not safe."

Nothing is safe. How will I protect her when I leave? I wonder if she could fit in my dead hooker bag. I'd give her food and water and take her with me wherever I went.

"I have to. She's by herself, Macs. She's probably freaking out. What if she's driving to me right now? How are the roads?"

She's pacing with the phone pressed to her ear. I notice she knows the number by heart and doesn't need to check her own phone.

The lights flicker in the studio. Fuck. The power plant. Fuck. Fuck. Fuck. This isn't good. She doesn't seem to notice.

"Mom!" she screams. "Are you okay? I'm fine. I'm fine," she says, responding to her mother's harried shouts.

I stand by the glass and try to tune out Teala's voice because hearing the pain that resides there makes me feel sick. I can't do anything about it, and I surely can't fix it. My hand automatically slides down to caress my weapon. Yes. There's one thing I can do about this situation.

I stretch my arms over my head as I eye everything taking place in the parking lot. The lights flicker again and then go out completely. Teala's apartment won't be safe. Not in the city, that high up, with a parking garage. That won't do. My house is in a neighborhood that's too clustered. Maybe her mom's place out of the city would be the best place to stash her while I'm gone. I pull another cell phone from my back pocket. It's slow, but I'm able to stay abreast on the attacks as they're reported. By this time, the news is about an hour behind. I see every gruesome target before anyone else knows, and I'm helpless.

"It's not even over yet," I whisper. "How in the fuck did we not know?"

"What did they say at work, Macs? Are you leaving?" Teala asks, the phone pressed to her ear, but eyes trained on me.

I nod. "I'll have to go. The primary focus will be securing the US, but I'm not sure where they'll send me first."

I skip the logistics part because she doesn't want to know what I'll be doing. No one does until it's finished and over. Then the news eats it up for breakfast and misrepresents everything. People will write books about this, and they won't have to make up any details because this is larger than life all by itself. With my thumb, I wipe at a tear on her cheek, right on top of her beauty mark.

"You should go to your mom's. I'll drive you."

"I need to get my stuff," she says.

Shaking my head, I squash that thought before it goes any further.

"Mom, I'll see you soon. Please stay safe," Teala says. "I love you, too. I love you," she says, but she's looking directly into my eyes.

It's too much. I look away.

"I don't have anything with me," she says.

She trusts me so implicitly she doesn't ask questions. Maybe she doesn't want to know, but she doesn't strike me as a woman who wants to live in the dark for the sake of her feelings. She's the type of woman who wants to know everything and stand among the devastation proudly. I nod to the rack of clothing she has for sale on the wall.

Without another thought, she pulls all of it off and shoves it into a tote bag with her studio logo on it. She goes under her desk and hunts out the zippered cash envelope. "What else?" she asks, meeting my eyes.

"The computer," I reply, glancing around. My gaze lands on her plants. "And anything you don't want to die."

She looks at me. "Then you're going to stay at my mom's, too? You're the one thing I want to keep breathing." Her eyes turn down in the corner, and it breaks my heart into a million pieces—a feat I would have laughed at if you'd told me it would happen only several months ago.

"I'm too stubborn to die," I reply, trying to keep my tone light. Death isn't something anyone wants to talk about, but in my line of work, it's a reality, and with what's happening right outside this door, I don't see a need to beat around the bush. "I'm always safe. Okay?"

She frowns, nods, and throws herself into my arms. It forces me to take a step backward. "My car is fine here?"

She can't see my face because she's wrapped around my body, which is good. "Take whatever you want out of it."

She inhales deeply, and my eyes flutter closed at the intense longing I feel at the simple gesture. I want to fuck her until there's no doubt in her mind that I'm coming back for her. She's mine. Nothing is taking her from me. Not my own ego, or what my brothers think of my reformed ways, and definitely not some fucking terrorists who want to steal everything. No one is touching her. The first thing I thought of when I watched a split screen of the conferences confirming this nightmare was her. I realize what that means.

I swallow down my flailing emotions and whisper, "Let's go."

Directing her to stand behind me feels odd. I'm in uniform, which usually gains respect, but right now it puts a target on our backs. As we exit her studio, a woman runs directly into me in a blind frenzy of tears and screams.

"They killed him!" she says, her eyes red-rimmed and wide. "They killed him!" the woman repeats and then runs off.

Teala clutches my back, and I'm made aware she's sobbing. I can't afford to comfort her right now. I may never be able to comfort her properly, but I'll keep her alive.

She told me before we locked the door she didn't have anything in her car she wanted. Teala is holding two bags with everything she collected from inside. I open the passenger side of my car and push her inside a little more roughly than I mean to. Teala doesn't say anything else, but she does whimper before I shut the door.

My phone rings when I take my seat behind the wheel. The doors are locked and we're safely stowed away, so I'm confident enough to answer the call from my friend. "I have her," I tell Tahoe before he can ask.

Teala peers at me with an indiscernible look of frantic love. It hits me so hard I take her hand in mine and rub my fingers over her knuckles. She soothes under my touch, and her bravado returns. I hand her a water bottle from the back seat and return my hand to hers. I reply to Tahoe at the appropriate times and try not to belie my true feelings. This is worse than anyone thought. I end the call.

This is WWIII.

I untangle my hand from hers and drive toward the freeway and try to remember the directions Teala gave me only moments before. She silences the static-filled radio and looks out the window as we go. She asks me questions as I drive. Not about anything she knows I can't answer. Simple things. Like where will she get food and clean water and what about electricity and normal living things and her bank and money and her apartment. I make up responses the best I can. She believes every single one, even though they were only things said to placate her. It's what I do for my parents, and maybe she knows I'm doing it because she's seen it firsthand, but she doesn't remark. She squeezes my hand tighter and leans her body as close as she can to mine.

Her mother's road is bare of cars when we arrive forty minutes later. I was right in my assumption. The melee isn't as severe out here. Or at least I tell myself this as a comfort tool. "You'll be safe here," I explain.

It's not a steel ball, but at least they'll have each other. The neighborhood is filled with older houses. This blessedly means residents have more property and can't hear their neighbors fucking like animals. She points to a tall red brick Tudor with a high, wrought iron fence surrounding it on all four sides. The gate is locked, and there's a box to buzz. Viola must be watching for us because the gate opens before I lean over to punch in the code Teala rattled off.

Her shoulders relax and her breathing evens as we roll down the long, black, winding drive. Trees line it on either side, and they meet each other at the top. A tree tunnel. "I like this more and more," I say, mostly for my own benefit.

I'm nodding when she asks, "Why?"

"There's only one point of entry, and it's locked. It doesn't mean people can't get in, but it may deter them."

I have no idea what to expect, and no one knows the extent of the damage still ongoing. I pull the car behind a red sedan and throw the shifter into Park. Sighing, I face her. "I don't want to leave you here, and I don't want to tell you what to do."

Teala is antsy. I can tell she wants to get inside to her mother. That's what I need. "I won't leave here. If you tell me to stay, I will."

I glare at her. "Not like this morning?"

She looks down at her lap, a small smile playing on her lips. It vanishes quickly. "I had no clue when you told me then. Had you said the world was ending, I probably would have listened," she explains, using her hands. "Or better yet, demanded you take me with you."

There it is. She wants what I want. Something I can't accomplish.

"I wish I could take you with me, Teala. The president is drafting orders as we speak. Martial law will go into effect shortly." I explain the basics. About how typically there will be a curfew and checkpoints on roads. No one will be allowed out at dark, and our military will take over completely. It's scary for civilians. Congress has never declared martial law. My mind whirs in a million different directions as I sort the information.

I help her out of the car and into the house. Her mother gives her a tearful hello, hugs me, and disappears out of Teala's room to leave us alone. My phone rings three times while I'm in the house. Each time it's someone telling me more bad news. I try to keep my composure for Teala's benefit. It's business as usual. I repeat that several times. I close the door behind us.

Teala is pacing back and forth in between her bed and the window covered in white, gauzy curtains. It's her childhood bedroom, and it looks as if it's untouched by all the years in between eighteen and now.

"Look at me," I say, my voice thick.

She stops pacing and spins on her heel. "How is this real life?" she asks. "I'm practical. I'm going to do the things you told me. I'll be okay. I will. That doesn't mean I can't wonder what in the ever-loving fuck happened, Macs. I think God is punishing the world because I'm happy. Why am I happy right now despite the amount of death?" She waves her arm to the window. "Don't leave me here, Macs. Please."

I swallow hard.

"God has nothing to do with this," I say. "Bad guys do. Ones that I have to take care of. If I don't, who will?"

"Someone else can. It's selfish and rude, and I feel like a heathen even requesting it, but I'd never forgive myself if I didn't ask. Do you understand? I want you to be with me," Teala says. "Don't leave me. Not like this."

Tears are pouring down her face, and I'm more uncomfortable in this social setting than I have been in a really long time. Explaining won't do any good when her emotions are so heightened. She wouldn't understand, and I can't fault her for that.

"I'm scared, Macs. Don't leave me."

I cross to her and take her in my arms. "You're going to be okay," I lie.

How can anything possibly be okay after this? Nothing will ever be the same. Catastrophes change people, which in turn shape the world. Instead of spinning in a nice round circle, it might hiccup here and there. It doesn't go away. It's a forever change.

"You'll be safe here," I amend.

I breathe in her hair. I kiss her neck, her collarbone, and the place where her ear meets her cheek. The truth is when I leave here, I have no idea when I'll be back. If ever. I love my country. I agreed to die for it. If I only get to feel this for the short time we've had, I'll die a happy man. She leans back to peer into my eyes—my soul.

Teala's stopped crying, but her face is wet, and I lose my breath. Her tears are for me, and that changes everything. She strips her tank over her head and steps out of her tight pants. I wasn't planning on having sex with her, but she's so sad and it might be the last time, so I don't fault myself for the delay. She hits her knees and unfastens my belt and unzips my pants.

"I've always wanted to fuck a man in uniform," Teala says.

She's hiding from the truth, and I won't deny her. Hell, I wouldn't deny her anything I could feasibly give her. It doesn't scare me anymore.

"And I just want you. Always, only you," I reply, cradling the sides of her face. She slides my boxer briefs down to my ankles and pushes me to awkwardly walk backward until the back of my legs hits the bed.

Teala crawls up me, her naked body a swath of warm, delicious skin, and I make a point of erasing my mind of everything but her.

It surprises me how easy it is. She is peeling off my skin, separating muscle, coiling around the untouched places reserved for darkness and depravity. Her light is inside me.

That makes her mine.

CHAPTER NINETEEN
Teala

THIS IS THE LAST TIME. Women can sense these things. Call it intuition, if you will. When I slept with men before, the sex always had a non-permanent quality. I could feel it all over my body. It's harried and vicious hands because tomorrow doesn't matter. Two hours into the future doesn't even matter, because I'd be left alone wondering what the hell was wrong with me and the things I desired.

Macs brings me back into the moment.

"Teala. Focus on me," he says, his hands on the sides of my stomach, caressing softly. He tossed his camo jacket off, but he still has on a white T-shirt, his pants are around his ankles, and his boots, with his feet inside, are on the floor. If anything signals a man leaving, it's when we have to fuck with our clothes on like we're in high school.

"I'm here," I whisper.

I'm straddling his hips. He's hard and waiting, and I want it to last forever. Maybe if I can live in this moment for as long as possible, everything else will vanish. Leaning over, I place my lips on his. The salty taste of my tears mixes in our kiss, and I can't help but cry a little at the bittersweet reminder. Macs shushes me and rubs my back, and I think maybe I can't have sex with him. The part of Teala who only wants sex and fucking and orgasms isn't anywhere to be found right now.

"I'm going to miss you so much," I whisper.

People don't know if their loved ones are alive, and I'm crying because the person I care about has to leave my side. I feel as guilty as the terrorists who stole so much from so many. Before he can respond, I deepen the kiss, placing one hand on the side of his head. I thread my fingers through his hair and open my mouth to allow his tongue to mingle with mine. The sweetness of the moment goes away when I reach between our warm bodies and adjust his shaft so he can enter me. He jerks as soon as we connect and moans out a small plea of pleasure. It feels good—right. He fills me with the next thrust, and his large hands tighten around my hips as he guides me at a pace he wants. Eyes closed and lips parted slightly, he continues his assault with controlled, manipulated thrusts. I can't even focus on coming because I'm too wrapped up in his pleasure. This isn't a face I've seen all day. It's been scowls and frowns, stoic reserve, and grimaces.

"You feel so good," he whispers.

Instead of responding, I kiss him and sniffle. He must have a face full of my snot, but he hasn't said anything yet.

"I want you to come," Macs says. "Please."

His voice is pleading and strained. His fingers are stroking my clit in a frenzied pace I know will get me off in no time if I can concentrate on nothing else. I slide my hands up his shirt to expose his abs and chest and let my fingers grip the mountains of muscle that reside there. I close my eyes and let the sensations take over. He's filling me, stroking me, and all my senses are overtaken by one entity—him. No sounds but skin slapping, and I smell his sweat and shampoo. My hands are worshipping him, and my heart—it's loving him.

Macs picks up the pace with his thrusts, and I come in a slow cycle of rapid-fire waves. I don't scream or call out his name. I merely concentrate on my breathing. As soon as the very last flutter of orgasm leaves, Macs slides me off his shaft and pumps his hand around the base of his slick cock and comes on his stomach. His face is chiseled from perfection even when he has no control over it. My core clenches in response. More. I want him to live inside me. I have a tissue box sitting on the bed because my mom shoved it into my hands when I came tearfully blasting in her front door. I take one and wipe his stomach when I see he's not making any fast movements to rid himself of the sticky substance.

"You don't want to leave," I say.

He keeps his eyes closed as he shakes his head to confirm my assumption.

"And I'm afraid that makes me unpatriotic, or less honorable in some way," he says, using a hoarse voice. "I'm sorry," he whispers.

I'm not sure what he's apologizing for, but it's a blanket apology, and I know all about those. My father tried them on me for the first several years after the divorce. It came to a point where an apology from anyone meant very little without action. Macs doesn't have anything to apologize for, and maybe that's why it means more than those in my past. I force him to look at me, leaning over his body. My breasts graze his chest, and that stirs him to life. His gaze flicks up to meet mine.

"You're going to leave, and you will be honorable and patriotic and do the hard things others can't. You're a good man."

He scoffs. "I don't know about that. I mean, I'm

awesome, sure. The adjective you used is a little loose," he explains, a grin gliding over his face. "Unlike you," he says, his hand winding its way in between my legs. He plays with the wetness for a moment or two, just long enough for my eyes to flutter closed in expectation. "This isn't how it's supposed to be." What he means to say is, *this isn't normal.* "I don't know what happens next, and I have no clue how long something like this could keep me away. There aren't rules anymore, Teala. This is war."

I probably look like a deer caught in headlights. He's giving it to me straight, which is all I could hope for from him. This is a little much to take in, but I nod.

He goes on. "And I don't want to ask you to wait for me, but I'm going to do it anyway."

I swallow down the terrifying words and brush the side of his face with my hand. "You don't have to ask."

He nods. "I do. You just called me a good guy." He smiles widely.

I laugh, in spite of the tears forming in my eyes and my pounding pulse. "It was a loose adjective. Remember?"

He sits up, his pants still around his ankles. It looks ridiculous now that I'm not riding him, and he's talking about his feelings. He pulls his pants up in one goddamn hot swoop and eyes me down so fiercely now I'm scared for another reason. He wills my attention by looking at me, a feat I never would have known was possible.

Taking my hands in his, he says, "No one is going to fuck you like me. Make you wet like me."

He's right. I'm sitting here sopping wet and ready even though it's been less than five minutes since he filled me. I smile at his statement. He doesn't return the gesture.

"No one is going to love you while doing it. Not like I will."

I choke on spit and cough—a most ungodly noise. He told me he loves me. Sure, it was in the same sentence as fucking, but that's been our way from the second we laid eyes on each other.

"You don't have a lot of confidence in me, do you?" I ask, finally relenting to the laughter that bubbles its way from the depths of my stomach. Which I think resides in my feet at the moment.

Sighing, he puts his hands on his hips. "It came out wrong."

I shake my head. "No, it came out perfect. I love you, too, Macs. Even if it means we're labeling it. Even if we said we wouldn't call it anything. When it feels like this," I say, laying a hand over my heart, "then you label that shit, put it in a jar, and keep it close. I love you. I'll wait for you. I promise."

If he knew how much my promises meant, he'd feel more exclusive, but as it stands, his reaction to my admission is enough to make me weak in the knees. He moves my hand and puts his on top of my chest, right over my heart, instead. It chills against my warm skin, still flushed in arousal.

He steps closer, and I lean up on my knees. "I never thought I'd like the sound of that," he says, leaning over to kiss me. Macs's hand slides down to caress my side and glides over my stomach as his lips work against mine. Sad eyes greet me when he pulls away. His lips turn down in the corner. "I have to go now, Tay." His neck works as he swallows.

"I'm not sure how to do this."

He steps backward and turns his eyes to the floor. "How to do what?" he whispers, rubbing both of his hands through his hair.

It's odd to see him without product coiffing his hair. It's not tousled or slicked back. It's sort of fluffy and perfect. Even though I want to cry some more, I smile instead. It confuses him enough to garner a grin back.

"How to say goodbye to you when you have this awesome hero hair going on," I reply.

Smiling, he looks up and hands me my shirt and pants he picked up from the floor. He hikes his thumb at the bathroom connected to my bedroom. "I can go do it really quick if it helps? You'd be shocked what I can accomplish with a little water." He turns away while I get dressed. "Watching you put on clothes only reminds me of taking them off, and we'll be in the same place we were ten minutes ago," he explains.

I wouldn't mind that. I want that. "I'm fully dressed," I say. "Albeit sticky."

He has one hand on a small black duffel bag he brought inside. Crossing to him, I hold my breath. The TV anchor drones on downstairs. I hear the hysteria, the panic, the confusion. It fans my anxiety flames.

Macs swallows hard. "I need you to keep this bag for me. There's another satellite phone in there, which you can use to reach me," he says, chancing a glance down my way, but looks away quickly. "I only ask that you use it in case of an emergency. The number to mine is programmed in there."

I nod, grateful for this lifeline even if I can't use it every waking moment. He goes through the bag and shows me things that I can use if we lose power to help with life. It's extra gear. Things he never in a million years thought he'd need to use or show me how to use. At the bottom is a handgun in a holster.

"This is only for emergencies, too," he says. "It's loaded." His voice is taciturn, demanding I know he's serious.

I pick the cool black weapon and turn it over in my hand. "I know how to use it, Macs," I say. "My dad taught me when I was a kid." I remember how important he thought the skill was. The older I got, the more I strayed from that logic. Guns kill people. I didn't want to have anything to do with them. When he left and I realized what a whore he was, I vowed to never pick up a gun in my life because obviously lunatics and selfish assholes use them. When I tell Macs the quick story, I see the tension in his shoulders relax.

"You'd scare someone with it, to be sure, but you don't know how relieved it makes me to know you can do more than that, you can defend yourself," Macs says. He's trying to talk over the television, I can tell. The volume is so loud I can hear that it's not normal news regardless. His efforts are misplaced.

"Here's a phone, but don't call me and here's a gun, but try not to use it?" I ask, laying it down on the top of the bag.

There's other stuff in there that lets me know he didn't intend to leave this here. Like his clothes and a dopp kit with grooming products. He walks over and shrugs his jacket back on. The uniform is identical to the one Tahoe had on, and the sight makes me sad. I launch myself into his arms and bury my face in his neck.

He clutches me tightly, but when he releases me a touch, I know it's time for me to put my grown-up panties back on. When my tiptoes hit the floor, I wipe underneath my eyes. "I lived without you once," I announce proudly. "And I can do it again."

My statement doesn't make him happy. In fact, I think quite the opposite happens, because his eyebrows knit together in anger.

"What? Do you hope I'm miserable without you?"

He scratches the side of his head. You can tell having fluffy hair is a distraction. "I guess not, no. But I don't want you to go back to being single either."

"Does this feel like I'm single?" I ask, leaning up and pressing my lips against his.

I will him to feel the passion through my lips. The love. The disdain for this situation. Everything I never said for fear of frightening him off. Macs groans into my mouth but holds me at a distance.

Keeping my eyes closed, I will the clash of teeth and lips to drown out everything else, so nothing else exists in this moment except what I give permission to. His hands are tender, more so than they've ever been. I bite his lip as I pull away and let my gaze find his. We're nose to nose, heart to heart, and it's the moment I break.

I sob into his chest.

"I believe you. That wasn't a single lady kiss," Macs says. "Don't get upset over it."

I laugh through a hysterical sob, and I feel like such a failure. Like the little girl who can't control her emotions. The more he sees me cry, the angrier I become. He tells me he's sorry, and it's not his fault, but I can't form coherent sentences to tell him that, so I just shake my head and clutch his jacket and let every fear take over my body.

When he says he has to go a third time, I release him with the intent of watching him walk out the door. Time has stood still since we entered the house. We've been in my room for less than thirty minutes. With a thumb, he wipes a tear from my cheek and pops his thumb into his mouth. It would probably make me laugh if there wasn't a constant stream of tears taking that one's place. He throws me a lopsided grin, his thumb still tucked between his teeth. A one-sided dimple appears. I shiver.

"From the back to the middle and around again," he sings, lifting and lowering his shoulders.

I do laugh now. "I'm gonna be there until the end," I whisper, completing his '90s song by Crystal Waters.

"One thousand percent. Pure," Macs says, raising his eyebrows in question.

"Love," I finish.

Macs kisses my forehead and walks out the door. I remember slamming that door a million times when I was a teenager. I remember tilting a chair under the knob to keep my parents out when I had a boy in my room. But I don't remember ever feeling such pain seeing a back disappear from it. He talks to my mother for a bit. I can hear that through the vents cut into the wooden floor. Macs walks out to his car in the same stride I've seen dozens of times before.

Slumping to the floor, I kneel, leaving my chin and arms on the windowsill.

Saying goodbye wouldn't be this hard if I knew when I'd see him again. If I could cross off the days on my calendar like a normal military girlfriend, it would be manageable, the pain wouldn't resonate so deeply, I'm sure. Macs doesn't look up at my window, and I know it's a purposeful move to regain some semblance of his other personality. He can be the SEAL. The man who will take care of a nation and serve his country well. He told me he loved me. He asked me to wait for him.

I want to know why the first man I've ever loved arrived during a skewed reality, twisted by enemies no one knew existed. It's the world's cruel joke. Give Teala what she's secretly wanted and then snatch it away before she enjoys it too much. I place my hand against the glass and peek through my fingers at his car disappearing down the drive. Even as I dwell with this agony, I hate myself for succumbing to the dramatics of it all. I did the same thing when my father left. If I'm being honest, the hollow feeling inside my bones feels the same way.

I turn on the clock radio on my nightstand and scroll

through the stations until I find a clear news station broadcasting the attacks. I turn the volume down and slide under my covers. I want to fall asleep hearing the atrocities that stole him away. The irony of where I'm at and what has happened isn't lost. I resolve to stay in this bed until I can put on a strong front for my mom.

For myself.

But mostly for him. And it's not the him you think.

CHAPTER TWENTY
Macs

THE DESTRUCTION IS fantastic in the most lowly, seedy way possible. The attacks were far-reaching and all-encompassing. Everyone I know was affected in some way. Martial law is being enforced by our military, the dystopian feel of it all being almost too much for even a seasoned government employee. Most days it's complete melee anytime you turn around. There are checkpoints set up on the back roads and highways, which means traveling anywhere takes forever, and it's rarely worth it. The news is broadcast twenty-four hours a day, and the President of the United States gives weekly teleconferences from the Oval Office. It's meant to reassure a country streaked by destruction and tainted by fear.

The SEALs are now being sent on missions unlike anything we've ever been assigned. We've been tasked to find the financiers and anyone connected to the attacks. It's hard because we aren't dealing with men overseas with an open agenda with guns pointed at our faces. We're trying to skunk out our neighbors with hidden agendas, ones we would never be able to surmise. The attacks hadn't been planned for long. Which is obvious to me, in a spot where intelligence is handed down, but

America refuses to believe this wasn't planned—or worse, a conspiracy theory. When citizens are finished reveling in fear, they move on to anger. I get it.

I am a step above angry. I'm fucking rage-tastic. I want to kill, and nothing is moving fast enough for my liking. My brothers have been spread out across the larger cities in the States.

"We're headed back to San Diego, bro. You gonna call her?" Tahoe asks, grinning scarily. His face is streaked with black paint, and he has a cut above his eye that was stitched by a medic with an obviously unsteady hand.

I wince. "That fucker had one job. One. That's gonna scar," I tell him, nodding at his gnarly gash. Our feet are dangling over the side of a chopper.

He laughs, a menacing sound. I'd hate to be on the receiving end of Tahoe's anger. He got the gash from cocking his fist back too far before knocking someone out. He lunged forward, and his head met the edge of a counter. I shake my head at the memory. Poor fucker didn't even have the information we wanted. That's our life these days. There aren't rules of war anymore. Not when our nation is bleeding uncontrollably.

"Not everyone cares about being pretty," he says. "There are those of us who care about doing our fucking job and not stinking."

I cut him off with a hand slicing through the air. "And there are those of us who appear after the frag smoke clears like a vision of fucking perfection," I tell him.

I give him some more imagery, mostly referencing my guns, both types, and when he's scoffing good and well, I stop with my daydream cocktail. He stops smiling when I do.

"I want to go see her," I admit, looking over his shoulder at the rest of the guys boarding different aircrafts in preparation to leave. My hands shake a little on my lap, and it's why I'm so unsure about visiting Teala. "I can't think of anything else."

It took weeks to get my head straight after I left her. My focus should be on my job, but she's there in every waking moment. She taunts me. She tells me I was wrong about myself all of this time. She tells me she loves me. My visions are vivid and heart-punching. Teala doesn't call me. Not even once. I suspected she would abuse the phone I gave her. I wanted her to. I merely gave the warning so I could sound like I wasn't a complete lunatic. I mean, I was giving her government property to borrow for a spell.

"Regardless if it's her or someone else, you have to get laid when we get back home. You're spun up like a fucking top. It's been nothing but work…frustrating work at that for a month now. Bars aren't open. Nothing is open. The only activity we'll have is fucking," Tahoe says, stretching out his legs.

Somehow I feel like he's going to have a hard time finding a booty call during these times.

"I'll have to leave her again," I say. Even now, my fucking chest aches with need. With desire. With fucking love. "I don't like it."

Longing. I'd never had to define that word before in my life. If I wanted something, I took it. Instant gratification. I didn't know what it would feel like to have another person inside you that was thousands of miles away. The desire was crippling. I miss her scent. The feel of her bare curves on my fingertips. I miss sex. What surprised me the most was that I missed her laugh. I missed talking to her and watching her face when she didn't know I was watching. I missed the way she could turn a conversation around regardless of what we were talking about. Her jokes. How sweat would bead along her hairline after she taught a class. The way her hair brushes her exposed shoulder blades when she wears her workout tanks. Everything about Teala Smart is what I long for.

"Who would enjoy leaving? You're fucking crazy to get hung up on one woman."

I'm not. I know that now. Tahoe will understand one day if he's lucky. I smile and shake my head. "I'm fucking crazy. Yep, that's me," I say, reaching behind me to dig through the small backpack I keep with me at all times. I drink the rest of the water in my canteen and roll the cell phone around in my hand. I check the screen. No missed calls or messages. I grind my teeth together and punch the satellite phone number into my phone quickly, glad I memorized it before I left it in her care.

I type out several messages and delete them. What is the proper greeting after so much time has passed without interaction? I'm in more new territory.

The chopper blades start up, cutting the air like razors. I hook myself in with one hand and slide my sunglasses down and over my eyes. The sun isn't as hazy here in the mountains. I think it's because we're closer to it. Some days and in some cities it looks hazy. That's what scares me. The smoke masks its true splendor, and I don't care who you are, that's fucking eerie.

Tahoe is playing Candy Crush on his cell phone, completely distracted by the colorful screen. I look back at the blank text box and think of Teala. Now that we're headed back, I've let myself think about her. I type out a rap song, then delete it again. I look out over the horizon, and this is commonplace for me. It's not for her, though. I swipe to open the camera and point it down at my ash-covered boots. You can see the world underneath me, small and insignificant. I snap the photo and send it before I change my mind.

Sighing, I try to enjoy the ride. I haven't been back to

my house since I left Teala. I have no idea what I'm going back to. The neighbor was supposed to check in from time to time, but everyone is self-involved right now. Grocery stores are just now beginning to get shipments again. The economy is in the shitter. Some semblance of normal life is beginning just by proxy of time passing and fear diminishing. The hospitals are overcrowded, and any place that can hold large capacities of people will be closed for an undetermined amount of time. I don't look at the phone. There's no way she'll respond right away. I bet the phone is still at the bottom of the bag I left in her bedroom.

It pings with a message seconds later. I lift it so quickly I almost drop it. It's not a photo like I fully expected.

It merely says, *I miss you.*

I didn't realize I was holding my breath until moments after I read her message. My mind is made up to go and visit her as soon as I land. Before I go check on my house or do any of the other million things on my to-do list. Teala telling me, using words, that she misses me is enough to tear my plans into shreds. I'll get over her again when I leave. The pain is something I'll deal with if it eases hers. If she feels a fraction of the mess that I'm dealing with, it's too much.

When I was a teenager, there was a girl I was pretending to date. I was really just fucking her on the weekends and after school in the bed of my truck. She had huge brown eyes with long lashes. People use the term doe eyes too frequently. This girl, though? She was the damn definition. She looked all innocent, convincing everyone I was tutoring her in physics, and then she tutored my dick instead. For a month or two I thought she could be girlfriend material. I had my eyes set on BUDs and becoming a SEAL, and she wanted to go to

San Diego State. Feasibly, it could have worked. I wanted her to be my girlfriend for all the wrong reasons. She could suck a mean cock and would be conveniently local. Oh, the naiveté I carried back then. When I discovered women throw their pussy at SEALs, I squashed all possibilities of Doe Eyes and commitment. Chapter closed. The end.

I want Teala for all of the right reasons. Overcoming a mindset embedded for years upon years was hard in terms of acceptance but easy because it was her. We're coming from the same mentality. We met on a level playing field. The game of fooling her friends into thinking we were dating was a farce. We both knew it was more than convincing her friends for a trip to Vegas. We were trying to convince ourselves we could do something hard—almost impossible. The depth this thing burrowed into my world was catastrophic. It changed me to my core. Then, the attacks changed everything else inside me. The importance of things and people shifted.

The phone vibrates in my hand, and I see that Teala sent another text message. *I'm back at my apartment.*

I didn't tell her I'm on my way back, but she must sense it because I reached out. I feel like an ass for not contacting her sooner. Would a quick text have taken that much of a toll on me? It's hard to say.

We're crossing over Los Angeles Stadium right now, and the ruins are shocking. It's black and leveled from one of the more severe attacks. Several car bombs exploded in the parking garage and underneath the stadium. It crumbled up in smoke in a matter of minutes. The air is loud out here, with the blades chopping the sky. It's a welcome distraction for everyone.

Turning to glance behind me, I see Moose. He's wringing his hands between his thighs while working his jaw left and right. He's been on edge since we left. Sitting next to him is Smith. And he's a ball of sunshine and rage since he broke up with his girlfriend. No one thinks the separation will last just because of how miserable he is. Tahoe breaks the moment by cursing loudly when he loses a level on his game. I text my mom to let her know I'm safe and home, and I have no idea when I'll be able to visit, and, no, she can't come visit me, and when the standard conversation is finished, we're landing at the compound at work.

Groups of people scurry as we arrive, and others rush toward our aircrafts to help unload. When my boots hit the familiar pavement, I sigh. It's relief tinged with grief, and I think that's how it will always be.

Ignoring the buzz of everything going on around me, I find my car in the lot. When I notice blood on my jacket, I remove it. It's not mine. I start my car and head toward Teala's apartment, settling in for a drive that is sure to be longer than I want it to be.

Entering her parking garage made me uneasy. Noticing an unfamiliar car in one of her spots forced even more emotions to the surface. I parked in one of the other spots and cleaned myself the best I could given the circumstances. I'm still pretty filthy and could use a shower or five. Our accommodations haven't been the best over the last few days. It's feast or famine. We're either staying in the nation's finest five-star hotels, or we're sleeping in fucking dirt with one eye open. I'm told it's part of our charm. The latter is why I just smoothed a deodorant stick through my hair and brushed my teeth using a bottle of water.

My fist is hovering over the doorbell, and I'm suddenly struck with a sense of unease—the notion I should have called first. I press the button before I lose all resolve. It's been a month, and one would assume another minute or two wouldn't break me, but I feel as if

I can't wait another second longer. My fist is about to slam on the wood when the door opens.

It's not her.

It's a man I recognize from our very first dinner out. As a man she described as someone who was a patron at her studio. Yoga Man's face goes through every emotion in the book. Surprise, fear, and then confusion as he takes in my appearance and half-assed uniform. I'm wearing the camo pants, but I left the bloody jacket and hat in the car. I have on a white tee that was probably white when it was issued but now has chosen to stay a nice shade of dusty gray.

"Hi," the man says, finally regaining his wits.

I don't return his pleasantries. "Where is Teala?"

He clears his throat, opens the door further, and I step through. I see her then. She's coming around the corner from the hallway to my left. She stops cold in her tracks when she sees me.

"Macs?" she whispers, my name a foreign object on her tongue. "Why didn't you tell me you were coming home?" Her eyes turn down in the corner, and I can tell the waterworks are coming, and there's nothing I can do to stop them.

I'm almost too stunned by her appearance to speak. I stutter a word or two. "I wanted to surprise you," I say. It's a lie, but it's also kind of the truth. I make a point of turning to the side to look at her male friend. "Looks like I succeeded at that."

"You didn't reply to my message. I wasn't sure what to think after all this time. He's here for a yoga class. I have a few friends coming over," she says, realizing I've intruded in on her new life.

My stomach grumbles, and it's not from hunger. It's from a fear I've never known the likes of.

"I'm not comfortable teaching in my studio yet, but I

figured it would be okay to start here at home for a class or two per week," Teala explains, using her hands.

I take another step into the room because the kitchen bar is blocking her, and I want a full view. I have a better memory than most, but it never quite does Teala justice. She's the Achilles' heel even on the subconscious level.

The guy closes the door behind me, and I startle. I'd forgotten about him during my study of her body. I send a quick glare in his direction, and he cowers into the living room, mumbling under his breath. I'd take care of him now if I didn't have larger things to worry about.

"Are you okay?" I ask.

She has deep, dark circles under her eyes. It changes her face drastically. Her hair is shorter. Much shorter. It looks like she took a hacksaw to it—one side more jagged than the other. She's always had a thin frame, but what I'm looking at now isn't healthy. "Tay-la." I enunciate her name to get her attention.

She's looking around the room. Anywhere but in my direction, and it's so intentional it forces my heart rate to speed. It's been a while since I've had to worry about the nuances of determining a woman's mood.

"I'm okay." She smiles weakly.

I'm not unskilled enough to know okay is a trigger word. It's almost never used when someone is okay.

"Do you mind coming back another day? I'm so sorry," she says to the yoga guy, her gaze flicking to the guy on the couch.

The awkwardness in the room ratchets up a notch, and I'm not used to being the interruption. I'm the interrupter.

Teala tugs the hem of her tank. She looks about ten pounds lighter. More than that? I survey her thin frame quickly so she doesn't notice. Yoga guy leaves without another word, and I lock the door behind him without taking my eyes off her. She reminds me of a caged animal that can't be trusted. How did I not know what was happening? Why did I assume she was okay these weeks while I was away? She didn't call me. No contact. The only logical assumption was she was fine. She gestures to the couch, but I shake my head.

I pinch my shirt. "I'm filthy. You don't want me on your furniture," I tell her.

Her hooded eyes appraise me very specifically. I recognize desire immediately.

She sits down instead. Running her hands through her hair absentmindedly, it's like a light bulb flicks on. Her hair. Her appearance. The disaster I'm seeing. If playing pretend was ever warranted, right now is when I need to make it count. I ask her what's going on using a look. Instead of telling me, she cries. Or what I perceive as crying. No actual tears arrive.

"I can't cry tears anymore. How fucking pathetic is that? I've used them all up!" She rattles on and on about inconsequential things she knows I don't care about to avoid the truth. I recognize what's happened straight away, and my heart seizes in panic.

My body tingles from my toes all the way up to my hair. "Shut up," I command. I'm not angry at her, but it's going to come off that way.

Her eyes turn down in the corner, and her bottom lip quivers. I run a hand over my face to keep from watching the emotions play across her features. None of them are the ones I was expecting to see right now. She's not flying into my arms or ripping my clothes off with the desire to love me. She's looking at me, knees pulled up to her chest like I'm the feral animal in her living room.

Tucking her hair on the side that's long enough to tuck, she says, "Do you know what it takes to admit he did this? That he has this control over my life without my permission?"

Her father. I'm able to piece together this disaster one abandonment issue at a time. Mix those with extreme anxiety, wait for a low boil, and watch for the explosion.

Through narrowed eyes she spits, "Don't ever tell me to shut up again." Teala is there, in her command this time. So be it. Anger is what needs to happen right now.

I sigh, kneeling down in front of her. Gently, I place my hands around her calves. It has dual purposes. The need to touch her is fierce, but she's so small I could snap her legs like twigs. Has it only been a month that has passed? Is this capable of happening in a month? My erratic behavior mirrors hers. I don't know how to relationship properly, and the one time I fuck up, I cause the worst possible scenario.

"I'm sorry," I whisper.

She doesn't meet my gaze, but her lip trembles again.

"I know you hate apologies that span multiple things, but that's what that was, and you're going to accept because I've missed you." Pushing my luck, I slide my hand up one leg and graze her face to bring a short chunk of her hair in between my fingers. I look at her and raise a brow in question. "Britney circa 2007?" I ask.

She smiles, and it's painful to watch. "Something like that," she responds. "Oops, I did it again. Maybe, one more time? I was upset, and I wanted to control something. Unfortunately I saw scissors and then realized my neck was sweaty. The rest is history." Her laugh is shallow as she runs her hands through her uneven haircut. She meets my eyes. "You know I can't be with a man who leaves. It's glaringly obvious." She waits for my rebuttal, but I don't waste my breath. What's obvious to me is that she's made up her mind. She continues, "Even if you come back every single time. I can't. This right here is proof." Teala motions to her body and face. "I'm not sleeping. Don't get me wrong. I'm in bed most of the day, but I'm awake not thinking about anything."

"You texted me," I say. I want to pull out the phone and shove the text in her face.

Her eyes are wild again. "I told you I miss you. Not come to me."

I wince. "Ouch."

My heart is combusting with the magnitude of what she's saying. She may not be in the right frame of mind, but my pride won't give her another chance if she does come to her senses and realizes what she's done.

She stands to get away from me. She walks to the bar and pours herself a glass of vodka.

"Why don't we get something to eat?" I offer.

"He liked women. Just like you. He was a professional at leaving. It was too similar," she explains, grabbing her hair.

I don't know what to say or respond with, so I ask about food again. She shakes her head and continues her explanation even though I don't want to hear another complicated word.

"I started yoga all those years ago to combat my anxiety." Teala laughs and turns to face me. "Fucking men helps too." She swallows the alcohol in a few large swallows while eyeing me over the rim of her glass.

My fists are tight by my sides and it takes a lot of effort to stretch my fingers out. It's painful. "I'm not your fucking father, Teala. I can be your daddy if that's what you really want." My stomach churns even as my dick hardens. "Have you been fucking other men?" I'll still fuck her right now if she replies in the affirmative, but it will be for the last time.

Finally, she smiles, and I'm glimpsing a piece of her from weeks ago. Her mind is twisted, and I don't even care. Suddenly I don't want to know the answer. It would change things even more.

I close the distance between us in a few steps and pull her into my arms. The glass in her hands clatters to the ground and shatters. I kiss her, and pure vodka sweeps my tongue. There's no trace of her sweet breath or the sounds of small sighs. Her hands are tight around my neck as she scrambles to climb my body like a rope at the gym. It's frantic, even for me, who sets a similar pace without realizing it. It's never been like this with her. I let my lips slide against her neck and close my eyes when a familiar scent hits my system. Now I have something to hold on to. I kiss her neck for a few more moments, leading her back to rest her against the wall.

"Fuck me," Teala growls. "Right now."

I haven't had sex with something other than my palm for a month. I want to fuck her. I didn't expect it to be like this and I'm surprised by the disappointment. I reach between our bodies and free my cock. Teala moans when she circles her hand around my shaft and pumps. I let her feet hit the floor long enough for her to strip off her pants. I bring up the mental image of her naked body from before. This isn't the woman I'm in love with in my arms right now—she's frail, weak, and devastated by a past come back to life. She hits her knees, and I have to remind her about the broken glass. She doesn't heed my warning and puts my dick in her mouth after she removes my dirty pants and boots.

It feels fucking amazing. Then I reach down to guide her with my hand in her hair, and I'm spiraling back into reality. When she stands up, her shins are covered in cuts and blood. I clear my throat to bring her attention to the issue, but her mind is only on one thing until her phone rings and she tells me she needs to answer it. Teala is all over the place, and I realize I'm just riding some foreign wave at this point.

It's her friend Carina on the line, and I listen to her play nice with her friend for several minutes. She's different. Normal. After she hangs up, I fuck her against the thick panel of glass. She clutches me as I thrust into her. I don't have to think about my grandma on a cold, wet day to prolong coming. I merely have to think about the woman I love to keep my orgasm at bay. Figures move in the building across the street, and it draws my attention, distracting me even further. Teala is screaming out in her release, her fingers laced in my hair and her teeth lightly grazing my shoulder and neck. I come by proxy after several more thrusts.

She collapses against me and makes no move to slide down, so I hold her, her weight light in my arms.

"I missed you so much," I whisper. I still miss her.

I walk her over to the bookshelf, far away from the broken glass, and set her down. Blood and cum are mixing down her legs in a streaking pattern an artist would love.

"Fuck," I say, closing my eyes and shaking my head.

"It's just a little blood," she says, grabbing her pants from the floor and cleaning her legs in a few swipes. "Never seen it before?" Teala smirks.

I don't return the gesture. Blood isn't the issue. I can wear it from head to toe for Halloween.

"Can I use your shower?" I ask.

Teala nods quickly, her gaze darting around the room like she's not sure what to do next. I don't want to be in front of the windows anymore.

"You really should get curtains in here or something," I mumble, heading into the guest bathroom.

Turning the knobs, I let the water get hot and stare at myself in the mirror. *What the fuck am I doing?* Showering and leaving. I get in and take my time, enjoying the hot water—a luxury I haven't had as of late. I know when Teala enters because she makes noise wherever she goes. At least that's the same.

"Did you know sloths aren't the sleepiest animal? They only sleep for, like, ten hours a day. There's a snail that can sleep for up to seven years."

That fucking sloth picture isn't going to make me smile today. All of my friends participating in a Bukkaka-lypse wouldn't make me smile today.

I rinse my body, crank the water off, and slide the door open. "You can't blow my heart open and then give me random sloth facts, Teala. That's not the way this works."

She swallows hard. "Blowing loads, not hearts, Macs."

I lose all the oxygen in my body in one giant rush and get a little dizzy and dark for half a second. When I gain composure, I raise my brows. "That's it then? I fucked away your issues for the time being, and I'm free to go?"

She bites her lip as she looks in the foggy mirror and uses her hand to clear a portion. "This happened when he left, too."

"I am not your fucking father," I scream. "I'm a goddamn Navy SEAL. With a job that takes me away. I don't leave for bitches with wet pussies. I leave because it's in my job description."

Teala winces.

"I've never given you any reason to think I would do anything to hurt you. I've never done anything to indi-cate I would never come back to you." I step out of the shower and grab the towel she's holding out for me. Seething doesn't describe how pissed off I am. I'm mad at myself for breaking my own rules.

"I gave up an entire life for you," I yell.

Her eyes widen briefly, but then she shrugs and draws a heart in the steamed mirror. "You shouldn't have."

I'm going to break something. Anything. The urge to throttle her rises, and I get the fuck out of that bathroom as quickly as I can. "I can't believe this is happening," I mutter to myself. "You're fucking crazy, Teala. Crazy." I hop into my dirty clothes quickly and rub the towel on my hair so it doesn't drip. I laugh when I glance at the mess by the bar. Water is the least of the problems right now.

"Where's your mom?" I ask when she ambles in to watch me.

She's still naked and dirty. Teala looks through me, her big gray eyes searching for something she'll never find.

"She's out shopping now. She'll be back," she explains.

Rushing past her, I peek in the guest room, and I'm relieved it does look like her mother is staying here with her.

"I'm not a child. I can take care of myself." She rustles around in a laundry basket next to her, searching for something to put on.

I nod. "Looks like it."

She seems unperturbed by my subtle dig.

"Do me a favor. Don't text me anymore. It's obvious you don't want anything of substance from me anymore, and that's fine, but I won't be your boy toy. I can't."

She crosses her arms across her chest and leans against the wall. She's donned a new pair of workout pants. "Fine." Crossing one foot over the other draws my gaze to the blood oozing through the fabric. "A relationship that began on false pretenses was never going to work out. You know that as well as I do."

"We'll never know now, will we?" I clap back, smiling wide, sending dimples and suave charm all up in her business. I'm pleased to see it still affects her. "You're your own worst enemy. Get help. Please." You can't save someone who doesn't think they're drowning, doesn't admit they need a life vest. I have to watch her sink, knowing the powerlessness I feel is preventable...by my own fucking hand.

"You've helped me. You could help me again," she says, licking her lips.

I don't answer her right away. I can't. Because my fucking heart wants to take whatever she's giving, but my mind knows better. The truth is staring me in the eyes.

"The world basically ended. Don't tell me I'm crazy. Don't tell me I need to talk to someone," Teala rattles on as she sweeps up the bloody mess using a broom and dustpan.

With anger subsided, I try a new approach. "Yes, everything is different. The world didn't end. I'm working on fixing it. A lot of people are. I know someone who you can talk to," I tell her. The team psychiatrists are probably overworked right now, but Teala needs help. Desperately. I keep my tone soft as I explain how I could take her to see someone, but she shuts down when I mention leaving again for another mission.

"I see it in my head anytime I shut my eyes, Macs," she says.

"The attacks?" I ask. I keep my distance. Her gaze is fixed on the floor.

She shrugs. "Kind of. Mostly you leaving in the midst of it. I stayed at my mom's for a while, but I wasn't getting better. I figured if I tried to pretend my life was normal and came back here, life would improve. It did for a little while."

We're getting somewhere.

"You knew what my job was. From the get-go. Before you told me how you felt about me. I was always going to leave. One way or another, I was going to leave."

"You forget I've never done this before, Macs. Let alone with someone who leaves for a job."

I suck in a deep breath. "I can't change that."

"And that's why we won't work. I wish I were a stronger person. I'm not. Maybe one day I'll change."

I shake my head. "I won't be here then. I'm here now. This is it." I raise and lower my arms.

"Then go," she whispers. "Solve this for both of us."

"Fuck you, Teala. I don't need anything solved for me. I came here thinking I was going to see my girlfriend. Assuming I was going to make love to the woman who I'm in fucking love with. The woman I'm fucking crazy about," I shout, my hands again fists by my sides. "I did get crazy. I'll give you that much." I snarl a breath and rake her body from head to toe in disgust.

She scoffs. "Awww. Is this our first real fight? Fuck you back. I am crazy. For thinking this would ever work." She smiles, but I see the overwhelming sadness below the surface.

I shake my head. There's no reasoning with her.

"I'm not leaving because you told me to. Or to solve anything for you. I'm leaving because I love and miss my girlfriend. And she's not here."

Teala collapses on the floor. I grab my shit, then turn to look at her. She's crying real tears now. I get the fuck out of there as fast as I can.

I run into Viola in the hallway as she's blowing out of the elevator, her arms full of bags. One look at my face tells her everything.

"She's talking to someone, Macs. I'm so sorry you had to see her like that." She speaks of Teala like she's a ten-year-old. Not a grown adult woman. She explains how the attacks triggered repressed memories and emotions. How the doctor thinks she needs time to sort through her issues. In the meantime, we're supposed to let her cope in any way she sees fit. What does that mean? Let her fuck her way through the remnants of San Diego?

I listen to Viola talk. I do. And I even try to pay attention and let her words sink in, but I've already made the decision to cut ties. It's not for selfish reasons. Not because I couldn't handle seeing her like this. I'm a strong man. I've buried more friends and brothers than I can count. Men have died while staring into my eyes.

I'm turning my back now because what if this is her forever? I'm not ignorant to the way things like this work. Quite the opposite. I've seen it too much: insomnia, mistrust, agitation, emotional detachment, self-destructive behavior. Many times it doesn't go away. It changes people down to their fundamental core. Viola is in tears as she explains how she watched it happen. How Teala got out of bed one day and wasn't herself.

I cut her off. "Viola. I'm sorry you have to deal with this. And as sad as it is, I can't stay around to watch it unfold. If I'm the trigger, me being around isn't going to help her. I'll be the reason for her grief personified. She made it quite clear about her feelings for me." My tone is even, stoic, utterly terrified. Not for myself, either. For Teala. "I'm so sorry. She doesn't want my help. She doesn't want anything to do with me."

"Don't apologize. I understand completely." Her smile reminds me of the genuine one Teala wears after she tells a joke. A lump forms in my throat.

I sigh, unable to keep my fucking mouth shut. "Keep me posted on how she's doing? I'll be in town for a bit before they send me away on another mission. I know everything is twisted, but if you need me. Call me. I can't see her, though," I say, wincing. I swallow hard. "It's too hard." I want to fuck her. And throttle her until Teala comes back. "For her," I explain when she looks upset.

She shakes her head. "You realize you're doing what she thought you would. Her worst fear realized. The scenario she concocted in her mind is coming true." Give her something to actually be upset about then.

Teala. Teala. Teala. No one understands I witnessed a fucking nightmare. One that will haunt me for the rest of time. This is what happens when you fall in love with fire and life douses it with water instead of gasoline.

CHAPTER TWENTY-ONE
Teala

HE LOVES ME. *He loves me not. He loves me. He loves me not. He loves me. He loves me not.* I tap my big toe on each book on the shelf as I alternate my truths. If I land on a book spine that contains green, I'll call him. *He loves me. He loves me not.* Red. Sighing, I roll onto my stomach and prop my chin on my hands. Mom isn't letting me leave the apartment. I don't want to anyway. It's so scary outside these days. My friends come over, and it's easy to pretend I'm normal when they're here. When I'm by myself, everything falls apart.

Something shiny catches my eye. I hop up and walk toward the sparkle against the dark wooden floor. It's a tiny piece of glass the sun is catching just right. After I put it in the trash, I return to the floor in front of my bookshelf. I chose a book with a pink, worn-out spine. It's my favorite novel. I thumb through the pages and stop on a page about halfway through and read a few random sentences. Tears prick my eyes. I throw the book across the room. The kitchen is tidy. Mom must have cleaned all morning long.

Everything in the world is starting to return to normal. Trash pickup resumed, and the grocers have produce again. The malls and shops are still closed but will open soon. I can't even think about opening the studio again.

I tried to teach a few classes in my living room, but it didn't feel right, and I couldn't focus to save my life. I can't focus on anything, actually. Water. I need a drink. Opening my fridge, I grab a water bottle and drain it completely. Zero calories. I don't have to worry about burning zero calories. I drink another one as fast as I can and throw the plastic bottles in the recycling bin. I slide the button on my tablet to bring it to life and check my email. Nothing new since I checked ten minutes ago. On autopilot, I go to my favorite workout gear online shop to read the message about being closed for the time being. No new pants or tanks to look at still.

I meander down the hallway and work my way into my closet. I sort through the clothing and organize it first by color then by shape. I run my hands over the soft fabrics and try to envision wearing them once again. It's impossible, and it frustrates me beyond belief. When my shoes are lined up on their shelves, dusted and loved, I sit in the middle of my bed. Macs's T-shirt is folded under my pillow. It doesn't smell like him anymore, but I still remember what he looked like when he wore it. It hugs his muscles in the right places and stretches across his broad chest enough to let any woman know what he's packing underneath.

I run it in between my fingers and get angry. Whenever I think of him, it ends in anger. Every time. He left me. I drove him away, sure, but he didn't even fight for us. He told my mom I'd be happier without him. He didn't want to cause me any more trauma by going on work trips. After I'm finished being angry at him, I get furious with myself for being so stupid. For giving my father permission to destroy me. Again. That man really is an asshole. My psychiatrist comes over twice a week, and my meds are regulated so that I feel like a normal person most days. Feeling normal only proves to show me exactly how much I lost while I wasn't normal.

It's a twisted game of Guess What Your Reality is Now! I did go out last week because one of our friends opened her salon for the first time since the attacks. I met Carina there. My hair doesn't look like Edward Scissorhands got ahold of my head. It's shorter than I'd ever want it, but I know it will grow back, and honestly, in the grand scheme of things, what the fuck does hair mean anyway? Nothing. It sits on your head. You can put products in it or leave it be. It grows. You cut it. Rinse. Repeat. Short hair is easy. I don't have to brush it. It exists all by itself. Like grown-up hairs taking care of themselves.

I lean back on my bed and close my eyes. Did you know it's impossible to will yourself to sleep? You can't do it. I can't take the drugs they give me to fall asleep because I don't like the way they make me feel. I greet the dark every night with open arms and hope it will pull me under briefly. It rarely does. When I open my eyes in the morning, I'm more exhausted than when I went to bed. If I sleep, the nightmares come. They're vivid and life-altering. I can't chance it, so I catnap during the day and play dark roulette at night.

I glance at my clock and realize it's almost time for my doctor's appointment. He'll come in using the key my mom gave him. He'll move the stool from the bar to the center of the living room and sit down like a man on a throne. I'll perch on the couch or lie down with my head on the nice blanket, and I'll spill my guts. All of them. My abs get sore from talking so much. It's my cardio for the week. The one subject that is quite off-limits is Macs Newstead. I don't go into any depths about my feelings for him, and the doctor knows not to broach it. He warned me we will have to talk about him eventually, but there's so much baggage with my father, I doubt I'll be alive by the time we make it to Macs.

I hear the door open and close, so I wait in my bedroom. When I'm sure he's set up in the way he always is, I enter, plastering a huge grin on my face. Absent-mindedly, I run my hand through the ponytail that doesn't exist. "Dr. Rhodes. How are you?" I ask, beaming. I offer him water, which he denies, like always, gestures to the couch in front of me.

I don't even want to know how much these in-home sessions are costing me. Luckily I was savvy with my money. Responsible.

"How are you feeling today, Teala?"

I tell him I'm fine.

"Doing some reading today to pass the time?" Dr. Rhodes nods to the book on the floor—the beautiful people on the cover peeking up at me, like they're ratting me out.

I shrug, leaning back on the couch. "It made me upset. It's my favorite book."

"I see. Why did it make you upset?"

I'm disappointed he went for the obvious question. How dense does he think I am?

"The man left his best friend and he shouldn't have. He knows she's in love with him. It's more than friend love. It's forever love."

He presses his lips into a firm line. It irritates me. "What does she do to let him know she loves him? Is it obvious to him?"

I sigh. "Of course it's obvious!" Then I think about it. Maybe it's not. "Well, maybe. I don't know. He's an idiot if he doesn't know, though."

"I see." It took therapy for me to realize *I* and *see* are the most annoying words in the English language. "Perhaps if she was more clear about her feelings, he wouldn't have left."

I smirk. "You've read it, haven't you?"

He smiles back in a genuine way that lets me know I've caught him. "They find a way back to each other," he says. "Eventually."

"Listen. I'm not ready to talk about Macs." Saying his name is painful. "It doesn't matter anyway. He doesn't do second chances. Hell, the man doesn't do first chances. I'm not sure how I squeaked by with that one." By lying to myself. It was never just a game or a bet for me.

"You can't let what you think he'll allow dictate how you feel."

I know exactly how I feel. Heartbroken. Scorned. Angry. "It's a moot point. It's the past."

"You know as well as I do that your past is pretty important. It affects the future whether you want it to or not. So do you think you're ready to leave the house? Begin teaching at the studio again?"

"Maybe if I could sleep." I throw an arm over my eyes to block out some of the light. I could take five or ten minutes right here and right now.

He clears his throat to let me know a nap isn't in the cards. "Nightmares still?"

I grunt to confirm.

"What was your last one?"

I'd like to nip this in the bud. I've already spoken *his* name. Something I'd rather not do, and I remember the last time Dr. Rhodes brought up the dreams. He asked if I would have a meeting with my father. I told him I'd rather stab myself in the eye a thousand times, but that niggling DNA thread that binds us forever won out, and I met with him. Right here on this sofa. Something miraculous happened during the time spent questioning him. I understood. He gave me what I needed. Closure. I never realized something that seemed so insignificant could make me breathe such a sigh of relief. Was I magically healed? Fuck no. I'm still muddled by a cloud of confusion and suffocated by the what-ifs with Macs. The nightmares of my father leaving are gone, though.

Was my dad an idiot? Yes. So are a lot of men and women in this world who let fleeting feelings guide them to their destination instead of clinging strongly to morals and promises. My life is a reflection of that, a mirroring image of what my father did without that one, very important facet. I never committed to anyone.

"Yes. Nightmares," I confirm.

"Not taking the medication? It might be the only way you get rest, Teala. You look better. You're putting weight back on again, but nothing can account for lack of sleep. You should try the pills again. Give them a chance to work. You may have a brand-new outlook once you wake after eight hours of sleep. The world will have a new hue." It makes sense, but he doesn't get it. Not fully, anyway. It's my fault. "Tell me what's bothering you right now."

"I guess I'm just upset Macs didn't check in on me after all this time has passed. It's like I meant nothing to him. Granted, I pushed him away. Thoroughly. But he knew how much he meant to me, and he didn't try."

"Ah, he didn't chase. That's not in everyone's personalities, you know? From the little you've told me it doesn't occur to me that Macs would be one to chase regardless of how he feels," Dr. Rhodes explains.

I nod. "You're right. I thought we had something more."

He scribbles on his little tablet with the end of a pen. "Would it change how you felt if you knew he did care? That perhaps he was checking in on your progress from time to time?"

Sitting straight up and staring my doctor down, I say, "Did he?"

He has no tells. I've tried before. You know? Trigger an eye twitch or maybe a movement in his neck or mouth. Nothing. I bet he could go on a killing rampage and pass a lie detector test with flying freaking colors.

He seems hesitant to kill my hope. "I don't know. You would find it heartening if he did, though."

Ugh. It was just a trick to gauge my reaction. He writes something else down.

"Things with Macs were always tedious because we're the same."

He clears his throat. "You were both promiscuous without need for committed relationships?"

"Just call me a whore, why don't you?" I smile. "Yes. And that we both wanted the same things to start, and when it shifted, we fell in love at the same time. It was hard and all-consuming, and I don't doubt if he never left, I'd be talking to him right now instead of you." I let my gaze flick back to the book on the floor. I pick it up and sit back down. "I'm not the same."

He nods. "You're better every time I see you. Look at the leaps and bounds you've made with your father!"

I shiver.

I smooth the cover of the book in my hand. "My friend has a book signing. Carina. I've mentioned her before to you. It's local. I think I'll go to it. It's walking distance. Down on Fourth." My poor friend is in rough shape as well. Her SEAL hauled off and broke her heart into a million pieces. She was able to have her revenge in the form of a novel. The title is *Never Forever,* and I'm sure it's going to be my new favorite story.

"I think that's a great idea. You have a clear head and a nice haircut now," Dr. Rhodes says, nodding at me, laughing. "You should go. It will be a great outing for you. Get some fresh air. You'll be surprised by how much has changed. Everything is different, but the things that remain the same will be comforting."

Immediately I cover my head in embarrassment. "I can't believe I cut my hair. Macs saw me like that, you know? He made a joke, like it didn't even bother him. I saw it in his eyes, though. He was terrified of me." I glance over my shoulder at the window. "He came here after being gone for a month, and I made him fuck me against that window. I was a walking disaster, and he did it anyway because I asked him to. He was scared. That big, muscled SEAL. Ha," I say, laughing to myself, yet grimacing at the memory. I barely even remember having sex with him. My frame of mind was skewed almost completely.

"Why do you think he was so scared?"

"He told me why. He missed and loved his girlfriend, and she wasn't there. It was akin to having sex with a stranger for him. It's pretty close to the truth, to be honest, but it hurts so badly. I know you're going to ask why, so I'll just keep going. It hurts because I had multiple opportunities to take him in my arms and tell him I loved him. Macs was waiting. He didn't just storm off at my first outburst. He took it all, swallowed it, and waited around for more abuse." This memory hurts the worst.

"You haven't spoken to him since he left?"

I shake my head. "Not even once." I look down at the pink, worn-out novel.

"Do you think he knows how you feel now?"

I meet Dr. Rhodes's gaze with tears in my eyes. "Of course he knows."

He smirks, and it's smug. I swear if he says *I see*, I'll knock him out. I may not have all the muscles I used to, but what I lack in biceps I make up for in pure fury.

"What's the worst possible thing that could happen if you told him how you felt? If he already knows, then it's not new information for him. He'll shrug it off, and he'll go about his business like he has been. If he's not aware you're still in love with him, well, then maybe it would sway his mind about chasing a woman. The very least you can do is apologize to him for the things you said and didn't mean."

It seems crazy. Implausible even. "I hate it when you're right."

Dr. Rhodes laughs. I smile. "I can't call him out of the blue. I don't even know if he's in town. Macs is busy saving the world. Literally."

"If he ever loved you at all, Teala, he will make time to listen to you. Perhaps you should email him? As a starter? Test out the waters. The internet is up and active everywhere again. There's no reason he wouldn't receive an email."

"Best-case scenario, he agrees to meet with me so I can tell him what an awful person I was and apologize. He's always going to leave, Doctor. I don't think I'll ever be okay with that."

"Leaving is in direct correlation with arriving."

"Or coming," I joke.

His face reddens, and he twists his short beard in between his forefinger and thumb.

"I'm joking. I'm joking," I chide, putting my palms up.

Dr. Rhodes sighs and scribbles on his tablet. "Anything worth having is worth losing. Sometimes having someone is just as painful as losing someone because of situations like this one. You have to decide what you're willing to accept and draw the line in the sand. If you can't handle his career, then it may be best if you don't get in touch with him. Let sleeping dogs lie." It's impressive he's able to recover from my dirty joke so quickly, but he has a sense for my personality by this point in our relationship. How easily he got me to talk about Macs. I can't even remember how he did it.

"Have you seen any men since our last visit?" he asks, changing the subject, but not really.

I walked right into this one.

Carina is sitting next to me at my desk. She's pulled up a cube that functions as a stool or a table.

"Help me make this sound better than it actually is," I whine. My head is in my hands as I scan the words in front of me on my screen.

"I can't believe you said those things to him. I don't think it's a good idea for you to bring them up again in this email. Especially because the title of it is 'I'm sorry.' My advice is to glaze over the finer details of what you're apologizing for, Teala. Focus on the bigger picture and the fact that you feel bad for the things you said when you weren't feeling yourself," Carina says, wincing. "I mean, gosh. You are like a man. Letters and emails are the worst things in the world," she goes on.

Smith, the SEAL who broke up with her, did it by a fucking letter. Don't get it twisted. It was more of a love letter than a breakup letter, which makes him that much more of an asshole. I don't tell Carina that, though. She's just getting out of her house these days, too.

Life will never be the same after the attacks. I will always watch my back or wonder if the parking garage is too full or if someone is lurking just beyond the corner, waiting to do bad things to good people. It's a sick feeling, but with it comes a sense of responsibility. The patriotism in our country is at an all-time high. Everyone is helping each other. We're all in the same boat. Carina endured a bomb that went off at a mall that morning. Thank God she lived and only has small scars as a reminder.

I hit the delete key and remove the nasty phrases. "I wish I were a writer like you. I bet if you wrote this, he'd forgive me."

She sighs. "Can't you call him? I heard they're in town still. Not for long, though. I was talking to Moose, and they're leaving on a mission soon. I check in on Smith because I'm a glutton for punishment."

I wrinkle my nose and pierce her with an ugly face. "You are, aren't you? Do you know when they're leaving?"

She shakes her head. Carina is the one who brought me his email address. She had to weasel it out of Moose, I guess. I type it into the "To" line and take a few deep breaths. "I need to finish this and get down to the studio," I tell her.

"You can do hard things, Teala Smart. He wasn't in the right either. You're being the bigger person by initiating the conversation."

"You sound like my psychiatrist. Are you sure you don't want to moonlight?" I ask. "Let me read you what I'm sending," she says.

Macallister,

I apologize for being an awful human being. I wasn't myself, but then again you knew that when you left and never came back to check on me. I don't fault you for that...too much. I wish things could have been different between us. I'm better these days. I'm back at the studio, my glutes and hammies came back to say hello. I met with my father and didn't kill him. I talk to a mysterious bearded man twice a week about my feelings, and I miss you a lot.

Not like, I miss you, but don't come see me, either. I hope you're well and driving the remaining female population wild with your dimples. Anyway, I'm just apologizing for everything. Blanket apologies are our thing, I suspect. Please be safe wherever your travels take you.

Love,
Teala

Carina sighs. "I like it. It's direct and to the point. You've accomplished your goal. You're sorry, and he knows it."

I wonder if he's sorry about everything that happened.

I hit send before my nerves cause me to sling my MacBook at the window instead. Once the message is confirmed as sent, I widen my eyes in horror. "What if I want more than to apologize? Was there enough leeway in there for reconciliation? Fuck!"

"Stop worrying. If he loves you, it won't matter what you said in there. You reached out. That's all he'll need."

He doesn't email me back.

CHAPTER TWENTY-TWO

Macs

I EXHALE, filling the air around me with a cloud of smoke. It's a nice bar—a really fucking expensive bar. The suit encasing my body cost five thousand dollars. When I leave here for the night, it will smell like I crawled out of a sewer. She watches my lips and licks her own. Grinning, I inhale another drag.

"You're playing tennis tomorrow?" I ask. Casually, I lean back and place my elbows on the bar, praying the bartender wiped down this section.

She nods, eyes rimmed in thick kohl open wide. She's fucking putty in my hands.

"What time?" I ask, leaning toward her on the barstool. "Who are you playing with?" Please fucking answer honestly. *Please.* I've been after this information all week. I ruined my suit for this. Please, Christ, give me what I need.

I let the scruff on my face brush against her cheek. "I love tennis," I whisper. "You know that." Completely in line with my character, I motion for the bartender to bring another round.

She flutters her eyelashes when I lean away. She's pretty. In the normal sort of way. Lots of makeup and lots of plastic surgery to make her lips look like they can suck a mean dick. "Doubles," she says. "My husband and his partner Pierre St. Croix and his wife," she adds.

Thank you, Jesus. I could kiss this bitch. The bartender slides us the drinks. Her a dirty martini, me a brown-tinged water in a lowball. The bartender knows me. He's also being paid well to keep his trap shut. I can't drink while I'm working. On something this important, I wouldn't dare. She crosses and uncrosses her legs.

"I wish I could play with you instead," she says.

I lick my lips because I know she's watching. Indifferently, I take out my phone and send the text.

"Do you want to get out of here?" she asks, running her long nails through her fake blond hair.

We could fuck right here on the bar and no one would say a thing. It's one of those places everyone rich and famous goes to have an affair. I saw her damn husband in here last week when she was out with her friends. It's taken two full months of wining and dining and playing interested to get Pierre's name from her lips and into my hidden mic. It's all we need to peg her husband, and the dominos will fall perfectly from there.

He financed the terror attacks—a very large portion of the attacks. He's big into gun smuggling. Law enforcement has been trying to take him down for years. Dirty money always stays dirty money.

"I should get going, actually," I reply, looking at my watch.

She knits her brows together, and I understand the look. Even though she has so many injectable fillers in her face, it shows no emotion. She's wary. I might have to fuck her after all. Take one for the goddamn team. Hell, celebrate this victory by fucking his wife. That would have a nice aftertaste, I think.

"I could probably push the meeting if you really need me," I say, tilting my head in question.

She stands from her stool and pulls me to her by jerking the lapels of my jacket. I go. She kisses me, and it tastes awful. Like drunk breath mated with vodka and plaque. I use the least amount of effort when I kiss her back. It's just enough. She moans into my mouth like a porn star. I roll my eyes. They're shut, so no one knows. If you'd told me I would be required to act when I became a Navy SEAL, I would have called you a liar.

Other people may be up for this particular job skills-wise, but the people we're after are dangerous, and those same people aren't up for that aspect of this game. SEALs are. So, here we are, sniffing around suburban house-wives with nefarious husbands spread across America.

I haven't heard from Teala. Not that it surprises me. Her mom gives me small updates every once in a while, and I try not to let them affect me or cloud my judgment. I've made the right decision in staying away. She's getting better, and I can focus on my career. I even tried dating a girl a month or so ago. It got messy because I was also trying to date stank-breath-bomber-husband at the same time, and even I have to admit, one chick is more than enough work. It was always going to be half-hearted, because try as I might, my heart beats for Teala. I don't remember the last time I saw the walls of my own house or felt like myself or wanted to do anything besides work. It's in the quiet moments that the fear slips in. It's terror because I might have made a huge mistake. Fear that I'll never have that feeling in my chest again.

I lost myself for a bit there after we broke up. The missions got weirder, and my head wasn't right to begin with, and I was too sad to realize I was better at acting than I was at real life. Obviously I hid my pain well, and no one suspects a thing. My parents asked about Teala, and it's the first time I had an honest conversation about what happened. They were concerned for her, and my feelings were pushed to the wayside. It's all so tedious. If she reached out at all, I know I would run with that shit, and I don't do second chances for anyone or anything.

"Want me to suck your dick? Let's go in the back," Alligator Breath rasps into my mouth.

I shrug, noncommittally. With a quick glance around the room and a nod to the bartender, I let her lead me to the back rooms. It's like a baby whorehouse. I finish off the cigarette right before she pulls me into the blue room. I started smoking to hide the fact that my breath never tasted like alcohol. I was surprised by how well it worked, if not completely appalled by how quickly I got used to it.

"Suck it while I'm standing this time," I command.

Dropping to her knees, she glances up at me. I hand her a condom because there is no way I want her tongue anywhere near my actual dick. She rolls it on like a champ and swallows my cock whole. It's a fumbling mess. I feign disinterest, because that's her thing and scroll on my phone.

I'm checking my personal email account when it finally starts to feel good. Delete a few messages. "Ahhhh, yes. Like that." Junk mail folder. Tap. Teala Smart, Subject: I'm sorry. Another one from Teala, Subject: Disregard my last message, and then another, Subject: You are a cruel man. "FUCK!" I roar. I tap to open the first email so quickly the phone falls out of my hands and lands on the bimbo with a solid thwack.

She falls back, clutching her forehead.

"I'm so sorry! I'm sorry!" I say. I have visions of singing *drop it down low*, but that would be too much like my real self, and right now I have to read the messages. They were from months ago. What have I done? Why didn't the message hit my inbox? My stomach turns, and my head gets light. I zip my pants up and rip the condom off. Grabbing a tissue, I wad the condom up and pocket it.

"Jesus, Will, what's up with you tonight?" she asks. Tears of pain fill her eyes, and her black makeup starts smearing down her cheeks.

No. This isn't good. I stoop to collect my phone.

"Disinterest is one thing. Being so tied up in whatever is on your phone is offensive."

Fuck. I slipped up. Literally and figuratively.

I cup her cheeks and try to wipe away the black streaks. Her head will have a large knot on it. There's no way around it. She must realize I'm panicked. "I'm clumsy. I fall all the time. Don't worry. He won't even notice. Kind of like you not noticing I was giving you the best blow job of your life."

I laugh. "That was not the best blow job of my life, sweetie. Nice try, though."

Her brows knit together. "You're a dick. Maybe I will tell my husband."

I don't have the heart to tell her a mass of people are heading to his business right now to lock him away... forever. Her too, if they find she had any intel of it. At this point I highly doubt it, but she knows her husband has been up to no good. I just don't think she knows how destructive he's been.

"I have to go." With the swift goodbye, I leave her on her knees in the blue room.

I nod at Moose in the corner of the bar as I enter the large, smoky space. He smiles widely and stands to join me. We walk outside together and hop into the large white SUV. The teammates in the vehicle cheer and slap our backs as we get in.

"It was mostly me," I say, correcting the raucous bunch, flashing a vain grin.

Moose disagrees, and the tone of the vehicle stays elated as we drive away. We're finished. This job is complete. No knife fights like last time either. Success.

I sit in the back seat and read the emails from Teala labeled as junk. The first email makes my chest hurt because I know what comes next.

Subject: Disregard my last message

I'm not sure what came over me. I never should have sent the last message. You obviously have no need for my forgiveness, so I never should have offered it. I'm mad at you. Now that I'm far enough away from the situation to see things clearly, I'm pissed as hell. You can't tell someone you love them and then never come back around regardless of their crazy status. I've decided you must have been mistaken. It wasn't love. It was something else. He's made me realize no one is irreplaceable. Consider yourself aware of my feelings on the matter.

Peace,

Teala too Smart to waste any more time on you.

My hands are sweaty, and I have to wipe them down my suit pants to get the slickness away. Who is *he*? Who made her realize? I grit my teeth and open the last message.

Subject: You are a cruel man

Not that I thought you would deign to respond to my lowly emails, but at least write back and tell me you got them. Are you dead? Or alive and cruel? I'm not sure which fate I prefer. Carina tells me I'll have to see you at her wedding. I'm not sure if I want to go. If it's worth the heartache, I'm sure I'll arrive at the sight of your fucking dimples. You aren't mine anymore. And that fact hurts more than admitting I'm not yours either. Do us both a favor and don't show up. We know it would only end in a pity fuck. I don't need that kind of bad karma in my life. Charlotte says there's a special place in hell for men like you, and for once I believe something she says.

Teala

I write out at least ten responses but end up deleting them. Which email would I reply to? I have the thought to reply to the first one and pretend I didn't get the other two. Yes. It's the only logical plan.

Teala,

I haven't been checking my personal email while I've been working. Please forgive me. I'm glad you are feeling better. Do you want to get together when I arrive home? Coffee? Smith and Carina are getting married, as I'm sure you well know. Perhaps I could accompany you to the wedding? I should be back in San Diego for a bit. I've been extremely busy, but you're always on my mind.

Love,
Macs

Sweat beads on my forehead as I hit send.

"Dude, are you defusing a bomb?" Tahoe asks from the seat beside me.

My thumb taps the button to darken my screen.

I swallow hard. How to explain that emailing Teala causes my nerves to fray, and conducting a national-level, dangerous mission leaves me cool and collected? "Checking mail," I say with a shrug, turning my focus out the window. Cruisers are speeding down the street, their lights flashing in harried dismay.

"Trying to patch things up now that we're heading back?" he asks.

It would make sense. I think it's what he does now that the dating apps are null and void. He makes nice with one of the women from his past to make sure he has sex lined up for his free time.

I shake my head. "That's over. You know that."

Tahoe laughs. "I've seen enough of this shit over the years to know when it's over. You haven't bagged any chicks since her, have you?"

I don't know anything about his history with any types of relationships. He's so secretive. I wish I had that type of superpower. There are whispers Tahoe got his heart crushed and that's what turned him into this monster.

I shrug again. "Trust me, it's over." Even if it wasn't, her last email made it perfectly clear what her opinion on the matter is. "I can't deal with that. Wouldn't you agree I have enough to worry about?"

Tahoe knows what happened. After I spoke with my parents about Teala's condition, I told him. Or better yet, he coaxed it out of me when we were drinking too much beer one night.

I chance a glance his way. He's smiling at me like a fucking bastard.

"This job is a no-brainer for you, you pretty asshole. That woman? A challenge that was too much to handle. You bit off more than you could chew."

I narrow my brows. "Are you telling me I failed?"

His laughter is loud, his head thrown back. "I would never tell you that. You might kill me," he says, eyes twinkling. "I'm saying she hurt you."

"Fuck you," I reply.

"Fuck you very much," Tahoe sings, still laughing. Then he goes on to explain how Teala is sort of his hero for doing what he couldn't. Fucking asshole.

He's one hundred percent right.

Teala doesn't reply to my email until later that night. I'm getting used to being in my house again. It feels more like a hotel than an actual hotel feels. My television is on, the news playing low in the background, when my laptop pings a new message. I starred her email address as VIP so I wouldn't have a gut-wrenching repeat occurrence.

Subject: Weddings and lies
Macs,

It's unfortunate you weren't checking your email. I saw they arrested people in NYC a couple of days ago. I'm assuming a way to go is in order. I'm keeping busy with the usual, trying to get acclimated to life after the attacks. It's taken me a while to feel this normal, and I'm afraid that any small shift will create a toppling of emotions and more life destruction. It's hard to believe how much was stolen from so many people, you know? I feel lucky when I think about it that way. My family and friends are okay. I'm scared a lot of the time still, but fear is just background noise instead of the headliner. Walking down the street, I can forget, even for just a moment or two, that anything happened at all. Honestly, you remind me of too much bad, Macs. Falling in love turned into something villainous. Like a virus taking over my body, it stole so much away. It's not your fault, but in the same token, there's nothing you can do about it. I should have guarded my heart better. It was foolish for me to think it could have been a normal relationship. You didn't respond to my emails, and those months gave me something you never could—not while my mind was twisted with love, anyway. Perspective. And mine is better without you in it. Stay safe, you fucking hero.

Best,
Teala
P.S. I'll see you at the wedding.

I don't mean to break my laptop. It finds its way to the floor on its own. I pace the room, focusing on random things as I go. The bright white molding. The handle on the glass doors. The clock ticking on the fucking wall, the television reporting on the same bullshit that's been on forever now, the coffee table. Avoidance. I can't think about her words and what they mean. It's one thing for her to break up our relationship when she wasn't thinking clearly. It's quite another to make a level-headed decision and still conclude we're not good together. The kicker is I can't fault her. She wrapped up her well-being around being away from me.

I want her happiness even if it means my destruction. I kick the laptop on a pace back toward my front door and curse loudly, pulling on the tips of my hair. I open a beer and drain it quickly. It doesn't erase anything, so I drink another. Then another. When Tahoe shows up with several of his friends, I open the door widely and let them pass into my space. I don't even question it like I usually would.

Teala made the decision for me.

CHAPTER TWENTY-THREE

Teala

"DEEP BREATHS, Teala. Everything is going to be okay," Dr. Rhodes whispers, leaning over.

I'd take his hand in mine for comfort, but he says it's not appropriate to have any physical contact, so I focus on my breathing and keep my face turned toward the large tree. I chose this chair specifically because it was so near the front of the flower altar and there was less chance he would sit in front of me and force me to look at him. Avoiding him completely is out of the question, but Dr. Rhodes even agreed limiting contact with Macs would probably be best.

It's a small wedding, only several white folding chairs on each side of the aisle and a podium covered by flowers for the officiant. I know the wedding will be quick, too. Carina and Smith decided to surprise everyone and hold it in Balboa Park last minute. After the success of Carina's novel and consecutive movie deal for *Never Forever*, there was a frenzy over their real-life relationship and reconnection. A wedding that is fast and dirty and unpermitted was how they were doing it.

I can't help the pang of jealousy that creeps in when I think of how happy my friend is. Their love seems so effortless even if I know for a fact it was also traumatic. What love is easy these days? I asked Dr. Rhodes to come to this thing with me because I wasn't sure I wouldn't self-destruct. Macs probably has a date here, as does most everyone else, including Charlotte. Dr. Rhodes comments on my friends, some funny anecdotes that make me forget why I'm nervous to begin with. He makes me laugh. He's safe.

My hair has finally grown out. It brushes my shoulders and is one length instead of fifty. I'm sleeping again, in part because I started taking the medicine prescribed to me and because I started to become…happy. With the support of my mom and without any vices. When you're messed up to begin with, relationships are a bad idea. My subconscious knew that even if I didn't. Add in the terror attacks, falling in love, and losing Macs to the unknown, and it was a recipe for disaster formulated just for me. What luck?

The wedding ceremony makes me cry, and I'm a blubbering mess as it concludes. Carina and Smith are this picture of stunning love simplified and magnified at the same time. She hugs me tightly in greeting as they make their rounds. There are already people bustling around, folding the chairs and putting them away.

Carina pulls back to look at me and says, "I'm so happy." Her words are watered down now, too. How can you choose the proper words at a time when mere words aren't enough?

I nod and sniffle. "I want to be happy," I whisper in reply.

"Then be it," she says. Carina nods hello to Dr. Rhodes and finds Smith standing next to his friends. She links her arm through his and leans her head to rest on his shoulder.

I know Macs is over there just from the sheer size of the men in the group.

I turn back to my date. "Everyone is heading to the restaurant for dinner. I think I would rather go home," I explain.

"Would or should?" he asks.

I smile. "I'm not paying you right now. You're my friend! Don't ask me vague, introspective questions."

He laughs, and his eyes crinkle in the corner. The sight makes me smile. I'm finally okay. This is okay. Even if I have to see Macs, I'll live.

A male clears their throat behind me. I read it on Dr. Rhodes's face. He knows who it is. His smile fades, but it doesn't vanish completely. His eyes narrow as he studies Macs. Perhaps he's finally sticking every story I've ever told him to the person it belongs with. It's fun to watch, but I know what I need to do.

"Teala," Macs says.

My name is all it takes for my body to respond. Every hair on my skin stands on end, and flutters invade my stomach—like little Stormtroopers readying for a battle no one wins.

I smile at the doctor and give him a wink to let him know I can handle this without hysterics, and spin to face Macs. His smile doesn't mirror mine. Not even close. "Well, if it isn't Macallister Newstead? How are you? It's been so long," I exclaim, keeping my posture relaxed and my smile wide.

His neck works as he swallows, and his eyes flick to the side. "Oh, I'm so rude. This is..." My voice wavers. Do I admit I brought my shrink as my date? How crazy would that look?

Dr. Rhodes strides forward and extends his hand toward Macs. "I'm Salvatore," Dr. Rhodes says, saving me from any and all embarrassment. "It's so good to meet you."

I knew his first name by proxy of the bills I finally looked at, but I have never referred to him that casually. I owe this man a lot. Macs grabs his hand, and they shake, Macs eyeing him up and down more than once.

"Nice to meet you," Macs replies as they're separating. "I'm Macs," he adds as an afterthought.

"Teala, I'll go get the car, okay?" Salvatore says, smiling.

He doesn't shrink away from the massive bulk of Macs, even though he's probably half his size. Confidence comes in all shapes, I muse. Nodding, I mouth a quick thank you out of sight of everyone else. I watch as Dr. Rhodes runs up the grassy hill toward the parking lot. A light breeze picks up my hair as I turn to face him.

"New boyfriend?" Macs asks.

I shrug. "Someone I talk to from time to time," I reply, twisting my hands in front of me. "You look good."

The excuse I've needed to let my gaze flick from head to toe. He's dressed in a crisp button-down shirt and dark navy dress slacks. He's so handsome he makes my mouth water. I wish I could take a photo so I could look at him longer than is socially acceptable in person.

Macs shoves his hands in his pockets and looks to the left. "Thanks," he mutters. He looks tired, his face a little more weathered than the last time I saw him. "I'm glad you're doing well."

"I don't like this," I reply.

He quirks an eyebrow. "What? The space between us or the small talk?"

I shake my head, smiling. "You never should have come over that day. Do you know how many times I've gone over that scenario? If you'd stayed away for longer and I had time to heal first? What if right now was the first time you saw me again? I wish I could erase that day and the things I said. I couldn't see past my nose." Things happen for a reason. The reason is usually that you've made a choice. He made the choice to visit me, and I made a choice I had no hand in. "Did you ever get any other emails from me?"

He shakes his head but doesn't meet my gaze. "I didn't. Just the one, and even that was too little, too late. I'm sorry," he says.

"You were busy. It's fine." I wave him off. "Someone has to save the world."

He glances behind him, over his shoulder.

I shudder. "Did you come with someone?"

I was okay when it was him assuming I'm dating Dr. Rhodes, but the notion he has a date here makes my skin crawl and my stomach roil. It's not okay, and I realize the possessiveness I feel toward him won't go away regardless of how much time passes. The people are thinning out, so it's easy to see who belongs with whom. There's a tall, thin, extra-blond woman standing next to one of his other friends.

I clear my throat. "I won't hold you up anymore," I say. "Bye, Macs," I whisper, finally letting my eyes find his. Still, his lips are pressed in a firm line. I smile at him, hoping for anything resembling his former self. When he doesn't reply, I turn to start up the hill.

"Teala," he calls out.

Looking over my shoulder, I raise my brows in question.

"I like your haircut," he stutters.

I laugh. "Thanks. I like yours too." It's the same as it's always been. Perfect. Not a stray hair out of place. I start walking again.

"Teala," he says my name again.

I stop and turn, placing my hands on my hips.

"I like your ass."

I laugh, covering my mouth with one hand. The beautiful blond woman walks up and takes Macs's hand in her own. I try not to wince or show how much it bothers me, but he knows. He tries to disentangle himself from her.

What more can he possibly say now that his girlfriend is standing next to him? When Macs doesn't make an attempt to introduce me, I start up the hill, my cheeks heating under her calculating stare. He calls my name again. Louder this time. I stop walking, but I don't turn around. The words I want to say are on the tip of my tongue. Half of those are swear words and insults, so I pin my lips together with my teeth.

"We were normal," he calls out.

Sighing, I spin on my heel. "What?"

He swallows hard. "You said our relationship would never be normal. It was normal. Because it was ours, and we made it. It was formed exactly how we wanted it. We were normal for us, and it was still extraordinary."

I must look like a deer caught in headlights because Macs doesn't wait for me to respond.

He blusters on. "You say I remind you of everything bad, that our love was villainous, and I'm calling fucking bullshit, Teala. Love is only villainous if you make it so. Me leaving doesn't cancel out everything else. Me leaving doesn't lessen the depth of feelings we have for each other. Me leaving is normal. So is me coming back. To you."

The blond woman scoffs, rolls her eyes, and stomps off in her heels that are too high for dirt.

"It was normal. We were good together. I'm sorry I didn't call you when I left, and I'm sorry for assuming all was well. I'm sorry I came by unannounced when I shouldn't have. I'm sorry the world is fucked up and you have to live with fear. You should know this. All of this. Once and for all." His strides are long as he approaches, and he's standing in front of me after several steps. He arrives, and his scent is strewn across every square inch of my body. I have to close my eyes to block out the memories.

I don't dare move. I should. I know Dr. Rhodes is waiting by this point. His words have glued me to the spot. Tentatively, Macs reaches for my face.

"Tell me you don't feel this," he says, cradling my head in his hand. "Tell me it doesn't matter anymore. I'll walk away and never look back. I'll go back to pretending I was happy, when in reality I was lonely. Tell me right now that zoo life should be left to the animals and monogamy to seahorses and penguins. Tell me." His eyes are pleading, and the tone of his voice is so sincere, the pit in my stomach threatens to swallow me whole.

The fact I've gotten this far into this conversation without crying is a miracle. "You didn't come back," I whisper, tears finally threatening. "I know what I said, and it's unconscionable, but you didn't even check in to make sure I was okay." All of the therapy and hard conversations about my father leaving are juxtaposed with Macs leaving, and this is what I couldn't get over. The niggling factor in the equation that just didn't line up.

I look up and meet his eyes, and the tears fall. He brushes them away with his thumbs, both hands now on each side of my face.

"Of course I knew how you were doing, Teala. Of course I checked in on you."

I shake my head, but he doesn't release his hold. "You don't have to lie. I'm sure you have reasons. It's as if your love for me died when the old me faded away. I'm back, maybe a little rough around the edges, but I'm better. You didn't check on me, and that's not…real love," I say, tripping over the last words. "I should go. Salvatore is waiting for me."

He releases me, a frown on his face. "Viola gave me updates, Teala."

I nod. It doesn't matter. "Whatever you say. I have to go now. Tell Carina and Smith I'm not going to make it to dinner."

Macs looks at the ground, disappointment touching every part of his body.

The hardest thing in the world is giving someone a half truth. What I didn't tell him was I'm still morbidly in love with him regardless of his attentions or lack thereof. Dr. Rhodes is waiting in the idling car when I find my way to the top of the hill.

Macs calls my name one more time. I turn, shaking my head. I throw my arms out wide.

"What?"

Macs shouts, "Tell Dr. Rhodes I said goodbye!"

I give him a thumbs-up, get into the car, stare out the window, make it out of the parking lot, then realize he didn't call him Salvatore.

CHAPTER TWENTY-FOUR

Macs

"YOU BLEW IT. You blew that load so hard all over her you'll never fuck her again even if you turned on the dimples," Tahoe rasps.

My date, if you can call her that, was pretty upset at my show after the wedding. She wasn't even an afterthought if I'm being completely honest.

I blow out a breath. "That makes no sense. I don't care if I ever see her again, anyway." The one person I do care about seeing is keeping her distance. She didn't call me after the wedding, and I checked my email incessantly for weeks after. She is well and truly finished.

Satisfied my gun is clean, I put it in the open case and move on to my open dead hooker bag. I'm unpacking from a trip inside my cage at work. Tahoe is already finished. He's here to annoy me.

"The op tempo is picking up instead of slowing down," I say, trying to change the subject. I can count the times I've been inside my house over the last several months on one hand. They've sent us to every imaginable city around the US. There are SEAL teams overseas working on restoring infrastructure and order side by side with allied forces.

"It'd be nice to stay home for a good bit," Tahoe admits.

I narrow my eyes through the cage into his.

"I'm getting tired," he says.

"You never want to stay home. What the fuck is going on with that?"

He growls in response. That subject is closed. "I'm thinking about taking up yoga," he says.

"Fuck you, man." The bag of dirty clothes that needed to be washed is now so large I've decided to drop it off at the dry cleaners instead of attempting to do it myself. "We're not talking about her. Don't think I don't see your subtle ways of trying to bring her up. I'm smarter than you."

He picks up his own bag and exits into the long, dark hallway. Locking my cage, I join him.

"I may have picked up your cell phone when it buzzed last night," he admits with a grin.

I push his shoulder so he slams into the cage across the way. He holds up his palms.

"What, what? It was a text from Viola. Which is a pretty fuckable name, by the way. She wanted to tell you about a class Teala was teaching tomorrow. Wondered if you wanted to show up and surprise her."

We're not allowed to have our cell phones on anywhere except in the cages. The buildings at our work require top-secret clearance, and loose ends aren't accepted. Cell phones are an ultimate loose end. Before we exit into the other building, I slide my phone out of my pocket and check my text messages while Tahoe chuckles like a child.

"You weren't lying. A fucking miracle," I say. My heart rate speeds up thinking about surprising her. I envision all the ways this situation could go. With my limited knowledge about relationships, I feel I've done all I can do. It's in her hands at this point. Facing my friend, I smile, using my dimples. "You're right. We should both take up yoga."

He throws his head back laughing, and we agree to meet at her studio twenty minutes early. I'm not sure why Tahoe wants to go, but I'm too excited to care. Any face time I can get with Teala makes me excited. I tap out a quick text to Viola, telling her I'm coming and I don't want Teala to know. She tells me she's risking her life texting me because Teala was upset when she found out we were communicating behind her back. I tell her I will defend her life if need be.

The gray bubble comes up to signal she's typing another message. *She's casually dating a guy she has no interest in. I think it's in an effort to dip her baby toe back in the world of relationships. He travels on business frequently.*

I stop in my tracks and swallow hard. Mentally I flip through the reasons Viola would have for giving me such information. If Teala is going to be with anyone who is *away frequently*, it's going to be me.

What does one wear to yoga when you have more muscle than most individuals? I decided on a pair of standard-issue black running shorts. I stripped off my shirt as soon as I got in the studio. Viola arrived early and let me in. When the front desk girl arrived, she looked at me like I was an alien. When I asked if she liked what she saw, she blustered an apology and explained she doesn't see *people who look like me* in here often. I laughed, and she tucked her tail and left.

Tahoe drank too much last night and texted me at four a.m. that he wouldn't make my tea party this morning.

It's better this way. Two of us would have drawn way too much attention. Teala isn't here yet, but this hot box of a room is filling up quickly—others unrolling their mats and stretching while they wait for class to begin. I tucked myself into a back corner by the mirror. It's dark in here, so my hope is she won't see me right away. I almost backed out, but the temptation to see her won out.

Every time the door swings open, my gaze flicks to the light to see if it's her. This time, it is. She walks in first, followed by a tall, slender man with a mat tucked under his arm. They both wear the smile of those who are in on a joke no one else knows. A sheen of sweat breaks out on my face at the sight of her and her obvious happiness. I should get up right now and leave—never look back for fear of rearview remorse. That's the condition you get when you look back on something and all it makes you feel is shitty. Typically I get rearview remorse about a mission—some small thing I didn't do and should have or vice versa. Teala's would be catastrophic, and I don't think I'd ever stop wondering what her life is like.

Teala starts the class and turns on the music. In the pike stretch, I put my head down and curse myself for being so curious. I curse Viola for telling me this was a good idea. I curse Yoga Man for taking what is mine, and with the last thought I know I won't be able to stay silent for much longer.

Teala stands in the center of her mat and speaks quietly, or what she presumes as quiet, and looks in the mirror in front of her. Her ponytail is long now. It's the only thing that marks time in my life. The phases of Teala Smart. It seems so stupid, but she's the only person I've ever been interested in long-term. Right now as proof, even when she's not mine, I'm still too intrigued for my own good. Her body is every bit as perfect as I remember it—the muscles in her legs and ass visible through the tight material of her pants.

I sigh and close my eyes. She's working her gaze through the large, hot room, and I hold my breath when she gets to my side. Her eyes flick to my corner a few times, but her posture doesn't change. There are probably thirty or forty people in here right now. She guides us through several flows, and I try my best to concentrate on something other than the back of yoga man's head and the way his eyes fix on Teala's ass.

"Take it to downward dog and stretch," Teala says, looking at her watch. She taps it a few times and heads back to where the music is coming from. She puts a water bottle to her lips, and I watch her drain it. Licking her lips, she puts the cap back on, and she finally meets my gaze. Her eyes narrow and then widen in shock. Her perfect lips pop open and she starts to say something, then realizes where she's at and closes her mouth.

The smile comes to my mouth all by itself. "Teala," I say, using my normal tone. It sounds like I'm shouting. "I need to talk to you."

Teala shakes her head no, furiously. "Not now," she whispers.

I stand, towering over the people in various arrays of stretching. I step over a few people using a large stride until I'm standing in front of her. "Yes, now. Now is the perfect time. I have your attention so fully, you won't be able to run away."

"Will she?" I ask the room. Someone has the audacity to shush me. I glare in the direction it came from. "I could rap you a song right now to tell you how I feel, but that would probably embarrass you."

Her hands perched on her hips, she avoids my gaze. "You're already embarrassing me." She apologizes to the class and whisper-shouts for me to get out.

I shake my head. "I'm not okay with you dating people, Teala."

She tries and fails to pull me out of the room. Her small hands slide off my slippery chest. I remark it's her fault for keeping the room so hot.

"Perhaps if it was cooler, you'd have a better grip?"

Tears spring to her eyes, and I think she very well may die of embarrassment right here and now.

"Forget them and talk to me, and I'll leave. Okay?"

She motions to the hallway, and with this small victory, I smile. I follow her out into the cool hallway and breathe out in relief.

"Go finish that class!" Teala yells, beckoning the desk girl to take over for her. She doesn't meet my eyes as she flies into the room. "I can't believe you did this in the middle of class. You just couldn't wait until the end? You had to be that selfish? Par for the course, Macs. Par for the fucking course!" She raises her voice at the end, and I wince.

I nod at the door. "You are so loud they're going to hear everything anyway. Better keep it down if you don't want your boyfriend to hear." I lick a drop of sweat off my lip.

She closes her eyes. "I don't have a fucking boyfriend." Teala opens her eyes to look at me like I'm insane. "Even if I wanted one, it would be pointless. Look at you, Macs. Look at you. No one would ever be you," she says, motioning to my body. "You're perfect in all the ways that draw me to a man. But you're bad for my health." She swallows as she sizes me up, one section of my body at a time.

"You're not dating anyone?" I furrow my brow. That's why Viola disappeared after she let me in.

"Of course I'm not! I'm in love with you, you stupid, selfish man."

I shake my head. "Why the distance? Why haven't you called? We're fucking adults. Staying away from you was the hardest thing I've ever done, and I've done some pretty hard things. Just for reference."

"I wanted to find myself, Macs. I wanted to be the person you fell in love with. I wanted to be the person you missed again. I will never be that girl, so I didn't reach out."

I can tell she's getting upset, so I grab her arm and lead her to the locker room in the back. She sits on the bench, and I sit on a bench facing her. Our knees touch.

"Plus, you had a girlfriend already. I do have some pride," she blusters on.

I scoff. "She was not a girlfriend. I don't even remember her name."

"Oh, gross. That's supposed to make me feel better? Why are you here, really?"

I should dime Viola out. She was counting on my alpha to come out and beat his chest. "I'm tired of staying away from you. I can't anymore." I shrug. "Take me as a friend if you must, but I can't stay away from you."

Teala furrows her brow. "A friend? You want to be my friend?"

I laugh. "I'd like to touch you, too. Define it however makes you most comfortable. I need to be around you."

"How do you know Dr. Rhodes?" she spits the question out. It's been on her mind since the wedding, I can tell.

I sigh. "I knew you were seeing him, so I saw him too. You shouldn't worry. He didn't tell me a fucking thing about your life, but I felt close to you by proxy. Your mom told me you were getting better, Teala." Using the smallest, most unoffending gesture, I brush her knee with my forefinger. "Without me. You were getting better, and I was away." I shrug. "It was easy to stay away, knowing you were happy." I'll let her define easy in any way she would like.

She shakes her head, unbelieving. "No one told me anything about that. Why? I wasn't happy...I was figuring it all out."

"Is it really that hard to believe I care about you? Admittedly, I got a little preoccupied with my job, and you can't fault me for that, but I can't not care about you. I tried that, too." I put another finger on her other knee.

She looks down at where we're touching.

"Looking at you. Seeing you," I admit, shaking my head. "You're everything that makes sense. I'm dead inside without you. Being next to you makes me feel alive." Love animates the soul in a way nothing else can.

She lays her hands on top of mine, and a shiver hits my body. "I can't be your friend, Macs," she murmurs.

I hang my head. The disappointment was expected, but the tiny fragment of hope that resides in my heart just turned to dust. "I understand," I whisper.

She tilts my chin up with one finger. "Because I'm madly in love with you, of course." Teala rolls her eyes.

I huff, exhaling a pent-up breath. "So, you are."

She nods. "I can be more than your friend, but not your friend in the normal definition of the word. If that's what you want?" Teala smiles through eyes brimming with tears. "You're sort of a whore, so I understand if you don't want that."

"You're awful. You know that? Playing me for a fool," I say. "I'm not a whore, either. I haven't had sex with a woman while we were apart. Apps were down." I give her a crooked smile.

She shakes her head. "It doesn't matter anyway."

I widen my eyes. "Uh, yeah, it does. Why wouldn't it matter? Were you with someone else? Multiple some-ones?" My breath catches in my throat. I will accept any answer she gives. I repeat that sentiment twice. I have to remember what my job has entailed lately and try to formulate a way to explain what I've been doing. That matters as much as this does.

"No. Not for lack of wanting, either. Dr. Rhodes kept me on the straight and narrow. It doesn't matter because the only way we can do this is if we start over completely."

I could kiss that man right on the mouth. I kiss Teala instead. I pull her into my lap, and she comes willingly, like she always has, her arms sliding around my neck as she straddles my lap.

"It wouldn't feel like this," she says against my lips. "And this is the only thing I've wanted more than my old ways. You."

With one arm around her waist pulling her close and the other on the side of her face, I live in this moment. One I never thought I'd feel again. Her scent. Her familiar yet foreign body against my bare chest, her lips are new and familiar at the same time. My head swims when I part her lips with my tongue and taste her. I could live like this—wrapped up inside her warmth. "I think the problem was the words. The emails. The black hole where sentiment is lost and emotions are fuzzed out and gray.

"Ask me again, what do I love?" I say, tracing her wet lips with my own. "Ask me."

She sighs, and a dreamy smile lets me know she remembers our very first date—tells me I'm in safe territory after all this time of uncertainty. She's receptive, and I can unload my weapons and sigh with relief.

"Give me the list, then," Teala says, clearing her throat.

I lean away from her and fish my cell phone out of my pocket. "I won't be your friend," I say, scrolling through my images. "I won't start back on date one either. I don't care what your friends think." That garners a scandalous grin for what it implies.

"Good. I'd hate to take you to Vegas as my friend," she replies, surprising me. "The list?"

"It's coming. It's coming. It's a hefty list, remember? I've been working on it for a long time." I tap on my phone, my fat fingers fumbling when I'd give anything to make them speedy in this moment. I find what I'm looking for and send it. She tells me the Vegas trip is a go, and I can't help but reminisce. It feels so long ago my only goal was to bag and bash, and Teala was nothing more than a conquest.

Teala's watch pings. Smiling, she brings it up to look. "A list of everything I love." She reads my message aloud and then brings a hand to cover her mouth. "The photo," she chokes out. It's the photo of her in my bathroom. She's tousled, red-faced, and more stunning than any woman I've ever seen.

"That's it. That's the whole list," I admit.

"A big change from the last list, huh? No hair products, shoes, or even your dick!"

Shaking my head, I bite my bottom lip and slide her down until her back is against this skinny bench. Her hands clutch my biceps to steady herself.

"My dick has missed you, though. You could probably say it loves you, too." I see a white flash of teeth, and then my lips are on hers. She's biting my lip and wrapping herself around me while kissing me like it's going out of style. Groaning, I melt into her touch, her lips, the warmth of her hot body against my skin, the small noises she makes that drive me wild. "On your mark?" I say against her lips.

"Get set," she confirms.

We both say "Go" at the same time.

CHAPTER TWENTY-FIVE

Teala

"I GOT what I wanted for it. I had to let it go," I tell Charlotte.

The housing market is finally back up after the slump, and my apartment sold in record time. It made the most sense to move into Macs's house because it has more space. Saying goodbye to this place is hard. I grew up as an adult here, found myself, lost myself, and put the pieces back together in between these walls. It's seen more than its share of men, and fights, and ups and downs.

"The realtors will be here soon. Ready to roll?" I ask, gazing out the window. I watch the figures move in the building across the way and wonder how much of my life they've seen. What do they know from the glimpses they've seen inside my world?

Charlotte sighs. "It does have the best view. I'll miss this place."

She's here helping me with the last few small boxes. Macs asked if I could stay away for the afternoon because he was working on built-in shelves in the living room. His friends are there, and beer is involved, and that was enough to keep me away without asking another question.

"My new place has an awesome view too," I remind her, spinning on my heel to face her.

She scowls as she picks up her handbag from the counter. "Yeah, because you live with a fucking *GQ* model, you bitch. God, what must it be like to sleep next to that every night? Do you hump his leg when you aren't actually humping? I would." Charlotte is bitter because her most recent boyfriend broke up with her.

After a quick peek down the dark hallway, I follow her out into the hall. "I don't look at it that way anymore," I explain.

She hits the down button to call the elevator. "Look at it how? Please tell me you know how lucky you are, Teala. Don't be that dumb bitch who feigns ignorance about her status in life."

I cackle. "You're so wrong. I know exactly what I have, and I remember what I had to go through to keep it."

Charlotte looks down at her shoes and apologizes quickly. Everyone forgets how bad of a time I had for a while. I hid it well, and most were surprised when I told them the extent of my problems. It was easily hidden because everyone was dealing with his or her own terrible shit at the same awful time. Charlotte lost an aunt and a cousin in the attacks. Jasmine lost two friends, both in separate cities, but in the wrong place at the wrong time. Carina got lucky and narrowly escaped with her life in a bombing at the food court of our favorite mall. My anxiety wasn't something anyone else should have to worry about given our current circumstances. I would never fault them for not being there for me. The thought brings me back to that day, and my stomach flips.

The elevator pings open to the garage, and we silently

make our way to my car. It's an unspoken rule about silence in parking garages now. It's another reason I was okay with leaving this place. I don't feel as safe as I used to. Things and places are tinged with grief and marred by the security stolen from right under our noses.

"We should go shopping for clothes or something," Charlotte remarks.

The engine purrs as I pull out into the sunshine of a perfect San Diego day. Agreeing with Charlotte is easy. We have an afternoon to kill. I dial my mom, and a comforting peace surrounds me when her voice sweeps the car speakers.

"Honey. How are you?" she asks.

"I'm good. Charlotte and I are heading to the mall to shop. Did you want me to see if I can find that top for you in a medium?"

The last time we went to her favorite store, they were out of stock. I've tried to tone down my needy habits with regard to calling and seeing my mother more than I should, but I do what makes me happy. Dr. Rhodes didn't think my relationship with my mother was unhealthy, per se, but he did mention I might rely on her emotionally too much. In light of all my recent self-discoveries, I can say he's probably right.

Macs gets the weight of my emotions these days. They're heavy and full, and everything I've ever dreamed of.

"No, no. Don't worry about me. Find something nice for yourself. I have a date tonight," Mom says, her voice lilting in excitement.

Charlotte whoops, and I giggle uncontrollably before we give her congratulations and ask if she wants any advice. Viola switches that conversation quickly, in no hurry to talk about men with her daughter. She should know I'm probably the only person with enough experience to give her advice on sex.

We say our goodbyes, and Charlotte starts in on a conversation about Smith and Carina and their impending baby. She says she feels left out because she's not making babies with a big, throbbing SEAL. Even though I tell her, all the time, she should probably find a man with a normal career and schedule, there's no talking sense into people on the outside. It looks glamorous and dangerous. It's shrouded in secrecy, and no one else really knows the truth unless they live it and breathe it. SEALs are hot.

We shop and buy things we don't need and drink coffee that winds us up, and we enjoy the easy afternoon. Our conversations are light and breezy, and the normalcy of it all hits me at once.

"I haven't thought about the attacks today," I admit. I think I blush, ashamed to admit such a horrible thing.

She shrugs. "I haven't either."

We both glance over at the food court across the way and take a moment to remember the beginning of a new life chapter. It wasn't just a new chapter for us. It was a new chapter for the entire world. Macs texts me a photo of the coffee table. I laugh, coming back into the moment.

"I think it's time I head back home. I'll drop you on my way." I take a photo of the bags I'm holding and text the photo to Macs.

As we walk to the car, I watch the gray bubble dance, waiting for him to reply. The anticipation is almost too much to bear. I think he'll send words back, but he may send another random photo I'm supposed to decipher. It's a photo. A pair of my panties. White ones, and they're lying against the dark maroon comforter of our bed.

"Oh, that's just not right," Charlotte wails, leaning over to be nosy.

I cradle the phone into my chest to hide it. "You shouldn't be so nosy. You're bound to see something you shouldn't when you snoop."

"You're always sending weird-ass pictures back and forth. What do they mean?" she asks, opening the passenger-side door.

She climbs in, and I follow.

"Sometimes they mean nothing at all, and it's just to confuse the other person. Other times they mean everything."

"How are you supposed to know which is which?" she asks.

I hear the accusation in her voice. We're playing a game no one else knows the rules to.

I shrug and pull into traffic. "Most of the time we just know."

"That selfie you sent on your very first date with him. Did it mean something or nothing?"

Okay, scratch that, now I hear accusation in her voice.

"Uh. That was something all right. I'm not sure what it meant, though."

She scoffs. "You had sex with him that night, didn't you?"

I laugh. "No. When? In the parking lot? You guys were at my house like little nannies!"

"I know you lied about something, Teala. I'll figure it out eventually."

This whole thing started with a stupid lie—a bet. It makes sense it should end with a final truth. "It started as a game, or so we thought. Play by your stupid dating rules and see what happens, and then go to Vegas."

"But?"

I shake my head, the smile falling from my face. "It was never a game, I don't think. Even when we were hashing out the details of the stupid bet, I wanted him more than I had any right. He wanted something more significant, too. It was the perfect storm, I guess you could say. We both started the relationship on the same foundation, and it grew on its own. We did wait until the proper amount of time to pass before we shagged it out—we followed your goofy guidelines. You should know that. Also, we paid for Vegas, too." I shake a finger in her direction. "You can't accuse me of cheating or lying."

"I'm beginning to think normal rules are goofy. I might need to go serial for a while and see if that lands Mr. Right. You paying for Vegas is what made me suspicious. You're never one to lose a damn bet," Charlotte says, shaking her head.

I watch her in my peripheral vision as she thinks back to the beginning.

"I knew something wasn't right. You were too perfect for each other."

It's insane that other people say this, but there must be some truth to it due to how much we're told something similar. "Perfect is a strong word, Charlotte," I say.

"And yet you've attained the pinnacle. I hope you'll finally accept his love and run with it. You put up with a lot of bullshit to land this man."

We pull into her drive. "It wasn't bullshit."

"It was, and you know it. The men and the dates and the avoidance. We all saw it, Teala. It's why we plied you with Vegas and trying something different to begin with. Look what happens when you listen to your friends!"

I take this moment to remind her how utterly annoying my friends are when they crash dates and act like teenagers.

"That's part of the Teala package. Have a good weekend," Charlotte drawls as she opens her door. She smiles in my face before she walks up to her door, and I'm left wondering what the fuck her issue is.

I send Macs a photo of my ear and start for home.

No one else is here when I pull in, and I'm surprised his friends aren't in the yard, half clothed and fully drunk. Macs is always doing one project or another, so the house always smells of sawdust or some type of building material. I open the door, and he's waiting for me.

Macs has me pinned with his gaze. I drop one of the boxes I collected from my apartment on top of the bed next to the pair of white panties. He's breathing heavy as he eyes me up and down like a panther stalking prey. You'd think I was naked, asking for him to bend me over and fuck me nasty for the way he's looking at me.

"I missed you," he says, walking into the room. With one hand, and more skilled ease than he should possess, he unbuttons and unzips his jeans. They fall to the floor, and he steps out of them.

"Oh, come on. Were you watching *Magic Mike* again? That move isn't even fair. If I tried that, I would have fallen on my face with my ass in the air."

Macs narrows his eyes. "Ass in the air. I like that."

His cock is hard. It's standing at attention, barely bobbing as he moves. If we had sex twice daily, I think I'd still be able to get him hard by smiling. It's why we work so well together. Our sexual appetites are similar. I slide my sweater off my shoulders. He stalks forward another step.

Turning, I pull a butter knife from the box of random, forgotten things from my apartment. I pick up my white underwear with the tip of the blade. Raising them in the air, I say, "I'm waving the white flag. You win. You win! This is me surrendering to your obvious lusty desires! White panties at the end of a butter knife."

Macs grins as he takes the butter knife out of my hand and sets it back in the box.

"I'm yours now. You don't have to work this hard," I tease. "I want to fuck you basically anytime you want."

"You're mine now? Just now?" He cocks his head in question, and the muscles in his shoulders and neck bunch.

I swallow. "Yes." I lean forward and trace his bone frog tattoo with the tip of my tongue. He shudders under the sensation. I smile.

"Here's the thing," Macs says, taking my waist in his hand. "You've always been mine. Since that first day I saw you. Argue if you must, but know I laid my claim on day one."

Arguing would be moot at this point. I want to be his. I grab his steel shaft and relish when he groans at my touch. Dropping to my knees, I put him in my mouth.

"Not too long. I'd really rather fuck you, but ah," he chokes out. "It feels too good," he groans. He's warm in my mouth, and his flavor is a blow directly to my core. That's all it takes. The chemistry of us is simple and maddening. I slide him to the back of my throat while keeping my gaze on his face. His eyelids flutter shut when I tease his balls in between my fingers. "Enough. Get on the bed," he commands.

It's a weak command, but I want him inside me, so I don't fight him.

I'm out of my clothes and sliding back on the large bed in seconds. He grabs me by the foot to stop me from moving any further. He leans down and kisses the inside of my calf, under my knee, the inside of my thigh, and then exactly where I'm telling his mouth to go. My voice is throaty and on edge as I give him orders and tell him where to touch.

"That feels good. Do that," I say.

Macs chuckles, and the vibrations set my teeth on edge. "Like that?" he asks, leaning up from his furious licking. Pushing his head back down, I let out a stream of curse words that causes him to laugh even more.

His hands are tight around my legs, controlling every tiny movement. The rough sensation of his scruff wars with the smooth gliding of his tongue and fingers, and I tell him I'm going to come if he keeps the pace up much longer. He knows my tells, and right when I'm about to come, he slides up between my legs and drives his cock deep inside me.

He grunts and groans and tells me he wants to live here—just like this. He starts moving eventually because the sensations are too deep, and I'm writhing against him to get the friction I need. His lips are on my neck, and my hands are twining in his hair. Everywhere his skin meets mine feels like electric, the greatest high in the world.

"You're mine," Macs growls in my ear as he bites the edge.

I moan in response, locking my legs around him at the same time. Skin slaps and limbs tangle. I come fast and hard, pulling his ass to me to keep him in as deep as he can go.

He leans his forehead on my shoulder and waits for me to finish before he slams into me several more times. "Where? Where do you want it?" His breaths are fierce as he demands fast answers.

"Come here," I say, closing my eyes and rubbing my nipples. I tilt my head back in case his aim misses.

Macs pulls out and comes on my small, rounded stomach. He apologizes for missing and slides down to kiss the side of my belly.

"Who are you apologizing to? Surely not the baby," I say, breathing out in a rush of adrenaline. "I said tits, and you missed. What kind of cummer are you?"

He laughs. "Well, I didn't mean to rain on his parade either," he explains, pointing to my wet belly button.

"He lives in wetness, Macs. A little rain wouldn't kill him even if you did want to come inside me every once in a while. You used to enjoy that, remember?"

It's the ongoing joke now that I'm pregnant—he refuses to blast the baby with semen. I understand his issue even if it makes zero logical sense.

Macs raises his eyebrows. "God, do I ever like coming inside this tight pussy," he growls, jutting inside me to drive his point home.

I sigh in pleasure, every nerve ending heightened by hormones.

"You're both mine," he says, kissing my neck.

"We are."

Nothing has ever made me this happy. "And you're ours."

"Good. Get dressed. I have to show you something right now," Macs says, leaning off me and hopping to the foot of the bed like a small child. "I'm serious. I even need to use the blindfold."

Epilogue

TEALA

"MACS, you're hurting my head. Please, for the love of everything holy, get to the point."

He has a tie wrapped around my head. It's his favorite thing since I forced him to watch the wildly popular BDSM movie he didn't want to see. It's punishment by hilarity. He also told his mom I made him watch it, and I thought I might kill him by a knife fight. Luckily she saw it too, and instead of a bloodbath, we talked about the movie.

"We're almost there. I want it to be a surprise, and I know how much you love to be bound and gagged."

"I'm not gagged. My eyes are covered. Brush up on your terminology, please," I say, trying to keep laughter out of my voice.

He was waiting for me in the hallway as I exited our bedroom.

We're in the office that seconds as a guest room. "I refuse to learn the terminology unless we get to act it out. Then I'll study like a demon."

I huff. "Macs. Please." I throw my hands down by my sides. "I've been gone all day. I just want to relax and see you, please."

He removes the tie. "Ta-da!" he says, rounding to stand in front of me.

I'm not sure what I'm looking at because the whole room is finally finished, so it's a lot to take in. The shelving is dark and hung on the long wall. My books and his books mix together. They're color-coded and arranged by size and width.

"You're not even seeing what I want you to see," he says, blowing out a breath. He has a streak of paint cutting across his cheekbone. He's shirtless, like always, and he looks devilishly handsome.

That's when I see the cluster of frames on the opposite wall. They're from floor to ceiling. Literally from the bottom of the molding to the top of the floorboard, housing every single random photo we've ever sent each other. My mouth drops open as my feet take me closer.

Hands, clocks, the sky, the interior of my car, his dimple—my favorite one on the right-hand side—an egg, a can of paint—randomness all brought together to make one huge collage of our life. Our love.

There are photos of just his chest and the back of my thighs as I'm in a yoga pose. There are photos I never remember seeing before and others that I cherish with all of my heart.

"This is the most beautiful thing I've ever seen," I exclaim. I stoop down to study the images at the very bottom.

"Photos mean more than words can, right?" Macs says.

I nod. My throat clogs with emotion. Words would fail me right now anyway.

"So, you go ahead and look at this wall for as long as you want, and when you're ready, look at me," Macs says, voice quavering.

Slowly, I stand fully erect and turn to face him. Macs

is down on one knee, the fear of God sparkling in his eye. His hands are both behind his back. He clears his throat.

"Here's the thing," he says as he brings his fists in front of him. "You have to pick a hand."

I smile through happy tears. "What if I pick the wrong one?"

His nerves seem to abate a little because he chuckles. "It's a win-win," he replies. The sun is setting through the window to my left, and the golden light shines in, highlighting him kneeling before me.

"Left," I say, pointing to his left hand. The vena amoris is in the left hand. It runs straight to the heart.

He opens his hand, and resting on his palm are two dimes and two pennies. I kneel in front of him so we're face-to-face.

"Twenty-two cents," I whisper.

He nods. "Twenty-two cents on forever."

Macs brings his other hand in front of his body and opens his palm to expose a diamond ring. It shines in the falling sun like a signal from a higher power. He raises his eyebrows in question and tilts his head to the side. Tucking my hair behind my ear, I try to gain some semblance of composure.

He slides the ring on the ring finger on my left hand without letting his gaze stray from mine. I grab the change from his other hand and slide it into the pocket of my sweatpants.

His lips crash into mine in excitement of my silent acceptance. I didn't have to say yes. Doubt isn't in our repertoire anymore. Clarity comes when you can't make sense of anything. You grasp what you want and forget everything else. His kiss takes over all of my senses. He only breaks to smile at me—no words are spoken, but everything is said.

Macs is my clarity. My family.
He's my hero.

A Look At Book Three:
THE DESTINED SEAL

Distance couldn't break it. Time couldn't touch it. Some things are *destined*.

Ben Brahms was the brainy best friend turned battle-hardened Navy SEAL—leaving behind his Ivy League dreams, thick glasses, and the girl he secretly loved when the world turned dark.. Now, he's a man forged by war and sacrifice. Saving the world is second nature. Saving himself? Not so much.

Harper Rosehall chased the life they once imagined—acing college, building a career across the country, and growing into the fearless woman he always believed she could be. But no amount of success quiets the voice that whispers his name...or pulls her back to the place where it all began.

Years apart. A broken pact. A connection that won't fade. As fate brings them face-to-face again, old wounds reopen, and the cost of what they lost might be more than either is ready to face.

In a world that takes everything, can Ben and Harper find their way back to each other . . . before it's too late?

AVAILABLE OCTOBER 2025

The list of things Rachel loves

I love my readers. For coming back time and again to see the new and inventive ways I can bring you to the brink of destruction and then pull you back into a warm, fuzzy hug of HAPPILY EVER AFTER. A huge thank you and shout out to all of my readers turned friends who hang out with me in my reader's group. (Rachel Robinson's Racy Readers) Dawn S., Suzy, Tricia, Jordan, Sophie, Julie W.—(and so many more!) You guys stick by me and cheer me on constantly. I love you for it and I wish we could be real life friends. That sounds creepy. I'm sorry. But, seriously, BE MY FRIEND, PLEASE!

I love my family and friends who listen to my ideas and probably think I'm insane half the time. You support me all of the time and that's what matters. My sister, Shelby, gets major kudos for reading rough drafts and telling me when I've gone too far. Someone has to temper my sadistic inclinations. Teala has a bump in the epilogue because Shelby is a sucker for pregnant heroines. (That doesn't mean you should get pregnant again, Belle.)

Kids. Speaking of those, I love mine so much. I love you, Everett and Blair. Hopefully by the time you read this, or understand exactly what it is I do on my laptop, I'm ninety years old and laughing in your face like a batty old lady. Visit me often. You guys are my world and I can't envision life (fictional or not) without you in it.

I love my husband. Without his support and knowledge, I'd never be able to write these books in a way that seems real. Critter, you're so good to me. You're the reason I know true love and romance exist in this cruel, twisted world. Without you I'd be a spinster with a sunroom full of cats. I love you. You have perfect fucking hair. There, I said it. Someone had to.

I'm clicking the shutter button right now. On my husband's face as he reads the last paragraph.

Rachel grew up in a small, quiet town full of loud talkers. Her words were always only loud on paper. She has been writing stories and creating characters for as long as she can remember. CRAZY GOOD and SET IN STONE, and TIME AND SPACE, three of her Navy SEAL novels are INTERNATIONAL BESTSELLERS. After living in San Diego, Virginia Beach, and then Fairfax, VA, she now resides in colorful Colorado with her badass husband, two children, her Sphynx cat, & her dog, Polly.

www.racheljrobinson.com
Rachel Robinson's Racy Readers